INNOCENT SHADOWS

THE SHADOW PATRIOTS
BOOK FIVE

WARREN RAY

This is a work of fiction. Names, characters, places and incidents either are products of the author's imagination or are used fictitiously. Any resemblance to actual events or locales or persons living or dead is entirely coincidental.

"A determined warrior can conquer
a whole army if he sets his mind to it."
Cole Winters

.

Thanks Muse For Continued Inspiration.

CHAPTER 1

JACKSON MICHIGAN

The cafeteria was empty when Scott "Scar" Scarborough came in for a cup of coffee. He found the machine shut off and the decanter empty, so he went about making a fresh pot with the last remaining packet of coffee. He was surprised to find no one there as it was late-morning but figured everyone was still recovering from last night in Grosse Pointe.

Scar sat down and stared at the coffee maker as it started to boil the water. His mind was occupied with last night's operation, which he could only categorize as one of the strangest he'd ever been involved with since they started the Shadow Patriots. They successfully entered Mordulfah's domain and rescued three people, but lost Cara because a woman she thought was her friend stabbed her with a knife. Scar let out a scoff as he got up and grabbed the half-full decanter. What the kind of person would do this? That poor girl. They must have lied to her from the get-go.

He sat back down and blew on the hot coffee before taking a sip. His thoughts shifted to Winters and what he must be going through. To watch your daughter die in front of you after you had risked your life to rescue her was beyond comprehension. How does one even try to get over something like that? Especially, after not seeing her for a year and to be so close to having her back, then poof, she's gone.

Scar shook his head not wanting to dwell on the unthinkable. The image of his own son, Scott, flashed before his eyes. He flew EA-6B Prowlers in the war out west. The military used these aircraft to pinpoint and neutralize the enemy's fire control radar. It wasn't too far from the realm of possibility that he could be killed at any time, but to successfully rescue your child and then have her die in your arms would be soul crushing. To be right there and then have it taken away was too much for any man. He didn't blame Cole for leaving. The man always carried the heavy burden for the group and it had been a hell of a week here in Jackson. From fighting the enemy and evacuating the citizens, to personally taking responsibility for the attack on the hospital, and then having his daughter killed. Was it any wonder he cracked and left the group?

Scar let out a heavy sigh because the burden of command would now fall on his shoulders until Winters came back if he came back. It was always a tacit thing that he was next in line. It was just something that happened whenever Winters was out of the picture, the men turned to him. While he never shied away from the responsibility, he never enjoyed it even though he was accustomed to giving orders. He had owned his own construction business and at one time had over fifty people on the payroll. However, having people's lives in your hands was quite a different thing. If he made a mistake in his business, it usually just cost him money. In this current business, mistakes cost lives. He took another sip and remembered his Marine Corps training. That training turned him into the man he was today. Thinking about it gave him a confidence boost and figured it would kick in when he needed it. Besides, this group was comprised of some tough and highly qualified fighters.

Scar looked up when he heard the door open. He raised his cup when Corporal Joshua Bassett walked in. Here was one of their most qualified fighters. His youthful energy, military training, and combat experience gave him an edge over the older members. Officially, he was still in the Army and had fought in the Middle East. This experience alone put him far above the rest with the exception of Nordell. His thirty years in the Corps was going to be invaluable to them in the future.

Bassett grabbed a cup of coffee and sat down. "Hell of a night."

"Yes, it was."

"You been up to see Elliott?"

"Just left him. Amber is hovering over him."

Bassett gave him a sly grin. "He'll like that."

"He deserves it."

"What about those twin girls? Did you hear their story?" asked Bassett.

Scar gave him a quizzical look and shook his head.

"That cop, Captain Vatter, is their cousin and was the one who gave them to Mordulfah."

Scar's jaw literally dropped.

"I know, right? It's pretty messed up. After we got back, one of the nurses scooped the girls up and took them away."

"Dammed despicable pig," said Scar.

Bassett took a sip of coffee and stared into the cup. "So, what are we going to do?"

Scar was waiting for it and now it had begun. Bassett was looking for orders. He was an Army man through and through. While he was quite capable of making his own decisions, his training told him to get directions first. Scar didn't expect Bassett to mention Winters' absence. For him, it just was, and now you moved forward.

"We'll continue moving the citizens out. Why don't you get with Nordell and make arrangements for a group tonight?"

"Sounds good, although I have a feeling he's going to be tied up for a little while."

"Oh?" asked Scar.

"He'll have Posey on the brain today."

With everything that had gone on, Scar had forgotten about the spy they captured last night. "Oh, yeah, forgot all about him."

"I can assure you, Gunny hasn't."

"I hope he doesn't make too big a spectacle of it."

"Don't count on it. I have a feeling we're talking about a big gathering. Think western movie style hanging."

Scar rolled his eyes. While he wanted Posey to pay for his crimes, he had bigger things on his mind than some grand execution. He wanted the group to continue as if nothing had changed. He figured the best way to do this would be an evacuation mission. Giving the men some purpose was the best way to keep their head in the game. There would be a lot of gossip today, which typically evolved into negative tones. Usually, there's a person or two that will think the worst and try to pull the group down to their level. He had dealt with it in the past and knew the havoc it could reap. It was the last thing he needed to have happen now.

CHAPTER 2

WASHINGTON DC

Staring into the salt-water tank in his office, Lawrence Reed watched the exotic fish swim back and forth with no particular place to go in their contained world. The big fish were kings of this world and weren't bothered by the smaller ones, all of whom gave way to them. There was a certain pecking order and everyone knew their place making it appear that everyone got along. Reed let out a scoff thinking how D.C. was relatively the same. The district was a big fish bowl with a few big fish in charge, with some medium ones striving to become big fish, and many little ones just going about their business in their own little fiefdoms. There was a certain order of things and it appeared to work. However, underneath the niceties, there was a constant struggle for wannabe big fish trying to reach the status of a truly big fish. Once in a blue moon, they legitimately earned a place among the big ones, but mostly they simply spent their time trying to manipulate other fish and events.

Reed got out of his chair, grabbed a container of food, and sprinkled the flakes across the top of the water. Most of the fish bolted to the surface and fought for their share while others patiently waited for it to drop to the bottom, taking what they needed without the hassle of fighting for it while staying unseen. These bottom feeders reminded Reed of those who liked to stay in the shadows here in the district taking what they wanted without anyone noticing them. These were the fish to watch out for because you never knew when or how they would strike. They were difficult to ferret out because sometimes they would use other people to do their dirty work or they worked in concert with other bottom feeders.

Reed plopped back in his chair knowing he had several bottom feeders working together. He rocked back and forth thinking about the chain of events over the last couple of weeks. The person who took out Pruitt must have gotten ahold of his laptop. There was no other way to explain the surfacing of the recording of Perozzi talking with Chinese officials. Reed cursed himself for thinking he had the only recording. He should have known Pruitt would keep a copy for himself. He should never have sent him to record that meeting in the first place. Reed shook his head thinking about his paranoia and how it was catching up to him. Perozzi was pretty pissed off listening to his voice on the recording. Of course, Perozzi knew about his paranoia, so there was no denying who ordered the recording. Besides, he was the only other one aware of the meeting.

Reed reached behind his chair, grabbed a crystal decanter and poured a scotch. He ignored the early hour of the day and took a large gulp of the burning liquid. It went down as it always did, burning his throat and clearing out his nostrils. He slammed the glass down thinking about what to do about Perozzi. He had pushed too far and needed answers before Perozzi decided he did not want him around anymore.

"Who the hell were these bottom feeders?"

He grabbed a pencil and paper and wrote down *Pruitt* and *recordings*. He then wrote down *Patrick O'Connor* who recorded their conversations of the bombings. Trying to control his anger at O'Connor, he pressed down hard on the pencil and the tip broke. He grabbed another pencil and wrote down *Allison O'Connor*, wishing again he'd killed that alcoholic bitch. He wrote next to their names, *recording* and *rescue*.

He leaned back in his chair thinking about her rescue and how whoever did it was able to kill two experienced men. Were they professionals? That possibility bothered him. He turned back to the fish tank and stared into it. As he watched a small fish swimming next to a big fish he realized what it was that bothered him. The shooter was a professional, but why did they need to rescue her? She shouldn't have been anywhere near the district

6

when they dropped off the recording at his house. They should have known in advance that he'd figure out where it came from. This had inexperience written all over it. He then realized he was dealing with bottom feeders all right but a bigger fish was involved as well, maybe even more than one.

He wrote down *work truck with fake license plates* and knew without question, this was the work of bureaucratic bottom feeders. This was not an easy task to perform, but could have been done by any number of people. He would have to send someone who would tear the place down, if needed, to get the information.

He looked at the list and figured there had to be at least five people in this cabal, possibly more. He tapped the list with the pencil eraser thinking about last night's interaction with Perozzi. It wasn't pleasant and a bit embarrassing having Perozzi know he was responsible for one of those recordings. It was interesting that this cabal sent him and Perozzi different recordings. These bottom feeders were clever to be sure and more than likely they were even now working on their next move.

He poured himself another drink making it a double. He started moving the glass to his lips but stopped when it reminded him of the double-shot he took last night. A new waitress called Stormy served it to him. You could not forget a name like that especially on someone as beautiful as she was. She was too pretty to be working at a restaurant and she had an air of confidence that was different from the rest of the girls there. No doubt she had modeling experience the way she walked and carried herself. Her smart-ass answer to his question bothered him the most. No one there dared talk to him like that. Why was she there and why now? That restaurant didn't have a lot of turn-over with the staff, so it was unusual to have a new girl there. The timing seemed too much of a coincidence while these bottom feeders were coming after him. He took the pencil, wrote down her name, and then wrote *background check*. He leaned back in his chair and after a few moments came up with a person whom he could assign to investigate. He picked up the phone and called him.

CHAPTER 3

JACKSON MICHIGAN

The sun shone through the window of Major Green's office in the Lafayette building. He sat in his chair and stared at the people in the park across the street. Their lives were far different from the rest of America. They didn't have the food or electricity shortages that everywhere else had to worry about. They also didn't have to worry about being killed by an enemy, either foreign or domestic. It was easy to ignore the hardships the rest of the country endured. Speaking of domestic enemies, the Shadow Patriots had gone on a mission to rescue Winters' daughter last night. Mordulfah was using her as bait, and since Green hadn't heard anything on the outcome yet, he didn't think the prince had been successful. Had they succeeded, the phones would have been buzzing.

Green shifted his mind to the meeting he had last night with Gibbs. He had gone at Gibbs' request not knowing his son's friend, Stormy, had spied for them. She took it upon herself to get a job at the Four Seasons, which was Perozzi and Reed's favorite watering hole. Last night, her first night there, she had waited on them and learned some valuable information. At first, the news of her escapades had angered him until he met her. Besides being beautiful, she seemed to be quite observant. So much so, she had even noticed Reed's tics when he lied. She was proficient in martial arts, so she was capable of handling herself and was downright gutsy to volunteer to do spy work. Since she was from Brainerd, Minnesota, and Perozzi was responsible for the damage there, she was also motivated. What Green did not know, was how far she would be willing to go to get close to Perozzi.

He reached over to his desk for his water bottle and took a sip. He then thought about Reed and the way he had lost control of his temper with Perozzi. Sending them each different recordings had certainly induced the effect he wanted. Now it was time to step it up a notch and start planning a fake assassination attempt on Reed. He would have to figure out a way to do this and make it look like it was Perozzi's handiwork. This would be just what was needed to drive Reed over the edge. He would instinctively respond and start working against Perozzi. They would then have to use all their resources to fight each other, which would expose their weaknesses. This would be better than just killing them outright because all the other players would still be out there jostling for power. Their elimination would be as if nothing happened. Green had to be patient and play the long game to get them all out in the open.

He took another gulp of water, which finished off the bottle. He got up and decided to get in touch with Kyle Gibbs. He needed more information on Perozzi and since Kyle had been monitoring him, he was just the person he would call. He left the office and headed to the Duxbury Coffee shop to get a latte and use the pay phone. The place never used to have a payphone, but with the collapse of the country, they were back in vogue. Most people didn't have cell phones anymore because the government was the only provider and the service was lousy, overpriced and monitored.

He entered the shop and ordered a latte before heading to the back to use the phone. He pulled out a slip of paper with a number written on it and dropped four quarters into the slot.

The phone rang a few times before Kyle answered.

"Hello."

"Kyle, it's John."

"Hey."

"You think we could get together anytime soon?"

"Yeah, sure. Why don't you meet me on the south side of the Reflecting Pool? I can be there in an hour."

Green grabbed his drink and headed out the door to the Reflecting Pool, on which the Lincoln Memorial stood at the south end. It was just a couple of miles away and he could use the walk. Besides, it was a great way to make sure he wasn't still being tailed. Even though Reed no longer suspected him of being a spy, he still wanted to be sure. He had learned a valuable lesson when Pruitt had been following him. It was unexpected and the results were devastating. Never again would he allow that to happen.

He took his time and enjoyed the cloudy summer day while sipping on his latte. He was glad he had thought to bring his nylon jacket as there was a slight breeze coming from the Potomac River, which made it cooler than normal for this time of year. He made several stops and diverted his direction several times until he was convinced he wasn't being followed.

Walking on Seventeenth Street he passed by the Washington Monument, the tallest structure in the district. He made a right onto the walkway and spied Kyle Gibbs up ahead standing with someone who was as tall as he was. It was Stormy, the former runway model. Her raven black hair stood out against the bright yellow running shirt she wore over black spandex jogging shorts. Green's heart skipped a beat as he realized she was joining them. He had become infatuated with her the moment they met and wanted to get to know her better.

"Major Green," said Kyle, extending his hand.

"Kyle," said Green, giving a firm shake. He then turned toward Stormy and shook her hand. "Stormy."

"Major."

"Please, call me John, both of you."

"Alright," said Stormy as she let go of his hand.

"Let's grab this park bench," said Green.

They walked over and sat down with Stormy in the middle.

"Thanks for meeting me on short notice."

"No problem. What's up?"

"I was wondering if you could help me with some information on Perozzi. Your dad told me you've been tailing him for the past couple of weeks."

Kyle nodded. "What do ya need?"

Green told them what he had in mind about pinning Reed's fake assassination attempt on Perozzi. "So, anything that might help convince Reed it was him would be valuable."

"I've kept notes. Let me go over them, I might even have a suggestion or two already."

"That would be great," said Green. He then confronted Stormy. "What about you? What are your plans?"

"Well, I have a feeling he's going to ask me out the next time he comes in," said Stormy.

"Will you accept?" asked Green.

"I don't know yet. Maybe. We'll see how it goes. Regardless, he'll need to ask several times before I accept anyway. Don't want him to think I'm easy."

Green cracked a smile hearing this. She knew how to handle men and had a lot of experience doing it. "We have a meeting out in Manassas late tonight. Can both of you make it?"

"I've got a short shift, so yeah," said Stormy.

"I'll be there. I'll bring my notes and go over them with you."

"Perfect."

They stood up, and Stormy took Green's hand. "Thanks for everything you've been doing."

Blood flushed his cheeks and he could only give her a nod. She let go of his hand, and then she and Kyle jogged away. Green watched them head toward the Lincoln Memorial for a few moments before heading back to his office.

CHAPTER 4

JACKSON MICHIGAN

Scar left Bassett in the cafeteria and headed outside for some air and to focus on what he needed to do today. He would have to give the men an update on Winters and let them know it would be business as usual. Scar decided to approach the situation as he did when he ran his business; he would hold a meeting. He'd need to get with his key players first, which included Burns, Meeks, Bassett, Taylor, and Nate if he was up for it.

He stepped outside and took in a breath of fresh air. The sun was out on a cloudless day and it was already hot. The pickup truck Winters had been driving for the last week stood in the middle of the parking lot. The old Chevy hadn't been washed in over a year. The driver's door had a dozen dents in it from where Winters had destroyed Reese's crutch and the windows were down as if someone had just parked it. Scar wished the man was still here, but knew wishes were for children. He set the thought aside and took another deep breath before heading back inside. Walking down the hall he bumped into Burns.

"Is he back?"

"No, he's not," said Scar, "and I don't expect him anytime soon."

"So, what are we going do?"

"Business as usual. But we need to get everyone together to discuss it."

"Probably a good idea. I'm already hearing the rumor mill cranking up."

"Doesn't surprise me. The sooner we set things straight the better. We should all get together and hammer out our strategy first. You think you could go get Taylor. I'll round up Meeks and see if Nate's up for it."

After getting a nod from Burns, Scar headed to Nate's room. He peeked in as he pushed open the door not knowing if he was asleep.

"I'm awake," Nate said in a gruff tone

"Hey, how ya feeling, buddy?" asked Scar.

"Pissed off," said Nate, as he put down an old magazine.

Scar raised an eyebrow.

"My best friend was almost killed last night. Captain Winters' kid was murdered. Now he's gone and I'm just sitting here and can't do anything about it. I feel friggin useless."

"Believe me. You're not useless. I'm going to need that gung ho attitude of yours."

"Oh?"

"The rumor mill is already kicking in. I'm going to need your help to keep the men in line."

"What the hell? Nothing's changed."

"Think about it. Lots of the guys here think Winters is bullet proof and now he's gone."

Nate shook his head. Yeah, I suppose. It does suck that he's gone. But we still got a job to do."

"I know that and I'm sure most of the men know that. We just need to show them a united front is all."

"What did you have in mind?"

"Gonna hold a meeting with everyone. Wanted to get us all together first so we could get on the same page. Didn't know if you were up for it, but I can see that you are."

"Hell, ya."

"Good. Let's say in about an hour."

"Cool."

Scar left to go find Meeks but he was nowhere to be found. He then decided to go check in on Elliott. The door was open and inside Amber helped Elliott drink some water. Both looked over when Scar walked in.

"Hey guys," said Scar.

Amber gave him a nod while holding a straw to Elliott's mouth.

Elliott finished drinking before acknowledging Scar.

"You're looking good," said Scar.

"Well, I actually feel pretty good, of course, Doc's got me on something to dull the pain. And I got this pretty angel fussing over me."

"You trying to make me blush again?" asked Amber.

"Always."

Scar let out a laugh. "Have you guys seen Meeks?"

"He was here about an hour ago," said Amber.

"Did he say where he was headed?"

"No. Why? What's up?" asked Amber.

Scar told them what he had in mind.

"Would you mind letting me in on this?" asked Elliott.

Scar gave him a surprised look. "Yeah, sure, we could do it right here."

"Thanks. I just want to be included."

Scar looked at Amber. "What about Reese?"

Amber gave him a grimaced look. "I don't know. She's pretty upset. She's sleeping right now."

"Okay, well, I don't want to exclude her."

"I'll check on her," said Amber.

An hour later, everyone started filtering into Elliott's room. When Nate showed up he noticed Reese wasn't there and wondered why.

"She's not up for it," said Amber.

"She needs to be here," said Nate.

"I told her, but she brushed me off," said Amber.

"All the more reason for her to be here. I'll go get her."

Amber gave Elliott a surprised look.

"He owes her," said Elliott.

Nate headed towards her room well aware of Reese's love interest in Winters and figured she was depressed about him leaving. Nate didn't want to be a jackass to her, but would risk it to get her head out of the clouds.

Nate's mother suffered from a bout of depression after his father had walked out on them. It took a couple of years for her to recover and Nate had to be the man around the house and take care of the fields as a teenager. It wasn't until he had an accident with the tractor that she snapped out of it. Nate had over-compensated a turn and rolled the tractor over in a ditch. He broke his leg and some ribs, which laid him up for a couple of months. The accident gave his mother renewed purpose, which forced her to break out of the fog of depression.

Nate would force her to do the same thing. Ever since the attack on the hospital, they shared a special bond. She saved his life twice that day. He owed her, and he knew she'd fight him on it, but he didn't care.

Nate reached her door and gave it a knock before entering. She opened her eyes as he walked in.

"Hey, kiddo."

She didn't answer him.

"Are you giving me the silent treatment? Nobody gives me the silent treatment," said Nate in a firm tone.

"I'm not in the mood," she grumbled.

"I know you're not in the mood. Why else do you think I'm here?"

Reese didn't respond.

Nate stared at her in silence and waited for a response.

Reese sat brooding for a half minute and then rolled her eyes. "Fine, what do you want?"

"Well, first off, I don't like it when pretty girls roll their eyes, it's very unattractive."

Reese jerked her head back startled by his scolding. "I'm sorry."

"That's better. Now…let's start over. How are you?"

It took a few moments before she answered. "Not good."

"Look kiddo, I'm not one to pussyfoot around, alright? I can see that you're hurting and upset, I get that. But, I also know how that feeling can take hold of a person and not let go. I've seen it happen to my mother when my dad walked out on us."

Reese's eyes lit up. "My dad walked out on us."

"Then you know what I'm talking about?"

Reese nodded.

"I'm not going to let you mope around here, alright. Now, I need for you to get up and come join us."

"Why do you care?"

"Reese, you saved my life…twice. Not only do I owe you, but I care what happens to ya," said Nate in a sincere tone.

Reese tried to deflect by saying, "But, I just don't want…"

"No," interrupted Nate.

Reese glared at him.

"No excuses. You need to come join us right now," said Nate, changing his tone to a harsher one.

Reese didn't know how to respond and flung off the sheet. Nate moved out of the way as she swung her legs onto the floor. He grabbed her red crutch and handed it to her.

"I don't think I like you anymore," said Reese, swiping the crutch from him.

"Good, cuz I can barely tolerate you," said Nate, giving her a sly grin.

Reese feigned insult. "Ah, now I see it, you're a jackass."

Nate let out a laugh. "Kiddo, that's common knowledge. Now c'mon, let's go, they're waiting for us."

Reese slammed the crutch onto the floor as she huffed out of the room. Nate chuckled to himself. As much as she'd gone through she was still a young girl and like every young girl he had ever known, could be obstinate at times.

They reached Elliott's room just as Burns and Taylor showed up.

Taylor gave Reese a hug. "Still feeling like a honey badger?"

"I thought you said there can only be one," said Reese.

"Well, I'd like to think I'm irreplaceable, but if it had to be anyone you'd be my choice."

"You're just the sweetest," said Reese. She turned to Nate and said in a taunting voice, "unlike some people."

Nate shot her a smirk.

After Elliott gave everyone an update on his condition Scar began the meeting. He talked about how the mission stays the same, and if they all stay on message, they can all help squash the rumor mill. Everyone needs to remain positive and to convince the others that nothing has changed. The end goal is still to bring down Mordulfah and save the citizens.

Because their forces were spread out all over town they couldn't hold a giant meeting, so Scar split his cadre into two groups to go visit with everyone and deliver the same message. Everyone was nodding their heads in agreement when Meeks entered the room.

"You guys are not going to believe what Nordell is doing," said Meeks in an excited tone.

CHAPTER 5

SABINE IOWA

The clanging of the shovel echoed inside the van as it hit the floor and dirt flew off in different directions. Winters slammed the back door shut and turned around to take one last look at the headstone of his deceased wife, Ellie. He breathed a sigh of relief knowing Cara was now with her. The fresh dirt sitting on top of their final resting place would eventually level off and no one other than him would know he buried Cara in the same grave. He reached down and grabbed the bottle of water sitting by his feet. He finished it off before getting back in the van.

He sat there with mixed emotions not sure what to think. He was no longer angry with Cara but couldn't shake his overwhelming sense of guilt. He grabbed a fresh bottle of water and took a swig trying to get the lump out of his throat but to no avail. He leaned his head back trying to come to terms with his part in her death. When did his responsibility begin? Did it begin years ago and could he have done something differently? He sat up straighter in the seat to try to fight off these thoughts. What's done is done. He couldn't change what happened, but he still wanted to crawl out of his own skin. Of all the mistakes he'd been making over the past few months, this one cut him the deepest. How could he continue to lead his men if he couldn't even keep his own daughter safe?

He cringed, remembering how she died in his arms knowing he'd never be able to forget that helpless moment. How insignificant you are to the reality of life and death's march toward inevitability. Thankfully, he had been able to forgive her. This was his only saving grace at this moment, a moment where he was teetering on the edge. Had he just gotten her forgiveness, he didn't think the loss would be so devastating.

Winters leaned his head back, slouched down in the seat, and dozed off in exhaustion. He hadn't had any sleep for more than twenty-four hours and had fought in a battle with devastating results. The drive back to Iowa and digging a grave was all his tired body could take.

Several hours later, the sun shined through the window and woke him up. He jerked up realizing he had fallen asleep. His body ached from the uncomfortable position of the seat. Reaching for the water bottle, he drank its contents. He looked around and realized he wasn't sure what to do next. He did what he came here to do and had little desire to drive back to Jackson. It took long enough to get here, and he didn't look forward to the reverse trip. The police van had guzzled fuel faster than he expected, and it took a couple of hours to find good gas because a lot of it had gone bad. Besides, he wasn't sure he could go back after the way he failed Cara. Her death was the culmination of all the mistakes he'd been making over the past few months. Every one of them had cost the lives of some of his men and the gravity of that responsibility bore down on him. Up until last week he'd gotten used to the weight, but then there was the attack at the hospital and now the death of Cara added to it in spades.

He looked across the cemetery and realized he hadn't noticed all the freshly dug graves when he first arrived. Several looked less than a week old and were still grass free. Some appeared to be as shallow as the one he'd dug for Cara. He dug down as far as he dared not wanting to disturb his wife's coffin. His fellow citizens seemed to be dying left and right. They must be filled with older people as they had a tougher time with limited resources, especially the lack of medicine. Or was it something else? He continued to stare when an idea struck him, and he started the van and headed over to his house. It was a quick ten-minute ride, and his heart began to beat faster realizing how much he missed it. They had lived in the same home for fifteen years, and it held many memories. He nodded his head promising he'd only think of the good times hoping that would help him get out of his melancholy. He might even stay the night and sleep in his own bed.

He turned onto his street and his eyes lit up as he recognized all the houses. The park across the street now had rusted playground equipment and the grass was overgrown. He remembered taking Cara to this park and pushing her on the swings. The place held good memories, and he tapped his fingers at their recall.

Approaching his house, he could only shake his head in disbelief. The place was burned to the ground. The houses on either side hadn't been touched, nor any of the others on the street. He gripped the steering wheel tighter and began to breathe fast as he stopped in front of the driveway. "Who the hell did this and why? Was it the government or his neighbors?" His short-lived sense of euphoria slipped away and he sank in his seat in growing disappointment. If he'd learned anything over the past few months, it was to not to count on anything. He should have known better.

As he continued to stare at the charred structure, he realized a couple of people across the street were staring at him. He recognized them as his neighbors, Edward and Judith Sherman. He opened the door to go talk to them but saw them scurry into their house. He let out a scoff figuring they didn't recognize him. He had lost weight and looked different from when he left. Besides, he was driving a police van.

He hustled up on their porch and banged his fist on the door. He could hear voices inside and knocked again.

"Ed, it's me, Cole Winters."

He waited a few moments. "Ed, please, it's Cole Winters. I just want to talk to you."

He strained his ears and heard murmuring. He scrunched his face in confusion. He had always gotten along with the Sherman's and had always been there to help them as they were older than him and couldn't always manage the place without some assistance. Their two sons were useless and never around to help and the grandsons were not much better. They were always getting in trouble with the law, and one of them even served time in prison.

Winters tried banging on the door one more time. "Please, I just want to talk."

He stood there waiting and hadn't noticed someone had snuck up behind him. The cocking of a pump shotgun prompted him to turn his head. He was startled to see a man boring down on him.

CHAPTER 6

JACKSON MICHIGAN

S car had been holding a meeting with the Shadow Patriots key members to discuss Winters' absence when Meeks came in and interrupted them with news about Nordell.

"Someone grabbed all of our prisoners and it looks like they're going to execute them."

"What?" said Taylor. "Those sons-of-bitches came in just as I was leaving to come here. They said they needed to question the cops about Posey."

"Where are they?" asked Scar.

"Downtown," said Meeks. "Something else you need to know."

"What?" asked Scar.

"The crowd is pretty riled up."

They all looked at each other and then at Scar.

"We'd better get down there," said Scar. "Corporal, you and Burns come with us."

They nodded and the four left Elliott's room.

Reese looked at Nate. "I ain't missing an execution. You up for it?"

"Oh, we friends again?" asked Nate.

Reese punched him playfully in the arm. "I suppose."

Nate looked at Amber. "What about you?"

Amber turned to Elliott. "Would you mind?"

"No, not at all, go."

"Don't forget about me," said Taylor. "They're my prisoners."

"Well, let's go already," ordered Reese as she hurried out of the room.

Nate leaned toward Amber. "Someone's out of their funk."

"Yeah, I see that," said Amber.

As he peeled out of the parking lot, Meeks saw Reese hobbling toward another SUV in his rearview mirror. It didn't surprise him knowing the personal hatred she held for the cops. He floored the pedal and headed downtown. Up ahead were two flatbed trailers parked in the middle of the intersection of Michigan Avenue and Jackson Street. A large boisterous crowd stood in front waiting for the show to begin. Thirteen gagged prisoners, six of which were cops, stood on the flatbeds with their hands tied behind their backs. Several armed citizens stood guard while Nordell yelled down into the large crowd.

"What the hell are we gonna to do?" asked Meeks.

"Damn good question," said Scar.

"We can't let them do this," stated Burns. "It goes against everything that we are."

"I'm with you on that," said Bassett. "Problem is, once a mob is whipped up, it's hard to settle 'em down. I've seen this before in Iraq."

"What happened?" asked Scar.

"Well, let's just say some innocents got killed trying to save the doomed."

Scar let out a deep breath knowing he was damned whatever he did. If he tried to stop them from executing prisoners, he'd anger the mob and lose control. If he didn't stop it, then it would be unforgivable in the eyes of most of the Shadow Patriots. Winters had laid down the law when they

23

first came together that all prisoners would be given quarter. These prisoners were under their protection and they couldn't let a mob take them. He needed to get down there right away and talk to Nordell.

Meeks parked the truck and all four of them got out and headed toward the flatbeds. The tension in the air was heavy as the crowd yelled up at the prisoners. A clear thirst for revenge electrified the mob. The citizens' eyes burned with revenge wanting these prisoners dead.

Scar jumped up on the trailer and could barely hear himself above the roar of the crowd as he approached Nordell who was center stage.

"What the hell are you doing, Gunny?"

"Having an execution."

"I can see that, but you're only supposed to execute Posey who's not even here."

"Yeah, I know, he's not well enough to execute, thanks to Winters."

Scar's eyes widened hearing Nordell's tone. Here, was the old Nordell they had come to know when they had first met. "What the hell is that supposed to mean?"

"He promised Posey to me, but he can't even get out of bed. How the hell are we supposed to execute him?"

"You can wait."

"I have no problem with that."

"You don't?"

"No, not at all."

"Then why are these prisoners here? Who told them we were holding them?"

"Hey, don't look at me. I didn't say anything."

"Who did?"

"Someone in your group spilled the beans about them, and next thing I know here we are."

"What?"

"You heard me. This morning, when everyone heard about Posey and what he had done, they were pretty pissed off. But when they saw his condition they knew they couldn't execute him. They were mad as hell when they found out what happened to him. So, this is Winters' fault for stabbing him."

"That still doesn't explain the prisoners."

"Someone in your group said something, alright." Nordell pointed at the crowd. "They smelled blood and now they want it."

"You need to stop this."

"You think I can stop this now. There's no way in hell I could. I can't and I won't. These people need justice and they're going to get it one way or the other."

"This isn't justice. It's revenge pure and simple."

"Whatever it is, it doesn't matter. These people want it and there's no stopping them."

"Bull-crap."

"Scar, don't do this. I'm telling you, this will not have a pleasant ending."

"Pleasant? There's nothing pleasant about this."

"I know that. But the people you're trying to help will turn on you. Do you want that? I sure as hell don't."

"These prisoners are under our protection."

"Look into this crowd."

Scar looked down at the crowd. Angry faces hurled insults up at the stage. The prisoners were standing behind Scar, and the crowd was now directing their hatred toward him. Even though they couldn't hear what he was saying to Nordell, they could tell he wasn't on their side. How could they be doing this to him? He was there to help them. Scar raised his hands and motioned the crowd to quiet down but they weren't having it. He grew frustrated and decided to take matters into his own hands. He pointed at Bassett to join him.

Bassett jumped up. "What are ya gonna do?"

"I'm taking these prisoners out of here."

Bassett looked at the men standing guard and shook his head knowing, as Scar started moving toward them, that this wasn't going to work.

All six guards rushed forward pointing their weapons at Scar and yelled at him to back off. Bassett grabbed onto Scar's big shoulders and suggested they leave.

"We're not gonna win this," said Bassett.

Scar looked at the guards, some of whom he recognized. He turned to

Nordell. "This isn't right, Gunny."

Nordell shrugged his shoulders and turned his back on him.

Bassett and Scar jumped off the trailers to jeers from the crowd as they pushed their way back through the mob to the SUV's. As soon as they reached their vehicles, shots rang out and four Jijis collapsed to the floor of the trailers. There was a hush through the audience before loud clapping and cheering arose as one sentiment.

CHAPTER 7

SABINE IOWA

Winters had come home to bury his daughter and take the first step on the long and difficult road to healing. Guilt and anger had overwhelmed him and he no longer trusted himself to make sound decisions. Everywhere he went death usually followed him but last night's death had been a tipping point.

After getting back to Jackson and hearing Elliott was going to be fine; the idea of coming home to bury Cara dominated his thinking. He hoped, in some way, it would begin the healing process.

"I got him, Grandpa."

Winters recognized the man who was in his early thirties and tried to remember his name. "Hey, careful with that, I'm not armed."

"Get your hands up so I can see 'em," yelled the man. "Grandpa?"

Winters raised his hands and opened his jacket to show the man he wasn't armed. The door then opened and out came Ed Sherman who wore a dingy white t-shirt that matched his yellowed white hair.

"What the hell's going on here, Ed?" asked Winters.

"You're what's going on," replied Ed.

"What do ya mean? C'mon you know me," pleaded Winters.

"Yeah, well, we thought we knew ya," said Ed.

Judith then came to the door wearing an anxious face and holding a revolver, which looked like an old Smith and Wesson .38. They all seemed determined to keep him there rather than chase him off.

"You raping murderer," Judith yelled in a disgusted tone as she came out on the wooden porch. Her short frizzy gray hair seemed to straighten out as she yelled at him. Spit came out of her mouth and drooled down her pink gingham apron that looked like a greasy abstract painting.

"We always knew you were just a creepy man," said Judith.

Winters took a deep breath knowing they had bought all the lies the government was saying about him. It didn't matter that they had been neighbors for fifteen years. As long as the government told the lies and told them often enough, people tended to put aside all skepticism and believe the lies. When it came to something like raping and murdering it seemed to give more gravity to the charge despite the lack of evidence.

"Timmy, keep your gun on him while I go get some rope," ordered Ed.

Winters then remembered Tim. He was the grandson who was always in trouble with the law. He had no morals at all and was as irresponsible as a toddler. He was short and his dark eyes were wide with the excitement of the moment. Winters turned to Judith who had always been sweet but was now a raving lunatic. Her eyes were fixated with irrational hate.

"What are you planning to do?" asked Winters.

"Are you stupid or something?" retorted Tim.

"I'm not sure I'm following," said Winters.

"Reward money," said Judith. "That's what we're doing."

"Seventy-five thousand dollars," yelled Tim.

Winters let out a sigh. He'd forgotten there was a reward on his head. He couldn't remember if that meant dead or alive."

"I see what you're thinking," said Tim. "It's a hundred thousand dollars alive and seventy-five thousand dead. That extra twenty-five sure would be nice, but we decided we'd rather string you up and hang you yourselves."

"That's right, Cole, you ain't worth the extra to keep you from a rope," said Judith. "A nice slow death for raping and killing those young girls, hell I'd bet anything you were molesting Cara too. The way that poor thing ran off."

A sharp pain formed in Winters' throat hearing that statement. His mind began to spin listening to these greedy people. The world had gone crazy, and here was an example of every man for himself. They didn't care if he was innocent or not. All they could think about was the money they were going to get. On one hand, he didn't blame them as it was tough eking out a living these days, but on the other hand, did they not have an ounce of honor. *Innocent until proven guilty.* Winters laughed at that quaint creed.

A few others were coming up the street and he didn't have much time before a crowd would gather to watch him hang. He began to think that perhaps he deserved the rope. Not for the reasons they thought but for failing to keep his daughter alive. Death would be so much easier than having to go back to Jackson to once again face the heavy burden of responsibility and death that had been all around him with more to come if he went back.

Winters began to accept his fate, but the reality of the moment began creeping up on him as he began to remember all the people who depended upon him and loved him. Reese must be going out of her mind that he left without saying goodbye to her. As tough as she was, she was still fragile and needed him to help her. He took a deep breath when he noticed a young girl among the people walking up the street. The child reminded him of Sadie, whom he missed more and more, especially now that Cara was gone. He needed to see her and soak in her spirit. A nice game of Cat's Cradle would do wonders for his soul and help him deal with the death of his daughter. He had made a solemn promise to her that he'd come back, and he didn't want to break that promise. A strong wave of determination swept over him and he knew what he needed to do.

CHAPTER 8

JACKSON MICHIGAN

A stomach pain shot through Scar knowing he had failed his first leadership challenge. He stared across the crowd and watched as the last three Jijis were brought forward and tied to the rail posts set into the bed of the trailer. He shook his head as Nordell commanded the guards to fire. The shots rang out and the audience responded again by yelling out in approval.

Scar turned to his friends. "Look at them eat this up."

"They deserve this," said Nate.

Scar shot him a glare.

"Hey, these bastards killed hundreds of people."

"I know that, Nate. But they were our prisoners and under our protection."

"After what happened last night, do ya think the captain gives a damn anymore?" asked Nate.

"He's not here."

"That's right, he's not. Besides, what were we gonna do? Give them a trial?"

"That's not the point."

"What is the point?"

Burns interceded. "It's our decision to do it the right way."

"Our decision? Please? Don't cha think these people earned the right to be involved in that decision, or at the very least deserved to know we were holding them?"

Scar shook his head in disgust at Nate's attitude. Does he not understand this is no better than murder, which puts us on the same level as the enemy?

On the trailer, Nordell split the six cops into two groups and had the guards tie them to the rail posts.

Reese shuffled over to Scar and pointed. "See those cops right there? The one in the middle, his name is Carter, he raped me six times, and the two next to him, liked to..." she paused for a moment, "Well, I don't even want to say what they did."

Scar turned to see the glee in her eyes. He didn't know what to say and only gave her a reaffirming nod. He kept staring at her as Nordell gave the command to fire and watched as a small smile appeared on her face as the shots rang out.

"It should be me pulling the trigger," she said to no one.

Scar glanced at Amber, who shrugged her shoulders.

They watched Nordell's men tie the last three cops to the posts. Tears ran down the cheeks of two of them.

"Poor Andy," said Taylor.

Scar turned to him.

"Andy Deeble, big time crybaby, he was literally asking for his mom."

"Yeah, well, he's still one of them," Reese said not taking her eyes off the stage.

The last shots rang out, and the crowd let out a big cheer while clapping. Nordell shook the hands of the executioners and jumped off the trailers to the waiting crowd. He received many pats on the back as he shook their hands.

Burns turned to Scar and asked in a cavalier tone. "Still feel like doing an evac tonight?"

The question gave Scar pause because he was angry at what had just happened. He looked out into the crowd and then realized not all the citizens were here, which meant not everyone agreed with the mob. Now that he was in charge, he needed to be the bigger man and look at the bigger picture. They still needed to honor their commitment and move these people to safety. He couldn't let something like this get in the way of that promise. Besides, he was more concerned with the cohesiveness of the Shadow Patriots. With Winters gone, it already had a different vibe and seemed more fragile. He just experienced some cracks in their unity and was fearful it would grow. It didn't surprise him that Nate and Reese would be for these executions, after all, they were in the hospital during the attack. It must have made a big impact on both of them, especially Reese with what she had gone through at the party house. What he needed to be careful of was to not let this come between them. Both Nate and Reese were important to the group as a whole, and he didn't need any bad blood infecting the group. It would only fester and become unmanageable. These executions were going to be an issue bandied about and he needed everyone to be calm and respectful in their conversations.

Scar made a quick decision and turned to Burns. "Nothing changes." He then looked at Nate and stuck his hand out. "What's done is done here, okay?"

Nate nodded and shook his hand.

Scar put his hand on Reese's shoulder. "Are you good?"

"I am now," she said too quickly.

Scar twitched his head back.

Reese considered her response and looked up at him. "I'm sorry, Scar. It's just that this was really emotional for me."

Guilt washed over Scar. He then realized it had been useless arguing with what was going to happen anyway, and he should have kept his mouth shut. "No, I'm sorry, Reese. I was being insensitive. I wasn't thinking about who these cops were and what they did to you."

"It's all good," Reese said as she put her arms out.

Scar moved in and gave her a hug then he pulled back and addressed the group. "Guys, let's just move on from here. We need to stick together no matter what."

Everyone gave him a nod and headed back to the hospital.

Scar leaned back in the seat while Meeks drove and let out a deep breath knowing he avoided his first conflict.

"Nice play back there," said Bassett from the back seat.

32

Scar turned in his seat. "It was needed. We can't afford any strife."

"I'm with you on that."

"Still, it wasn't right," said Burns sitting next to Bassett.

"I know, but it's done. I'll tell ya what though, Nordell's attitude was back to what it was when we first met him."

This got everyone's attention.

"You mean, arrogant jackass," said Meeks.

"Yep. He blamed the executions on Winters."

"How so?" asked Meeks.

"Said it was because he stabbed Posey and that he's too laid up to be executed."

"Well, dumb ass must have bragged to everyone about Posey and worked everyone up about it," said Meeks.

"Yeah and when he couldn't pull through he offered up the prisoners," said Burns.

"He swore to me that one of our guys spilled the beans about the prisoners," said Scar.

"And you believe him?" asked Meeks.

"I can't believe one of our guys said anything," said Burns.

"Well, it doesn't really matter now," said Scar.

"Yeah, it does, because we might not be able to trust Nordell," said Burns.

Scar reflected on this for a moment. "You got a point."

"With Winters gone, he might see it as a way to take over," said Burns.

Scar hadn't really thought about the fact they were both in the Marines, only he was there for just four years and come out a Lance Corporal. "Well, Gunnery Sergeant does outrank a Lance Corporal."

"He just might see it as a slight that he's not in charge," said Burns.

"Is this more Sun Tzu," asked Meeks.

"No, I've just seen guys like this in the corporate world."

"I'll get with him and see what's up," said Bassett.

"Okay, do that, but in the meantime let's get into our groups and make sure everyone is ready to press on," said Scar.

CHAPTER 9

SABINE IOWA

Winters' blood began to boil thinking how he did not want to disappoint his new family of Patriots. Not only would they never even know he was dead, but they would think he just ran off on them. He couldn't let that happen. The noise of the crowd became louder as it came closer and grew in size. He took a deep breath knowing what he was about to do wasn't going to be pretty and would only cement what everybody already thought about him. He'd never be able to come back to this town again, but at that moment he didn't care as he felt Mister Hyde bubbling back up. He was being forced to kill old people, but he didn't have any choice.

"I've got me a hanging noose," said the old man carrying a long thick rope and another smaller one. "Bring him down here, Timmy."

"You heard 'em, get down here."

Winters glared at him. "Screw you."

Tim raised the shotgun aiming it right at Winters' face.

"Get. Down. Here."

"Go to hell...Tiny Tim," said Winters in a taunting voice knowing the grandson hated the derogatory name.

His face turned red and he stomped up on the porch. He swung the shotgun using the butt end to strike Winters in the gut.

Winters tightened his stomach muscles knowing what was coming. He hoped Tim would come at him and try to knock him to the ground. The blow hurt but didn't cause him to lose his breath. Winters keeled over in exaggerated pain and reached down to his ankle for the Ruger SR-22 that Sadie gave him. He pulled the small gun out and waited for Timmy to grab onto him.

"Get your sorry ass up," said Tim, grabbing Winters' jacket collar.

A determined expression formed on Winters' face as he got up on his knees and pointed the hidden Ruger into Tim's groin. He pulled the trigger as he rose up to meet Tim's eyes. Excited eyes turned to bewilderment. The gun report sounded like a firecracker and confused Judith who stood behind them. Ed was still on the walkway and backed away after hearing the bang and his grandson's screaming. Winters grabbed the smaller man by the throat to hold him up as he pulled the trigger again. The bullet ripped into his stomach and he began to cough up blood. Tim began to go limp, but Winters forced him to stand up to use him as a shield. He spun them around just as Judith raised her .38 and without hesitation, Winters pointed the Ruger at her face. A small mist of blood splattered against the screen door as she crumpled to the wooden floor.

Ed let out a blood-curdling scream while dropping the hanging noose to pull out a Taurus 9mm from his waistband. Winters let go of his shield and aimed at the slower man. The old man's hand shook as he pulled back the slide. Winters had him beat and ordered him to stop. The old man didn't and managed to fire a round that went wide. Winters shook his head and fired a single shot into the man's forehead. The impact tossed him on his back and he shook for a moment before dying. Winters bent down to pick up the 9mm and heard Tim crying in pain.

Winters walked over to him. "Ya should have just pulled the trigger."

The wounded man tried to spit at him, but only managed to hurl blood on himself.

Winters aimed the 9mm at his head and squeezed the trigger. He then jumped off the porch to the approaching crowd. Some ducked for cover while others pointed weapons at him. Mister Hyde was in full control as Winters marched toward them with confident strides. A few more peeled off, but a couple of foolish ones stood their ground. Winters raised the old man's 9mm and fired off a few shots. A round hit a man in the leg, and he fell to the ground. Winters continued toward them without hesitation. The crowd sensed he wasn't going to stop and picked up their friend to drag him to safety.

Winters willed himself to stop. It was pointless to continue as he had already made the statement that he was not to be messed with. He stopped mid-stride and tried to slow his breathing down. Everyone hid from him except for the little girl and her mother who stood their ground and stared at him. The girl was about Sadie's age, and she didn't avert her eyes when he met them. That she had to witness the shootout caused a pang of regret to sweep over him, but then he rationalized that it was her mother's fault for bringing her.

Winters smiled at her hoping she'd return it. It took a moment, but she did, and he was surprised by how much it meant to him. A child gave him back a glimmer of humanity, and Winters ate it up as he turned around to go back to the van.

He got in the van and watched the crowd disperse. They were no longer interested in him. Everybody was leaving except for the mother and child who had begun to walk toward the van.

"What the hell are you doing?" Winters asked aloud.

The young mother held onto her daughter's hand and stopped fifteen feet away. Winters stared at her realizing thinking she looked familiar. She wasn't scared of him and it appeared she wanted to talk.

Winters looked around before opening the door. He shoved the 9mm in the small of his back and walked over to her.

"Mister Winters, it's me, Ashley."

Winters tried to remember where he knew her from. The long brown haired girl was five-foot four and probably didn't weigh but a hundred pounds. She was gaunt in the face and looked like she needed food. Her daughter appeared to be much better fed, and Winters figured she had sacrificed to make sure the little girl had enough to eat.

"I used to baby-sit Cara."

Winters tilted his head to the side. "Of course, Ashley. I'm sorry, it's been a long time since I've seen you and you've grown up. And is this your daughter?"

"Yes sir, this is Kaitlyn."

Winters knelt down to the young girl, who looked just like her mother. "Hello, Kaitlyn."

She moved behind her mother.

"She's a little shy." Ashley looked at her daughter and said, "Say hello, honey. He's not gonna hurt ya."

"Hello," she said in a weak tone.

"And how old are you?"

"I'm nine."

"Wow, you're practically a lady," remembering the quote from his daughter's favorite movie.

She broke out in a big grin.

"I'm sorry you had to see all of that," said Winters to the shy girl, but directed it toward Ashley.

"I heard what was happening, which is why I rushed up here. I wanted to try to talk some sense into those fools. I know you didn't do what they said you did."

Winters stood back up. "You do?"

"Of course! You couldn't do those things, but some people like the Shermans will believe anything. Tim was nothing but white trash anyway, and he helped spread the biggest lie around town."

"Which lie?"

Ashley hesitated. "That you killed your wife."

Winters shook his head at the lie Cara bought into as well. It was the one lie that bothered him the most, which is why the government used it.

"We all know you wife died of cancer, but that fool said it was BS and that he knew because he lived across the street."

"So, who burned my house down?"

"The Shermans and a bunch of others. They made it into a big party. I'm really sorry about all of this," she said sincerely.

Winters was curious if she was doing okay and wanted to find out about her husband.

"May I ask where your husband is?"

"He's off fighting in the war. Haven't heard from him in eight months, so I'm not holding out much hope."

Winters was shocked to hear her talk this way in front of her daughter.

Ashley noticed his concern. "It's okay. I'm very up front with her. It's been really rough around here so we need to stay in reality."

"What about your parents?"

"Dad left for the Patriot Center six months ago, and mom died of a heart attack shortly after."

Winters fought to control his eyes when he heard about her dad knowing he was already dead. At this point, it didn't do any good telling her about the Patriots Centers. She had no brothers and sisters to depend on, and it didn't appear she was getting along well. She looked malnourished and in need of a good meal. If she didn't stay healthy her daughter wouldn't survive.

"Ashley, I too, want to stay in reality and I have to say you don't look well."

Her tone changed. "Like I said it's been pretty rough here."

"I can see that. How have you been surviving?"

Ashley's face went ashen, and Winters suspected something was going on.

"Well, it's been hard you know, I mean, we all got to do what we got to do to survive."

Winters put a hand on her shoulders. "What exactly have you been doing?"

Ashley looked at her daughter and then toward the ground. She had something to get off her chest. He wasn't sure if she was struggling to say it in front of her daughter or just saying it at all.

"I, uh, you know, I uh, I get, like, passed around."

Winters raised an eyebrow. "You do this for food then?"

"Yes, sir." She looked back up at him. "Please don't judge me."

Her eyes were full of shame but the poor girl had a daughter to feed and would do anything to make sure that happened.

"Ashley, I would never judge you. You do what you have to do for your daughter, okay?"

Tears began to form in her hazel eyes and ran down her cheeks.

"It's okay. You've done nothing wrong, okay?"

She gave him a half nod.

"Ashley, I need you to tell me, who is doing this to you?"

She nodded and began to tell him the story of what was going on in the town of Sabine, Iowa. Winters fought to control his reaction to hearing how his hometown had fallen into the abyss.

CHAPTER 10

JACKSON MICHIGAN

S car needed to talk to Gunnery Sergeant Nordell to find out where he stood. The men were angry at what happened this morning and had begun to question his loyalty. He and Bassett had been looking for him for a couple of hours and then he ran into him quite by accident. The mob from the executions had dispersed and the streets were once again empty except for Nordell, who was crossing the street heading toward city hall.

Nordell surprised Scar when he greeted him in a friendly way. "Scar, hey, hope you can forgive me for this morning."

"Wasn't the right thing to do, Gunny," said Scar not convinced of his sincerity.

"Hey, with Winters leaving and the way the town was out for blood? Let's just say it's been a crazy couple of weeks and leave it that," said Nordell, holding his hand out.

Scar was taken off guard. He certainly hadn't expected this from Nordell but was glad for it. He needed him on his side and didn't want him infecting any of the citizens or his men. He grabbed his hand and gave it a firm shake.

"Semper fi," said Nordell.

Scar gave him an acquiescent nod. "You on your way to see the mayor?"

"I am. Why don't you join me? We need to talk about the current food supply or lack thereof."

They headed up the stairs and found Mayor Simpson at his desk going over some papers. The mayor waved them in and got up to offer them coffee. He appeared as frail as ever and looked even more tired than usual. Scar considered bringing up the execution but decided against it having just gotten the feeling Nordell was going to cooperate again. There was no sense in getting into an argument over something that wasn't going to happen again.

Mayor Simpson ambled around to get their drinks before sitting down.

"It's used grounds. I'm afraid we're running low."

Nordell turned to Scar. "We're running out of a lot of things."

Simpson poured each of them a cup of lighter than usual coffee.

"How much food do we have left?" asked Scar.

"Roughly fifty boxes of canned goods, but only five hundred pounds of wheat," said Simpson. "That's barely a thousand loaves."

Scar gave him a curious look.

Simpson noticed and said, "I used to own a bakery."

"I did not know that," said Scar setting his cup down.

Simpson started punching numbers on a calculator. "I'd say we only have three maybe four more days of bread left."

"The rice and beans will run out just a few days after," said Nordell.

"Any suggestions?" asked Simpson.

Scar moved his head from side to side. They still had over a thousand people to move to safety. It was going to take much longer than three or four days. What they needed was a new supply of food and a way to get it to Jackson. He thought about the mission in Grosse Pointe and being out on the water when an idea struck him. They could take boats across Lake Saint Claire into Canada and bring back some supplies. Because of the fuel shortage, it would be easier than driving north through Michigan into the UP before crossing into Canada.

"What if we could get some supplies out of Canada?" asked Scar.

"I've given that some thought as well," said Nordell. "Those boats you guys took. They'd be able to bring back quite a load of flour."

"Yes, they would," said Scar.

"Can we not just get everyone out of here?" asked Simpson.

Nordell shifted in his chair. "It's taking too long."

"I agree," said Scar rethinking the mission tonight to move citizens.

"Then let's take a boat ride tonight," said Nordell.

The three of them looked at each other and agreed.

Scar left City Hall with a clear goal of what to do next. Instead of moving more citizens out, they would set off for Canada. He'd have to get with Burns and Bassett to go over the mission. Burns's experience with boats would make him the best choice to lead the expedition to Canada. He wasn't sure how many people should go or who else to send. Would they need money? Perhaps once they got into Canada, they could call General Standish in Winnipeg and ask for assistance. He'd be happy to get a status report and help them out any way he could. Maybe even get word to Major Green on their status as well. What he also hoped for was to get an update on his activities. The last he'd heard was that Green had put together a group of well-connected people and was trying to take down two characters named Gerald Perozzi and Lawrence Reed.

CHAPTER 11

WASHINGTON D.C.

Picking up the phone, Lawrence Reed was pleased to hear Lieutenant Wagner's voice on the other end. Reed had asked him earlier to look into who could have falsified Motor Vehicle documents and to do a background check on Stormy Robinson. Wagner was in his early thirties and worked for the National Police. He had entertained Cara Winters while she was in town and was quite proficient in doing investigative work. He had come up the ranks in the ATF and transferred to the National Police when the ATF was eliminated.

"What do you have for me, Lieutenant?"

"Not much from Motor Vehicles."

"Oh?"

"It's a tough nut to crack over there. There are so many different departments with numerous staff members and any one of them could have forged those docs."

"Government at its best, I see," said a disappointed Reed.

"I can keep digging, but I think it's a waste of time."

"What about the girl?"

"Now she's more interesting, at least to look at anyway."

Reed sat up straighter in his chair.

"New York model. She did runway and high fashion work for a while.

No problems that I can see. Cycled out after ten years. Ended up doing some photo shoots for sports magazines, that sort of thing."

"Where is she from?" asked Reed.

"Let me look here…Minnesota, Brainerd, Minnesota."

Reed's face went flush. He tried to remain calm and didn't respond right away. Not many people, not even in the National Police, knew the full story on Brainerd, or any of the other goings on in the Midwest, and he wasn't sure if Wagoner was one of them. He liked to keep things compartmentalized as much as possible. Few people knew about the Patriot Centers and only a select few knew who was responsible for the bombings in the Midwest.

"Where does she live?" asked Reed.

"Don't have a current address on her."

"Find out and make it a priority," ordered Reed. "Also, find out who her friends were in New York. I want them interviewed."

"No problem."

Reed hung up the phone and leaned back in his chair thinking about Stormy. It was too much of a coincidence that she was from Brainerd and now working where he and Perozzi frequented. Reed grabbed a glass and poured a drink from the crystal decanter. He swished the Scotch around a few times before taking a sip. How did she even know? And who in the hell is she working with? He took another sip, finishing it off. He started to pour another one but stopped once he realized she was the key to all of this. If he was right, then this was the best lead they had and she could point out all of her accomplices. He laughed to himself thinking how easy it would be to get such a pretty girl to talk. She wouldn't be able to take any pain and would give up names in no time. He would have Wagner bring her in for questioning as soon as he finished her background check.

Reed finished pouring the second drink and began to take a sip when he started to fidget and tap his fingers. What if she caught wind they were investigating her? It wouldn't take but a phone call from a friend in New York to tip her off and then she'd go into hiding. They'd never be able to find her. It was amazing how well they'd been able to hide so far. He decided to have Wagner pick her up right away. He knew where she worked so they wouldn't have to bother finding out where she lived.

He grabbed the phone and called Wagner back.

"Yes, sir."

"I want you to arrest this girl tonight at work."

"Where do you want me to bring her?"

"To the Hoover building and make her uncomfortable. You understand? I want her scared out of her mind before we interrogate her."

"I understand."

He hung up the phone knowing Perozzi would be pissed at him for taking his favorite new waitress into custody. He was already in enough trouble with him but he'd have to take the chance. If he could force a confession and get the names of the other conspirators, then he'd be able to make amends with Perozzi. It was a chance worth taking and besides; it would embarrass the billionaire at the same time. Reed rocked in his chair at the prospect of being right at Perozzi's expense. He tightened his grip on the glass thinking about the way that girl smart mouthed him and embarrassed him in front of Perozzi. It was already bad enough Perozzi had yelled at him and then to have her mouth off to him was too much. If she knows anything or not she was going to pay for her smart-mouth regardless.

CHAPTER 12

After having a gun pointed at him in an attempt by his former neighbors to kill him, Winters scared off the rest of the developing mob. Everyone took off except Ashley, a girl who used to baby-sit Cara when she was a toddler.

Winters listened as Ashley told him about a group of men who took over the town's food supply. They began by promising to ration the food equally but ended up using it as power over everyone. After convincing everyone to bring all their food in, they then went through all the abandoned homes looking for more food storage and brought it to one central location for distribution.

For a while, it was all working out. Everyone got their rations with no problems, but little by little, they started asking for small favors, which only got bigger and bigger. Soon, they forced the females to perform sexual favors in order to get their rations.

Winters could only shake his head at the irony. The Shermans wanted to hang him for supposedly raping little girls and yet here was a group of thugs doing the exact same thing right under their noses. Over the last few months, Winters had learned a few things about social order. When left unchecked, it always plunged into some form of anarchy and human politics abhors a vacuum. Winters had seen it play out in several different ways over the time he had spent fighting the results. Fortunately, or unfortunately, there was always someone to fill the void. In some of the areas it was altruistic, like in Jackson, but in too many areas it was not. Here it was not, and the players didn't have the best reputations, to begin with. They didn't have the honor to volunteer for the war. Instead, they took advantage of the women who were left behind by their husbands and fathers.

By the time Winters had left Sabine, ninety-five percent of the people were already gone or had plans of leaving, which meant there were only a few hundred people left in the area. Like all the other small towns the Shadow Patriots had come into, most were filled with women, children, and the elderly. Not many brave souls to stand up to a bunch of bullies.

All the worries and melancholy weighing Winters down began to vanish as enthusiasm began percolating through his veins. He couldn't leave his hometown to a bunch of bullies. Using food as a weapon was a new one to him, but it was the perfect tool to get what you wanted. What didn't surprise him was that they used it to solicit sex, which always seemed to be a common denominator among all the bad guys he had encountered. One way or the other, it always seemed to boil down to sex.

Ashley had put herself in danger by telling him this because some in the crowd that came to watch the hanging were part of this group that controlled the food. They would know she talked to him so she couldn't go back home, which meant he'd have to find her a safe place for her.

"C'mon, let's go."

"Where are you taking me?"

"Somewhere safe."

"Then what?"

"I'm gonna have a word with these bullies."

"But they have guns."

Winters led her to the back of the van and opened it. Ashley's eyes grew wide looking at all the guns and ammo sitting in the back of the van. Winters was grateful he had the wherewithal to grab a cache of weapons before leaving Jackson. In his state of mind, he wasn't sure when, if ever, he'd be back and didn't want to be empty-handed.

"But those stories about you?"

"Get in and I'll tell ya all about it."

Ashley had Kaitlyn sit on her lap in the front seat and buckled them in. Winters cracked a smile knowing good habits are difficult to break. There wasn't any traffic for hundreds of miles, but still, you felt the need to strap in.

He pulled the van around and headed out of town to a house he knew was off the beaten path. It belonged to his friend, Paul, who had talked him into coming with him to the Patriot Center. The place was empty and was out of the way enough not be found.

Winters glanced over at Ashley. "Did you ever wonder why those stories of me are even out there?"

"I didn't really believe any of them."

"They're partly true."

Ashley stiffened.

"It's true that I lead the Shadow Patriots, but what isn't true is what we do."

Now both Ashley and Kaitlyn stared at Winters as he told them about the Shadow Patriots and what they had been doing. He decided he couldn't tell her the whole story without telling her about the Patriots Centers. Her reaction to the news didn't have the result Winters thought it would. She probably had already come to terms with the fact that her father and husband were more than likely dead.

"So, you see, I can't in good conscience leave my hometown to a bunch of bullies."

"But you're only one person."

He looked at her with a thoughtful expression. "A determined warrior can conquer a whole army if he sets his mind to it."

Ashley didn't seem convinced. She had no idea of what he was capable of doing, which didn't matter to him because he knew what to do. These past months had taught him much, certainly enough to take on a bunch of thieving bullies. He would also use his pent up anger, of which he had plenty to spare and unleash hell on them.

Winters glanced over at them as they stared straight ahead. Looking at her reminded him of Cara, who she had babysat many a time. An interesting idea came over Winters on why he was back home. Was the death of his daughter some kind of a calling? Winters' face began to heat up thinking that in some way he was supposed to come home and that her death had a deeper meaning. A girl who used to baby-sit her was now under his protection. Winters shook his head in order to stop thinking about it. If he dwelt on it any longer, he'd break down in tears and he didn't want to do that in front of Ashley. For now, he took comfort in the fact there was a mission to complete, one that had a purpose. He'd contemplate the deeper meaning later.

CHAPTER 13

JACKSON MICHIGAN

Scar was about to turn the corner of the hall when he heard the thumping of a crutch hitting the carpet. He pulled up short just before running over Reese.

"Well, hey there, Reese."

"Hey Scar," she said, as she put out her arms to give him a hug.

Scar moved in and squeezed hard.

"Hey, are we still good?" asked Reese.

"Of course we are. What makes you think we're not?" asked Scar, keeping his arms on her but pulling back.

"I don't know. I, like, feel weird about this morning is all. I mean, everything just seems different now. And I think I was being a bitch to you and I feel bad about it."

Scar's heart sunk realizing she was depressed and not doing well. "Honey, you don't need to worry about that okay? It's all good."

She nodded and a couple of tears ran down her cheeks.

He pulled her closer and gave her another hug. "I'm sure you're depressed over Cole being gone. We all are, but I know it affects you more."

Tears continued to fall down her face and Scar decided to lead her into an empty room so she wouldn't feel self-conscious about crying in the middle of the hallway. He guided her inside and sat her down. Pulling up a chair next to her, he waited for the tears to slow down. She needed to get this off her chest and hoped he could be of some help. He grabbed a tissue from a box on the table and handed it to her. Scar watched her wipe her face and realized he had never taken the time to talk to her on a personal level. He didn't know how she had been able to handle everything she had gone through. Now that he was the leader, he was responsible for her and wanted to show her that he cared.

"You know Reese, you are without a doubt the toughest girl I've ever met. And if we're to be honest, you're tougher than some of the guys here, well actually, most of the guys here."

Reese let out a small laugh, which encouraged Scar.

"Who else can say they saved Nate's butt twice and not hold it over him."

A hint of a grin spread across her lips. "It's in my back pocket."

"Really?"

"Yes, I just let him think he's free and clear."

"Oh, you are good."

Reese shrugged her shoulders in a non-committal way.

"Well, I hope to be there when you exercise your prerogative."

Reese didn't respond and they sat in silence. Scar didn't want to rush her and waited for her to speak.

Reese finally looked up at him. "Do you miss your wife?"

Not expecting this question, Scar leaned back in his chair. "I do. I think about her every day, you know, wondering how she's doing."

"Is it hard?"

Scar figured she was confused about her feelings for Winters and wasn't sure about what, or how, to think about them, or him.

"It's hard. I'm not gonna lie to ya, Reese. We haven't been separated from each this long since I left for basic training." Scar took in a deep breath before continuing. "I just have to keep reminding myself of what we're doing here and how important it is."

"That helps?"

"Yeah, it does. It's a big sacrifice, but we've all committed to it. You know, everyone here has someone they miss."

Reese gave him a blank stare. "I don't. Well, not until Cole left anyway."

"You don't have any family?" asked Scar in a sad tone.

Reese shook her head. "I only had my mother."

The cops had killed her mother and she had no other family. She was alone in more ways than most people. How hopeless it must be to know her mother had been murdered on top of being tied up and abused for ten days. It explained why she was so torn up by Cole taking off.

Scar grabbed her hand. "Reese, you've got more family here than you know. We all care about you and love you. Both you and Amber are like our daughters and you should know that you are a part of us now. You have a bond with all of us that can never be broken."

Tears began to stream down her cheeks again and Scar fought hard to hold back his own. He'd never talked to anyone about his wife the way he just had with her and it was making him melancholy. He looked into her big watery brown eyes and could see she really was stronger than everyone here. How many people could go through what she did and come out the other side fighting while clinging to their sanity?

"I'm sorry, Scar, I know I'm being a baby."

"No, you're not. Don't even think that."

"It's just so hard. Cole and I were, like, just starting to hit it off and, you know, one second he's here and then the next he's gone. And I feel so guilty about it because, you know, he lost his daughter and here I am being selfish about him being gone. Like I have a bigger loss than he does?"

Scar squeezed her hand tighter. "It's perfectly natural to feel this way, Reese. And, it's not a competition, both are important, so don't go down the road of feeling guilty."

Reese's chin quivered while she gave him a weak nod.

"Listen, Cole will be back."

Reese let out a scoff. "Don't be so sure about that."

Scar tilted his head. "Why do you say that?"

"He never said it, but I know he wants to be done with all of this and has since the beginning."

Scar didn't give that much weight knowing they all wanted to be finished. "Trust me, he is not gonna leave someone as pretty as you behind."

Reese covered her mouth to hide a smile. "You think so?"

"You're definitely a catch, so yeah."

"Even though I'm a little on the psycho side."

"A little?" cracked Scar.

Reese crossed her arms and tilted her head back. "Okay! Fine! Full on psycho."

"Hey, what girl isn't a little on the psycho side."

She raised an eyebrow and curled her lip.

"Oh, I'm just kidding."

She broke out in a smile, which relieved Scar knowing she was in better spirits and was thankful he was able to pull off this feat. He raised a son, not a daughter and didn't have much experience with them. He had been honest with her, and it had been the right approach to use. She may be young, but she had been forced into being an old soul and could detect a lie a mile away.

CHAPTER 14

SABINE IOWA

Winters started to prepare for the night's foray. He had arrived at his friend's house to find someone had vandalized the place despite it being off the beaten path. Kitchen drawers were ripped out and cabinet doors left open. Whoever it was must have been in here looking for food. He laughed to himself knowing that before Paul left he made sure his wife and kids took all the food for their trip south. Other than the kitchen being ransacked the place looked just like he remembered it, although a bit dustier.

After settling in, Ashley gave him a rundown on everything that was going on. She spent thirty minutes going over everything from who they were and where they lived. Billy Gamble, a known drug dealer, led the group. He had three partners that controlled the whole group of guys who ranged in age from their early twenties to late forties and some of them were even married.

The way it worked was for a week's worth of rations; you had to perform once a day to whomever you were assigned to on a schedule. She wasn't sure how many girls were involved but thought it was around thirty or so of various ages. Her daughter wasn't one of them but knew a couple of the girls who were just as young.

Gamble kept adding to the food supply by offering the girls as payment for any food that was brought to him. This encouraged some of the non-members to scavenge the countryside for more food.

It started a couple of months ago and grew bigger as more guys got in on it. There had been some protesting, but Gamble killed two of the protesters. Both were grandfathers of some of the girls. Afterward, Gamble managed to confiscate all the guns and whatever gasoline was left in town in order to keep everyone from leaving. Some of the girls did manage to run away with their families in the dead of the night.

Winters was familiar with a few of the names and unbeknownst to him, he had already killed one of their members today. It didn't surprise him that Tim Sherman had been participating. He and his friends were worthless and some of them were not the kind of people you messed with. Winters shook his head thinking how Judith Sherman accused him of doing things that her own grandson was doing.

Winters sat on the bed and studied the list of names and addresses. He decided to visit one neighborhood where two of the members lived. Both of them were drug addicts and low hanging fruit.

Winters walked into the kitchen where Ashley was feeding her daughter with the food he had brought with him.

"I'll be back by morning," said Winters.

Ashley gave him a worried look.

"If for some reason I don't come back by tomorrow night, take the food and head north into Canada."

Ashley stood up and gave him a hug. "Thank you for doing this."

Winters looked down at Kaitlyn and gave her a high-five before heading to his van to check his weapons. He then went into Paul's garage, who was quite the handyman and found some zip ties. He wasn't sure if he needed them, but he didn't have all the names of those involved, so if he could, he'd try to interrogate a few of them.

Winters pulled out of the driveway and ten minutes later was within a mile of his first destination. Knowing the police van stuck out like a sore thumb, he drove it into a barren field and hid it in a small wooded area. Powering up his night-vision goggles, he set out to the first house. He took extra care as he moved through the quiet neighborhood. No one was outside, and he didn't expect to run into anyone, but still took his time and kept alert. His pulse quickened the closer he came to his destination. He was operating alone and hadn't done so since he had raided the train station. Of course, since then his skills and confidence had increased a hundred fold.

He entered the small neighborhood and looked at the dark houses, which all looked abandoned, but he couldn't be sure. Since the town had no electricity, it was difficult to know who was still around. As he walked down the sidewalk, he heard the familiar sound of a generator. It was a small one, which wouldn't put out a lot of power, but enough for some lights and a radio.

He followed the sound and wasn't surprised when it led to his first target. Randy Stratton, a thirty-five-year-old, who was a known drug addict and low-life. At one time, the kid played high school basketball but was kicked off the team for fighting. The fighting was only a symptom of a larger problem that had started with drinking and eventually led to using Meth.

He moved in closer to the one-story house where a dim light shone through a window. Winters bolted across the lawn and tightened his grip on the Colt M-4 rifle as he reached the side of the house. He flipped up his goggles to look in the window and let out a scoff. Inside, Randy Stratton hovered over a young girl who he had handcuffed to the bed.

"So, he likes to tie them up as well," thought Winters.

Before turning away, he noticed a pistol on the nightstand and decided not to take any chances with him. Winters flipped his goggles back down and crept to the back porch where the small generator chugged along. He nodded his head knowing his next move.

.

CHAPTER 15

Not wanting to wait until he finished with her, Winters found the switch to the generator and flipped it off. The motor stopped and the lights went out. Winters pushed the switch back to the on position knowing that Randy would think it was out of gas. He then moved off to the side and crouched down behind a bush to wait for his target.

He didn't have to wait long before Randy came out onto the porch in his birthday suit holding a flashlight. He moved the beam of light around before pointing it on the generator. He took off the gas cap and looked inside.

"Damn piece of junk," said Randy, pulling on the cord.

The generator started back up and Winters jumped into action. Randy turned to open the screen door as Winters decided to do what had been done to him earlier in the day. He used the butt end of his rifle and smashed it into the small of Randy's back.

The crack echoed in the air as Randy buckled to the floor and cried out in pain.

Winters pointed the M-4 to his face and said in a calm manner, "do something stupid and I'll pull the trigger."

Randy's eyes grew big and he nodded.

Winters took out a zip-tie and cuffed his hands behind his back.

"Now get up," said Winters, as he pulled him up off the floor.

"What the hell," he protested.

"Get inside."

"Hey man, you can't do this to me, alright."

"I can and I am."

Winters pushed him down the hallway to the bedroom. The girl's eyes grew wild when they entered the room, and she flailed her arms against the handcuffs.

"I'm not gonna hurt you, okay?" said Winters.

The girl nodded hesitantly.

Winters looked at Randy. "Keys?"

"So, like what, you want a turn with her?"

Winters balled up his fist and belted him in the stomach. Randy fell to the ground, and Winters bent down to pick him up. As he grabbed him under his arm, Randy spit at him. Winters backed way and wiped the slime from his cheek before swinging at him again landing a blow across his face.

Randy toppled over and let out a laugh.

"He's as high as a kite, Mister," said the girl. "He ain't feeling anything."

"Certainly explains the bravado. Do you know where the key is?"

"On the dresser, I think."

Winters picked up a blanket up off the floor and draped it over her. Her shoulder length brown hair was tousled and strands came down over her dark thick eyebrows. She had a few small butterfly tattoos on her thigh. "What's your name?"

"Finley."

"Finley, I like that, how old are you?"

"Sixteen."

Winters gritted his teeth remembering the party house when he rescued Reese and the other girls. He remembered how angry he was then and the vow he made to never let anyone hold a girl for a sex slave. This young girl like the others in town did it for food. Food! In some ways, this was even more devious as you weren't being forced into the exchange, you joined by your own choice. It wasn't a great choice, but still, one you made.

Winters needed to let off a little steam so he moved back over to Randy and kicked him in the face. Blood splattered out of his nose as he let out a loud yell. Winters fumbled around on the cluttered dresser looking for the handcuff key.

"Got it."

He moved back over to Finley and took the cuffs off. "Does your mother know?"

She nodded while rubbing her wrist.

"Why don't you put your clothes on."

"I can't go home."

"Why not?"

"Because I can't."

Winters waited for her to finish.

"I have to go to see Jarvis later."

Winters was confused because Ashley told him it was one person a day and asked her about it.

"Sometimes I do double duty to get more rations for my sister so she doesn't have to work."

Mister Hyde started crawling around inside Winters' gut. He struggled to maintain control and asked how old her sister was.

"Kayley is twelve."

Winters moved his hand over to the hilt of his knife and squeezed hard. He needed to let off more steam and turned toward Randy before turning back to Finley.

"Do you know all the guys involved and where they live?"

Finley nodded.

Her answer gave Winters a perverse pleasure knowing he no longer needed to interrogate Randy for more of the names. "Honey, why don't you go and put your clothes on and meet me in the living room. We'll figure out how best I can help you and your sister."

She got up and reached for the pile of clothes on the floor before scooting down the hall and into the bathroom.

Winters waited for her to leave before moving over to Randy who appeared to be zoning out. He grabbed him by the hair as he pulled out his knife.

"It's your lucky day, Randy."

He looked at him with blank eyes.

"I'm not gonna interrogate you," Winters said putting his hand over Randy's mouth before sinking the blade deep into his throat. Air gurgled out as Randy's eyes grew frantic while his body twitched on the carpet.

Winters let out a deep, gratifying sigh and casually cleaned the bloody blade on the bed covers before shoving it back into the sheath. He grabbed the Glock 17 off the nightstand and tucked it in his waistband. He looked at his watch and saw that it was ten o'clock. The night was young, and he had much to do before it was over.

He shut the bedroom door and tramped down the hallway to the living room. The bathroom door opened just as he was passing by. Finley came out wearing jeans and a yellow Iowa football t-shirt with the number sixteen on it. She noticed the door was shut and asked him about Randy.

"He won't be bothering you again," said Winters.

She gave him a knowing nod and asked who he was.

"I'm Cole Winters."

"Oh, wow, so it's true. They said you were in town and that you killed Tim Sherman."

"News gets around fast."

"They say you rape little girls."

"They do say that now, don't they?"

"Well, I'm little and you didn't rape me, so I'd say that's all just a pack of lies."

"Then you would be correct."

"Are you gonna stop what's going on here?"

Winters glared into her brown eyes and nodded.

The revelation seemed to put her in a good mood, as Winters noticed she was in better spirits than before. He needed more information from her and asked about her family. She told him that her two older brothers and father were fighting in the war. That her mom begged her not to participate in the food exchange, but she had no choice when they ran out of their own secret stash. Her mom tried to take her place, but the men laughed at her because she was old and overweight. It was Finley's idea to do the double duty to protect her sister.

She told him that her next stop was a few blocks over and she needed to be there by midnight.

"There's another one just up the street. Do you know who it is?"

"Oh yeah, that's Jimmy Boyd."

"Would there be a girl there now?"

60

"No. He's at home with his wife right now."

"Does his wife know?"

Finley let out a nervous laugh. "Of course she does. I mean she's in on it. Like the whole town knows."

"I see," said Winters, noticing a slight change in her. She began blinking her eyes rapidly and fidgeting. "You alright?"

"Well, you know, I don't want you to think, like, I'm a slut. I mean, I do this to, like, help my mom and sister."

Winters put a hand on her shoulder. "Finley, I don't think that at all. You're doing what you have to do to feed your family and that's all. If anything, I think you're pretty damn brave."

"Really?" she asked in a sincere tone.

"Oh, gosh yes."

"Alright, cool."

Winters let out a short breath seeing her happy with his response. It was interesting to hear how she didn't want him to judge her even though they had just met. He put the thought out of his mind for now and focused on the situation at hand. He bobbed his head from side to side while considering his next step. He had a list of people he needed to eliminate tonight. It was crucial to take out as many of these bastards as possible. By tomorrow it was going to be much more difficult. The problem he now had was a passenger who lived several miles from here and he didn't want to leave her alone now since he had killed her *John*. There was no sense in taking the chance of getting her in trouble with the rest of the gang. Besides, it was becoming clear he'd be picking up more passengers before the night was over.

A loud bang came from the front door sent a shiver up Winters' spine. He spun around just as Finley jumped into action.

CHAPTER 16

WASHINGTON D.C.

S tormy's eyes sparkled as she plastered a big smile on her face while approaching Gerald Perozzi's table. Because of the importance of what she was doing, she had to practice this several times in the ladies room. It helped to psych herself up and it was not unlike prepping for a match in the ring. Only here, she'd be receiving sexual advances instead of blows from an opponent.

"Well, hello there, Stormy," greeted an overexcited Perozzi.

"Gerald, how are you, sir?"

"Now that you're here, I'm doing exceptionally well."

Stormy chuckled to herself. "Are you flirting with me, sir?"

Perozzi nodded. "How am I doing?"

"Better than most, I would say. At least you're honest about it."

"I do my best."

"At flirting or being honest?"

"Flirting, of course, there's no fun in being honest."

"But isn't that an admission of honesty?" she asked with raised eyebrows.

Perozzi let out a laugh. "You are one quick witted girl."

"Yes, and as I told you before, it gets me into trouble all the time."

"Which means you're not the boring type."

"I don't know about that. So, what can I get you?"

"My usual."

"Is your friend joining you?" asked Stormy.

"Oh, no, he won't be joining us for quite some time."

"Hmm, too bad," she responded with a smirk.

Stormy returned to the bar and put in his order. Her breathing relaxed a little bit now that she was back into the swing of things with Perozzi. She laughed to herself, wondering why she had been nervous, to begin with. The old man was putty in her hands and couldn't keep his eyes off her breasts. He wanted her and would do anything to get her, which was how she wanted it in case anything came up.

She placed his drink on the tray and headed back to his table when she noticed out of the corner of her eye that two cops in suits were approaching. She could spot undercover cops anywhere. She took a deep breath and hurried to Perozzi's table trying to remain calm.

"Here you go, Gerald."

"Thank you, Stormy. It's too bad you couldn't join me."

The cops were almost to her, so she took advantage of his offer. "Well, I get off at ten."

Perozzi's eyes widened at her response.

The two cops stopped at her side.

"Stormy Robinson," said Lieutenant Wagner.

She turned toward them. "Yes, that's me."

"I need you to come with me."

"Excuse me?"

"You are to come with me for questioning."

"About what? I haven't done anything wrong."

"I didn't say you did."

Perozzi slammed his drink down. "What's the meaning of this?"

"Excuse me, but this doesn't concern you," said Wagner.

Stormy backed away from the table, and the other cop grabbed her arm. She fought off her first instinct, which was to twist his hand around and punch him in the face. She didn't want Perozzi to know what she was capable of, so instead, she let the cop manhandle her to the next table. He threw his weight on her back while twisting her arm up behind her. Her right cheek hit the table as she waited for him to throw on the cuffs.

"You let go of her," yelled Perozzi as he stood up.

"Back away, sir," said Wagner.

"Do you know who I am?" asked Perozzi.

"No sir, I don't, and it doesn't matter because she's coming with me."

Perozzi puffed out his chest. "I don't think so."

Three large men came running toward them with guns drawn. Wagner reached for his own gun and pulled it out.

"You might want to rethink that one," said Perozzi.

Perozzi's bodyguards started yelling at Wagner to drop his weapon and he did as he was told. Another bodyguard grabbed the other cop's gun and then pushed him to the wall.

Stormy breathed a sigh of relief and was glad she had decided to let Perozzi handle this.

"Now, exactly who are you?" demanded Perozzi.

"I'm Lieutenant Wagner, and I've been ordered to bring her in for questioning. And who may I ask are you?"

"Who gave you these orders?"

"I'm not at liberty to say and I suggest you unhand me and let me do my job."

"Son, I'm Gerald Perozzi and you'll answer my questions or you'll find yourself at the bottom of a river."

The color drained from Wagner's face. "I...I didn't know, sir. I'm sorry, sir."

Perozzi stared at him with impatient eyes.

"Mister Reed ordered me."

Perozzi shook his head. "I should have known it was him."

"Lieutenant, you've been dealt a very bad hand tonight. Mister Reed is...let's just say he has a personal vendetta against this girl. So, I would suggest you take those cuffs off and leave while you still can."

Wagner gave him a humble nod and approached Stormy while pulling his key out. He took the cuffs off and asked if he could go.

Stormy started to rub her wrist and made a big act out of it while watching the two cops walk back down the hallway. She didn't have much trouble acting nervous and started to shake a little bit. She hoped Perozzi would rescue her, but wasn't really sure he would, so she had already developed a backup plan of escape once they were outside.

"There, there, you okay, Stormy?" asked a concerned Perozzi.

"I...I'm a little shaken is all."

"Nothing to worry about," said Perozzi as he put his hand on her back.

She cringed at his touch but needed to let him be the big protector.

"I just can't believe Mister Reed would be this angry with me," said Stormy.

"Yes, well, he's gone too far, I can tell you that."

"You won't let him hurt me will you?" asked Stormy, playing it up.

"Don't you worry about that."

Stormy's boss, Robert, came waltzing in asking if she needed anything.

"I think Stormy needs the rest of the night off," said Perozzi.

"No, no, I'm okay. I just need to splash some water on my face."

She turned and hurried to the ladies' room. Pushing the door open, she let out a sigh of relief and then turned on the faucet, cupped her hands, and splashed water on her face. The cold water refreshed her senses. She looked in the mirror thinking about her next move. Perozzi would offer to take her home, which she didn't want to have happen because he would insist on coming inside. She shivered at the thought of the old man touching her let alone hopping in the sack with him. Besides, having to go to Manassas tonight, she didn't want him to know where she lived. However, she needed his protection from Reed, and if she offended him, he might not be so forthcoming. She kept staring in the mirror, and then it dawned on her why Reed wanted to talk to her. He must have done a background check on her, and if that was the case he would know she was from Brainerd. "Not good, sweetie," she whispered at the mirror.

An idea struck her and she started breathing in hard and fast working herself back into hysterics. She exited the bathroom and snuck into the kitchen to find her manager in his office.

"Robert, I'm...I'm really shaken up. I need to go."

"Yes, of course, but what about Mister Perozzi? He's going to want to see you."

She sat down on a chair next to him and put her hand on his arm. "Could you do me a favor and tell him thank you, but I just needed to get out of here."

Robert gave her a firm nod. "No problem, I'll take care of it."

She squeezed his arm and scooted out the back door of the restaurant hurrying to her white BMW. She looked all around making sure no one was watching. She started it up and took off satisfied with her exit strategy. Perozzi would just think she was too scared to stay, which would make him even angrier with Reed. She let out a laugh knowing Reed, with little effort, had helped prod Perozzi a little closer to their goal.

CHAPTER 17

SABINE IOWA

The banging on the front door startled Winters and he jerked his head back as Finley leaped into action. She put her finger to her lips and motioned Winters to move behind the door. He slipped into position as she pulled it open.

Finley locked the screen door as she called out, "Jimmy Boyd, why am I not surprised to see you here? And where's your wife?"

"I'm right here, sweetie."

"Wanting a threesome now do we?"

"You know we do,"

"Well, I'm sorry, but Randy is dead tired, so he can't join ya."

"Ha, ha. You know it's you we want," said Jimmy, as he pulled on the screen door. "Now, unlock the door."

"It's against the rules, Jimmy."

"You never complained before and we got some food here for ya."

"I don't want your food, besides, I've got to get over to see Jarvis."

"You got a couple of hours before you need to be there, now open up."

"No."

Winters raised his eyebrows impressed by her bantering with these fools. She had the same kind of smart mouth Sadie had. She could outwit anyone, and this girl was just as good if not better. Of course, Finley knew who was backing her up on the other side of the door. Good. She deserved this moment of empowerment. Winters found it surprising to learn the wife was just as guilty as the husband was. He hadn't been sure about what he was going to do with her but now made up his mind on her fate.

"What the hell's gotten into you? Where's Randy?"

"I told ya, I wore him out tonight. He is dead tired," said Finley in a humorous tone.

Jimmy grabbed the door handle and started shaking it. "Open this damn door, Wannabe, you hear me."

"An odd nickname," thought Winters.

"If I have to rip open this screen, Wannabe, I'm gonna beat your ass."

"Finally, something you're good at, cause it sure as hell isn't screwing."

Winters formed a lopsided grin and nodded his head. "That was a good one."

"You little bitch. I swear I'm gonna beat the hell out of you."

Winters flipped down his goggles figuring the show was about over.

The sound of the generator got louder when the back door opened. Jimmy's wife ambled through the dark kitchen toward Finley, who was oblivious to her presence. She wound up her right arm when Winters stepped forward and met her with his right arm throwing her off balance. In one swift motion, he covered her mouth, pulled out his knife, and sliced her throat from ear to ear. He laid her down in the darkness and whispered to Finley to let Jimmy in.

"Okay, Jimmy, you win," she said unlocking the door before stepping backward.

He stormed inside and wrapped his hand around Finley's throat squeezing hard.

Winters grabbed onto the back of Jimmy's hair and pulled him off her. He tripped over Winters' foot and screamed out as a knife plunged into his stomach. Jimmy's blood began soaking his dirty white t-shirt as Winters jammed the blade into his throat.

Finley stared through the darkness wide-eyed and didn't say anything as Winters stood up. He couldn't decide if she was surprised or in shock as to what just happened.

"You okay?"

"That was awesome. I mean you just took out those two slimy jackasses and you did it, like, really fast and without, like, any kind of bother. Mister Winters, you are a badass."

"Oh, well, I thought you might be in some kind of shock or something."

"Hell, no. Those two deserved it, I mean, let me tell ya something, I've been, like, having to put up with these two dirt bags because, Randy was, like, always trading out his time with me for drugs. I mean, these two aren't even on my list and they smell, I mean they really, really smell bad. And, I swear they never brush their teeth, their breath is disgusting.

Winters scratched the side of his head and started laughing to himself at how fast she was chatting. A big weight had lifted off her shoulders, which opened the floodgates of non-stop chatter.

She continued as she waved her hands around. "Did you hear how I was mouthing off to him? I swear I was laughing so hard on the inside. Like, I thought I was gonna pee my pants. I mean, I have been dying to say these things in, like, forever, but I couldn't, cause I mean, you know, I had to act all meek and mousy and pretend I was really enjoying myself. Oh man, I just can't stop talking."

"I can see that. Why don't you splash some water on your face and maybe take a couple of deep breaths?"

"Okay, yeah, yeah, I'll try that," she said while turning on a battery operated lamp sitting on the counter.

Winters flipped the goggles up and curiously watched as Finley splashed cold water on her face a few times as she danced at the sink.

None of the girls he had rescued before had acted like this probably because the situation was different from the others. These girls were not being held captive and even lived at home. They had crappy choices, but still, they made them. What an odd thing. Did they understand that even though they didn't have physical chains, they still wore them? Winters shook his head figuring it was for psychologists to debate.

Finley grabbed a towel to wipe her face and then put her hair in a ponytail. "Hey, let's go get Jarvis now. I guarantee you that boy is stoned out of his mind right now. I can help you out too, okay? I mean, you know, I can help with any of them really, I mean I can totally help you stop these suckers."

Winters nodded. "Okay, but on one condition."

"Sure, anything, I mean I'll do anything," said Finley, who hadn't stopped moving around.

"When we get outside, you need to stop talking, okay?"

"Oh, yeah, I'm sorry. I talk a lot when I'm nervous." Finley looked down at Jimmy and his wife. "I mean, I've, like, never seen anyone get killed before, but wow, what a rush."

"I understand. Are you going to be able to handle yourself?"

"Mister Winters, I'm totally up for this. I hate these bastards for what they've been doing to us."

"Good, now just do me a favor and call me, Cole."

She nodded twice. "Okay, Cole."

Winters wanted her to settle down and decided to ask about the nickname he heard.

"So, can I ask why he called you, Wannabe?"

"Yeah, cuz, you know, I supposedly want B's, so, you know, Wannabe."

Winters gave her a confused look.

"You know, B cups, you've seen me, I'm flat-chested."

Winters' face turned bright red and he didn't know what to say.

"It's okay, Mister Winters, I mean Cole, I don't really care."

Winters couldn't change the subject fast enough and asked her to write down all the names and addresses of the guys involved. She took the list Ashley started and completed it in a few minutes. Winters studied the list and nodded in satisfaction. He then escorted her outside. He put his hand to his lips when she started to ask him another question. She raised her hands up and whispered an apology. They scurried through the darkness to Jarvis' house. When they arrived, Finley grabbed his arm and told him Jarvis had company.

CHAPTER 18

After checking Randy and Jimmy Boyd off the list, Finley led Winters to her next stop. He was intrigued by the spunky girl who took a bad situation for what it was and dealt with it as best she could. Despite the fact that what she was doing would be frowned upon by any civilized society, she was providing for her mom and little sister. Anyone desperate for food could rationalize that it was acceptable and use it to get through a bad situation. However, her enthusiasm for helping him was evidence enough that she didn't like what she was doing and wanted it to change.

They arrived at Jarvis' house and found a couple of vehicles in the driveway. Finley whispered to him that he was having a party with his friends. Jarvis also had a generator running to power the house.

Winters escorted her across the street behind an overgrown hedgerow. He scanned the area with the night-vision goggles and didn't see anyone outside.

"How many do you think are there?"

"Definitely three, maybe four," whispered Finley.

"More girls?"

"Oh, yeah, two maybe three."

Winters continued to look across the street.

"Hey, can I try those?"

Winters took the goggles off and helped her put them on.

"Oh, cool, you can see everything, and it's all green."

Winters remembered the first time he had tried them on and of having the same reaction. It was like looking at a TV screen or being in a video game. He'd been using them long enough now to not give it a second thought. He let her keep them on while he asked more questions.

"Will any of them be armed?"

"Hmm, probably just Derek. He usually has, like, a gun on him."

"What does he look like?"

"Tall and skinny. He'll be the only blond haired guy. But I wouldn't worry too much though, because I guarantee you, like, everyone in there is already stoned."

"Even the girls?"

"Yeah, I mean, you know, it helps you through the night."

Winters understood and brushed it off. If anything, it was going to help him accomplish what he was about to do. The last thing he needed was a bunch of girls screaming and getting in the way. He wanted to make sure she was correct with her assumptions and came up with a plan. She agreed and took off the goggles before running across the street. He watched her enter the house and sat there waiting for her signal.

It took five minutes before a pen light turned on in the middle window. The light blinked four times signaling there were four guys and then two longer blinks for two girls. Winters' heart quickened as he ran across the street. He had decided if they were stoned then there was no need to turn off the generator, which would only alert everyone. He wanted them in there as relaxed as possible. He would just go in the front door that Finley had promised to leave unlocked.

He reached the handle and let out a breath as he opened the door. The door opened into a small foyer where the smell of marijuana was obvious. Mixed in were various odors from incense and candles. Winters heard soft music coming from the living room. He peeked around the corner. A lamp was turned on low and there were a few lit candles scattered around four people, two of which were in the throes of sex on the couch. Winters pulled out his knife and approached a couple who were sitting together on a smaller couch. The man, who looked to be in his late twenties, had dark hair and was wearing headphones listening to his own music with his eyes closed. The teen girl also had her eyes closed and didn't notice Winters cover his target's mouth before pressing down to slice his throat. The victim's arms reached up for a moment before falling back to the cushion.

This kill reminded him of his first ones back at the train station. He had snuck in on sleeping men who had been drinking. He had been scared and unsure of how to do it. Of course, now he was an experienced killer and didn't hesitate or question what he was doing.

The girl next to his first victim never moved a muscle. The other two across the room were still going at it and Winters decided to wait on them. He wanted to know where Finley was and heard voices over the soft music coming from the back.

He started down the hallway and slid against the wall to the first opened door. He took a quick peek to find no one there. He looked at the half opened shade where Finley had signaled him. Voices came from the back bedroom where the door was open and a low light spilled out into the hall.

"C'mon, Wannabe, take it."

"I don't want it, Derek."

"Take it," yelled another.

Winters crept in closer and figured the other one was Jarvis. They didn't sound too stoned, but then he didn't know much about it.

"Wannabe, you've got a long night ahead of you, so don't be testing me."

"Testing you? Don't make me laugh, Derek. Have you ever passed a test? I mean, I heard you even flunked your GED."

Winters struggled to hold back a laugh. He then heard a slap and Finley curse aloud. Then another slap as Winters came through the door to find a blonde man knocking Finley to the ground. The blonde, who had to be Derek, fell on top of her and grabbed her arms. The other one cheered him on. Winters swung his left arm around Jarvis, covered his mouth, and sliced his throat. The man went limp in his arms and Winters let go of him. He fell to the carpet with a loud thud, but not enough to alert Derek.

Winters then stepped over the dead man and grabbed onto Derek's blonde hair pulling him backward off Finley.

"What?" Derek yelled out confused.

Finley kicked him in the face before Winters thrust his knife into the side of his neck. Blood ran down Derek's neck as he floundered on the carpet before taking his last breath.

Winters looked at Finley's red face as she stared at Derek. "You alright?"

She nodded and got up off the floor. Her eyes lit up under her thick eyebrows. "Did you hear my GED joke? That was so worth the beat down, I mean, his jaw, like, about hit the floor."

"Keep it down, I've got one more."

"Who?"

Winters shrugged his shoulders. "They were getting it on."

"Oh, that's Laney and Owen."

"But he's one of them, right?"

"Oh, gosh yes, he's like thirty and she's only seventeen."

Winters shook his head in disgust. He padded back down the hall to find Owen still on the couch with her. Finley followed and scurried around him as they came into the living room. She grabbed a tall wooden candle holder that held a lit candle and swung it at Owen. The blow landed on his back as the candle went flying.

"What the hell?" yelled Owen as he turned around to see Finley holding the makeshift club. "Whaddya go and do that for, Wannabe?"

Finley swung it again, but he blocked the blow and jumped off Laney. He stood up in his birthday suit and hadn't yet noticed Winters, who stepped back having decided to see just what Finley was made of. She stood five-foot-five and was full of energy. Did she have the nerve to follow through with her mouth? He would let her have another minute or so before taking Owen out.

She swung again but missed as she wasn't close enough to him. He then rushed her, but Finley stepped to the side and landed another blow on his back as he stumbled past her. He came at her again and she danced to the side again. His reflexes were dulled by whatever he had taken.

"What the hell you doing, Wannabe?"

"What I should have done a long time ago."

Owen puffed his chest out. "You're dead. You hear me, dead."

Finley started laughing while swinging the club back and forth. "No,

Owen, you're the one who's dead."

"Brave words, little girl."

"Are they?" she asked pointing the candlestick at the bloody corpse on the loveseat.

Owen turned to see blood running down his friend's neck. His jaw fell open as he asked, "Is he dead?"

"Damn right he is."

Winters looked over at his handiwork and grimaced at how much blood had oozed out after he left. It looked gruesome enough to shock anyone. He then caught a movement in the corner of his eye. Laney, a five-foot-two light brown haired girl, jumped on Owen's back and wrapped her legs around him while pulling his hair. The quick action surprised Owen and Finley took advantage by charging him. She used the candlestick holder as a battering ram and belted him in the stomach knocking out his wind. He collapsed to his knees. Finley swung at him but Owen managed to grab onto the makeshift club. He pulled hard to wrestle control away from her as she leaned backward while still holding on. Laney got off his back and started punching the side of his head with little effect. All three began screaming at each other.

Winters stepped back amazed as he watched the struggle unfold before him. The two girls were battling a common foe and appeared to be in control. Winters figured they both needed this, and he decided to allow them to take it as far as they could.

With her blows not having much effect, Laney reached for a vodka bottle that was sitting on an end table. After grabbing it, she wound up and hit him across the head. Liquid splashed out as it landed with a loud thud, but it didn't break. Laney tried again, striking him on top of his head. Again, more liquid drained out, but the bottle didn't break. The blow caused Owen's arms to go limp, and he let go of the candlestick making Finley fall over backward. She scrambled up, and both girls looked encouragingly at each other before striking him again. Their blows landed one after another. Laney finally broke the bottle on the next try. Glass and vodka shot out in different directions as blood poured down the side of Owen's head. He fell over and Finley gave him one final blow.

CHAPTER 19

Winters wasn't sure if he was surprised at either the viciousness of these two girls or the eagerness of the attack on Owen. He had only met Finley, but she didn't seem to be a violent person. However, escaping the bonds of slavery is such an overwhelming sensation that it puts you in a different frame of mind. He'd witnessed it with Reese when she killed three of her oppressors as soon as she was released. These two didn't seem much different from Reese. Winters had been confused when he learned what was going on and how the girls handled it. He wasn't sure if or how much it bothered them, but having seen these two in action, he realized they hated it.

Winters stepped into the living room where the two girls were breathing rapidly over their victim. His movement startled Laney and her eyes grew wild as she flung her hand up using the broken neck of the bottle as a defensive weapon.

"It's okay, Laney," said Finley. "He's with me."

Laney swayed from side to side while keeping the jagged glass aimed at Winters.

Finley dropped the candlestick "Laney, this is Cole Winters."

She darted her eyes between Finley and Winters and began nodding in recognition. She then realized her state of undress and dropped the bottle before using her arms to cover up. She stared at Winters as he bent down to check on Owen.

"Is he dead?" asked Finley.

"Not yet, but he will be."

"Oh man, did you see us? I mean, I can't believe we just did that. And Laney, the way you jumped on him, I mean, like, that was so friggin awesome. I knew we could get him, and Cole, I'm so glad you, like, didn't stop us. I so wanted to do this."

Winters closed his eyes and shook his head slightly at how fast this girl talked. Of course, she had good reason to. It wasn't every day you had an opportunity to beat on someone who has been tormenting you.

"Laney, I mean, wow, what gave you the courage?"

She looked at Finley. "I didn't want him to hurt you. And the way you were standing up to him, it, like, gave me the courage to do the same."

"Yeah, but Laney, I knew Cole was there, like, the whole time, but you didn't, I mean you were so awesome to do what you just did. You're the brave one here."

Winters stood up. "Girls, believe me, you're both incredibly brave. This isn't even something a lot of guys can do."

"Seriously, Cole, you're not just saying that?"

"Oh, no. You two remind me of a couple of girls who fight with me and believe me, they're both bad assess."

"You hear that, Laney? We're a couple of badass chicks," said Finley in an excited tone.

Winters wanted to get out of there and head to the next place. He looked over at the sleeping girl, who still hadn't moved. He would need to get her to safety before going after his next target.

"Finley, can you wake her up?"

"Probably not."

"Well, give it a try, okay? Cause we need to get out of here."

Laney grabbed her things and ran to the bathroom while Finley attempted to wake the girl, whose name he hadn't learned yet. He now had three passengers and decided to take one of the vehicles in the driveway. He'd have to take the sleeping girl back to where he was staying and have

Ashley look after her for the night. In the morning, he'd have to find out where everyone would want to stay while he took out the remaining bad guys. The faster he moved tonight the less difficult it would be to take out the rest tomorrow. He considered hiding the bodies, but there was so much spilled blood to clean up that it wouldn't be worth the effort.

"Blair isn't waking up."

"Okay, I'll carry her then," said Winters learning the girl's name. "We need keys to one of those cars. Can you help me?"

"Yep."

Winters trotted down the hallway and rifled through the bedroom looking for keys. He knelt down beside the dead bodies and went through their pockets coming up empty. He found Derek's pistol, a Sig Sauer .380, on the dresser and put it in his jacket.

"Found 'em," yelled Finley.

Winters headed back to the living room where she handed him the keys. They were to a blue four-door Impala, which would be perfect to get them out of there. He heard Laney come out and saw she was dressed in jean shorts and a checkered pattern tank top. He hadn't realized just how small she was until then. She looked dainty and underfed, which surprised him since she had been able to do what she had just done. Finley's extra three inches over Laney made a big difference. She also had small butterfly tattoos on the side of her leg. Winters hoped it wasn't some kind of a slave brand.

After picking up Blair and putting her in the back seat, Winters went back inside to finish off Owen, who still hadn't died yet. He didn't want him to somehow survive and tell the tale.

Winters powered up his night-vision goggles and drove the Impala back to where he left Ashley and her daughter. The two girls chatted non-stop about what they just did and how much they wanted to keep helping. Winters wasn't too sure he should involve them any further, but both continued to work him over.

"We won't get in the way, and besides, we know who everybody is," pleaded Finley.

"And you could use the lookouts," said Laney.

Winters shook his head knowing he was about to give in to them.

Their pleading reminded him of when Cara would work him over. He had a weakness for her wishes and always gave in when she was younger. He decided to make it conditional, however, because he wanted to know about the butterfly tattoos.

"Alright, I'll let you guys come along," said Winters.

"Yes," said Laney from the backseat.

"I swear, you won't regret it," said Finley."

"But."

"But what?" asked Finley.

"First ya gotta tell me about the butterfly tattoos."

Laney leaned forward. "That's easy."

"Yeah," said Finley.

"They're a reminder for us," said Laney.

"That we can, like, have a rebirth when all of this is over and leave all of it behind us," said Finley.

"And…to not give up hope that it will end," said Laney.

"Yeah, and something tells me we're gonna have our rebirth tonight," said Finley.

"I'm already feeling it," said Laney, grabbing Finley's hand.

"Me too. I mean, it's like we're already starting to come out of this disgusting cocoon that we've been, like, locked in."

"Right," said Laney, "it's why we want to help you. It means everything to us to help."

"Does everyone have them?" asked Winters.

"No, not everyone, just some of us," said Laney.

"A friend of ours did 'em. They're not fancy, but we like 'em," said Finley.

"Well, I like 'em too," said Winters. "A good reminder to hang tough and to stay united.

Winters leaned his head on the backrest absorbing everything they said. They had great attitudes and looked forward to the future figuring their current situation wouldn't last forever. They were hopeful and in the country's current situation, sometimes hope is all you have to rely on.

They arrived back at the new hideout and Ashley was happy to look after Blair and any others that might be arriving tonight. He kept the visit short and ushered his new *fighters* back into the car. He was glad to learn Laney knew how to shoot. Her father had taken took her hunting at an early age, and she had done considerable target shooting as well. Winters handed her the Sig Sauer. She did a proper check of the weapon when he handed it to her much to Finley's amazement. Finley was the more athletic of the two and played soccer. She also loved watching football, which was why she wore a yellow Iowa football jersey.

Winters headed back to town toward their next target and took a right turn just as a pickup truck sped past him. A shock zipped through his body when he looked in the rearview mirror. The truck had stopped and Winters was supposed to do the same.

CHAPTER 20

JACKSON MICHIGAN

Bassett was running behind schedule for getting tonight's operation together. He hurried down to the cafeteria to grab something before heading out again. He chose a ready-made sandwich and coffee then sat down to eat.

He thought about Scar's suggestion that they take Nordell with them tonight. Scar had told him the man apologized for what happened this morning at the executions. Bassett took a bite of the peanut butter and jelly sandwich before washing it down with some coffee. Of course, if Nordell came with them, it would ensure he wouldn't have a chance to cause any more trouble here. No telling what could happen if all the leadership was gone.

Nordell was proud and perhaps thought he was better suited to command than Scar. While Bassett had no doubt about the man's experience and capabilities, he didn't have the same rapport with the men that Scar had. He was still too new to everyone and besides; he had held a gun to Winters' head when he first came on the scene. This was not something you forgot. While he had made up for it over the past week, some of the men didn't care and didn't trust him, and now that he had been the ringleader this morning, he would be even more distrusted.

Bassett finished his sandwich and headed outside. He exited the hospital and looked across the parking lot for his SUV. He noticed the old Chevy pickup Winters had been driving still sitting in the parking lot with the windows down. He hoped Winters would find what he was looking for back in Iowa. Bassett's mind drifted to his own family who were in Florida. After the Chinese invaded California, his parents took his two younger sisters down to Fort Myers where his grandparents lived. They had a home right off McGregor Boulevard, which ran along the river with easy access to the Gulf of Mexico.

Bassett had just come back from a tour in the Middle East and was only able to visit with them in Yoder, Indiana, for a couple of weeks before he received orders to report for duty at the Rock Island Arsenal, in Rock Island, Illinois. This was unusual as he was in the 101st Airborne Division and there was no active army unit he was aware of at Rock Island. Besides, the Army had been shipping most of its soldiers out west to fight the Chinese. The orders had given Bassett pause making him question why they were putting a unit together in the Midwest. Not trusting the new government, he suggested to his parents that they get to Florida while they still could. His mistrust of the government proved right and he was thankful they headed out of the area when they did. There had been a Patriot Center in Indiana and many volunteers had reported to it, of course, they were all now dead.

Bassett jumped into his vehicle and started it. As he pulled out of the parking lot, Major Green came to mind. Before being assigned to Rock Island he had never met the man, but quickly recognized him to be a stand-up soldier and was grateful he had been picked to help with the cause. Thinking back to their assignment in the Midwest now, it didn't add up, but at the time with the country in the throes of chaos, it seemed plausible. The government wanted citizens to join the military, making perfect sense then because there were bands of marauders roaming the countryside killing innocent Americans. It was a sickening feeling to discover you were part of an evil plan to kill the volunteers. It was a just cause when Green killed Colonel Nunn. He never came right out and admitted it, but everyone knew he had done it and didn't care. They were all glad he did it and would no longer have to be a part of the slaughter of patriotic volunteers. Bassett shook his head knowing the guys were reassigned out west and no doubt were at the front lines because they knew the truth about the Patriot Centers.

CHAPTER 21

SABINE IOWA

There were pros and cons of driving without headlights. The pro was no one would see the car unless they drove right by it, which was also the con. Winters didn't expect anyone to be driving around and was surprised when one sped by without him noticing it beforehand. The truck had stopped, so knowing it was expected, he did the same. The truck didn't back up and was waiting for Winters to move. With no other vehicles around it would be normal to approach each other's side windows, which meant he'd be having a shootout. The last thing Winters wanted to do was shoot someone here. It would be loud and could possibly draw unwanted attention, which would also alert their targets that something was wrong.

"That's one of them," said Laney.

"If he sees me, I'll have to shoot him, which I don't want to do here."

"I'll go talk to him."

"You sure."

"Yeah, I know him."

Winters didn't like his options but this needed to happen fast. Before he could give the okay, Laney jumped out of the car. Winters turned to the rearview mirror and watched her run to the truck. She was talking and laughing with him. The occupant put his arm out and started to paw at her, which made Winters take a troubled breath. Not seeing any other passengers inside the truck Winters decided to take him out.

"Stay here, I'll be right back."

"Do you need help?"

"No, Laney seems to have it handled."

Laney noticed him approaching and kept talking to the man. Winters jotted around to the other side of the pickup and could hear his voice through the open window.

"C'mon Laney, I'll be real quick "

"You know I want to, but Derek is over there waiting for me."

"That douche-bag isn't even on your list."

"Neither are you."

"Yeah, but he doesn't have what I have."

Winters had heard enough and pulled out his knife before he opened the door. As he jumped in, the startled man turned his head. Winters backhanded the knife into his stomach before pulling it out and slashing his throat. The man moaned before his head hit the steering wheel.

Winters pulled him over to the passenger side before getting out and walking around the front of the truck.

"You did good."

"Wasn't sure what to do at first, but then remembered I've got what he wants."

"Never forget that, kid," said Winters, getting into the driver's seat. He put the truck in gear and looked across the street. "Do you know if anyone lives there?"

She looked over. "I don't think so."

Winters drove it into the driveway to the very back of the house before turning the truck into the yard. He got out and jogged back to Laney who was waiting for him at the end of the driveway.

"If someone does live here, they'll be in for a heck of a surprise in the morning."

They got back inside the Impala and Finley began asking them questions.

"That was Brian Beckett," stated Laney.

"Really?" asked Finley in an excited tone.

"Yep."

"Who is he?"

"He's one of the dirt bags in charge," said Finley. "As a matter of fact, he's Billy Gamble's, right-hand man."

Winters nodded in pleasure knowing he just knocked off one of their head guys. The night was turning out very well.

"What did you say to him?" asked Finley.

"Told him I was with Derek and he had his lights off cause he's stoned. This is Derek's car by the way," said Laney.

"Good to know," said Winters.

"What happened next?" asked Finley.

"Oh, he got all handsy feeling me up, and, like, wanted me to come with him. But then I saw Cole getting out of the car, so I knew I wasn't going to have to put up with him much longer."

"Hell ya, that was sweet," laughed Finley.

Winters put the car in gear and continued to their next destination as Finley and Laney talked about what just happened. The two chatterboxes never seemed to settle down when they were together.

The next stop was at a big house where Eric Pendleton lived. Before the country collapsed, he worked at a convenience store and could never have afforded such a house. However, he appropriated it months ago when the owners had left town. When Winters pulled up, he recognized the house since he'd been in there many times. The Williams were old friends and had left for Florida.

Winters parked the car on the side of the road. With no streetlights, it was easy to disappear into the darkness. He looked around the quiet neighborhood through the night-vision goggles and didn't see anyone moving about.

"Is there anyone else in there?" asked Winters.

Laney leaned forward from the back. "No."

"You know this for sure?"

"Yep. He's on my list and so are those others," Laney said, pointing to three other houses.

Winters took out the list of names and handed it to Finley. "Do me a favor and check off the ones we've already eliminated."

"What are you gonna do?"

"Add to the list."

"Oh, yeah, of course," said Finley.

"Do you need help?" asked Laney.

"Either of you guys know how to drive?"

"I do," said Finley.

"Get in the driver's seat and be ready to go. Laney, keep that pistol close by, okay? Remember, red is dead."

Laney nodded,

"I shouldn't be too long, but if trouble comes your way, honk the horn one short beep, okay?"

Winters scrambled across the road and entered a home he knew quite well. Dave Williams was a co-worker and often hosted poker parties here. He had retired before the country fell and had planned to move to Florida for some time. His two sons had joined the service before the war out and were now in the fight. He and his wife had left before winter set in and didn't appear to be coming back.

Winters checked the door to find it unlocked, which did not surprise him. A lot of people in the area never locked their doors and with so few people left in town, why bother?"

He stepped inside and listened for a few moments before climbing the staircase to the master bedroom. He entered the room and found his next victim sound asleep. He approached the sleeping man and without hesitation, sliced his throat. Confused eyes looked up before they went blank.

Without ceremony, Winters climbed back down the stairs and shut the door behind him. He looked across the street where the two girls waited for him in the car. He was glad they had come along and had already been a big help. Their knowledge of who everybody was and where they lived was saving him a lot of time. So much so, that he might be able to take everyone out in one night. He entered the next house, which belonged to another couple he knew, but he didn't know where they ended up after the collapse. The back door was open, and Winters again made quick work of the sleeping occupant.

The third house was more of a challenge because he had to force the back door. His heart started beating faster when the door creaked open. He stepped into the kitchen and took a moment to scan the room. Dirty dishes littered the countertop with discarded freeze-dried food packages mixed in.

Winters found two bedrooms empty before locating his next victim who was also sleeping, but with headphones on. The music was still playing when Winters approached the man who looked to be in his early forties. He shook his head at him before putting his knife to work. Like all the others, he assumed a surprised look and then nothing.

Winters exited the house and ran across the lawn to the next one. He looked at his watch before entering the unlocked back door. It was just approaching one in the morning, which wasn't too bad, all things considered. After all, he had already taken out half of the group, and still had four or five hours left.

Entering through another kitchen, he noticed this one was cleaner than the last one. He cleared a couple of rooms downstairs before hearing voices coming from the upper level. He took his time climbing the steps. Winters didn't know how many would be there but assumed at least two, a male and a female. He reached the door at the top of the stairs where candlelight spilled out into the hallway and then a female began to whimper.

CHAPTER 22

MANASSAS VIRGINIA

The evening air was cool enough for Green to have the windows down as he drove out to Manassas, Virginia. He and his mother were on their way to meet with their secret group. The wind carried the scent of pine trees into the car as they traveled along the quiet road that traversed through the thick woods.

Captain Vatter, the station commander in Detroit, had briefed Major Green earlier in the day. It had taken him until the afternoon to report on the disaster that befell Grosse Point. Instead of giving up, Winters had stormed the mansion and rescued his daughter. While on the phone with Vatter, Green had to fight to control his joy on hearing the news. Either Captain Winters was the luckiest man alive or had become a most skilled operator to execute such an audacious plan. But then again, Mordulfah wasn't the most skilled tactician. After all, he had allowed his mansion to be successfully attacked twice and had lost over half his men in a week's time. These are the consequences of having rabble instead of trained soldiers. Still, how do you not keep the upper hand to retain such a valuable hostage, especially one that was willing to help you?

Winters must know by now his daughter had been conspiring against him. This begged the question; had he known beforehand, would he still have risked his life to save her? Not having any kids himself, Green could only speculate on that.

Regardless, Mordulfah had miscalculated and suffered severe humiliation, which, for a man like him, was always personal. Green had no doubt he would seek retribution in the harshest way he could conjure up.

Green pulled into the long driveway of Senator Abby Seeley's house. It was situated in a secluded area with woods surrounding the property and didn't have any nearby neighbors to bother, or spy on, them.

"Is this Stormy girl going to be here, John?" asked Sarah Green.

"I believe so."

"She sounds like an interesting girl, I can't wait to meet her."

Green's mother wanted to find out if she was her son's type. After all, he was thirty-five years old and she wanted grandchildren. He didn't blame her as she was a widow and could use someone new in her life to spoil.

He rounded the curve in the driveway and came upon three parked cars. There was one he didn't recognize but figured it belonged to Kyle Gibbs. Sam's car wasn't there as he had another commitment, which couldn't be rescheduled.

They reached the door just as Abby Seeley came out to greet them.

"Sarah, you're looking as pretty as ever," said Abby, the retired senator whose outgoing personality had always been her biggest asset, especially on the campaign trail. The heavyset sixty-year old had been divorced for the last ten years and had dated sporadically since then, but nothing serious. She liked her freedom and didn't want to further complicate her busy life.

"As do you," replied Sarah.

"John, you're looking especially handsome tonight, any particular reason?"

Green rolled his eyes as she and his mother laughed conspiratorially.

"Is she here?" asked Sarah.

"Yes, she is," said Abby in almost a singing tone.

"Oh goody," smiled Sarah.

Abby ushered them inside her five thousand square foot home and down the hallway to the living room at the back of the house. The place was decorated with an obvious women's touch. Frilly curtains hung against dark yellow walls where paintings of flowers finished the look. They reached the oversized living room, and everyone stood up as they entered. Abby walked over to Stormy and introduced her to Sarah Green.

"It's a pleasure to meet you," said Stormy as she extended her hand.

Sarah took hold of her hand. "The pleasure is all mine, Stormy. My, but you are a beautiful girl."

"Well, thank you, and you must be so proud of your son."

"Yes, he's been very brave and we're fortunate to have his leadership," said Sarah finally letting go of her hand.

Green let out a sigh knowing what his mother was up to. She was trying to impress Stormy and be coy about it. Green stepped forward and greeted her before it got awkward. He then greeted everyone else, which included Kyle Gibbs and his father Jacob, the former FBI man. The state department diplomat, John Osborne, stood next to Alison O'Connor. Green approached and gave her a big hug, as did his mother. He noticed Alison's complexion was much improved and she no longer looked like the depressed alcoholic he'd first met when she had opened the door with a cigarette in her hand. Ever since they had rescued her from Reed's men and brought her out to Manassas, she had been steadily improving.

Before Green could start in on the update, Stormy got everyone's attention by telling them what happened to her a few hours ago.

Green was slack jawed listening to the details. "It was Wagner who came for you?

Stormy nodded.

Green shook his head realizing this event would help to poison Perozzi's mind and further deteriorate his relationship with Reed. A flash of adrenaline rushed through his body as he realized the significance. "I think congrats are in order for, Stormy."

She blushed as everyone gave her a round of applause.

After it settled down, Green continued the meeting by giving them an update on what he thought had happened last night at Grosse Pointe. In reality, though, his briefing was lacking, as he was unaware of the death of Cara Winters. He then told them he wanted to move as fast as possible against Reed. He turned to Kyle and asked if he'd had a chance to look over the notes he'd been taking on Perozzi.

"Yeah, dad and I went over them together. We didn't find much of anything that would indicate what Perozzi might do to make an attempt on Reed's life."

"With that in mind," said the elder Gibbs, "we know that Reed is a drinker and I was thinking we could poison him."

"Wouldn't really tie Perozzi to the attempt though," said Green.

"We could blow up his car," finished Gibbs. "Can't be too many people that know about the bombs."

Green's eyes lit up. It would be pure irony and one that not many people could pull off. "I like that idea, but do we know anyone who has EOD experience?" Green's use of the anonym EOD was referring to a military term for Explosive Ordnance Disposal.

Gibbs tilted his head side to side. "Yes, but it would mean bringing someone else into our group, which brings its own risk."

"Is there anyone that you trust completely?" asked Green.

"Let me think about it."

"But won't Reed think it was someone connected to me?" asked Alison.

Green hunched forward in his chair and looked at her.

"I mean it was my husband who did the bombings, so won't he think that?"

She was right. The last thing Green wanted was for Reed to think it was anyone else but Perozzi. He turned back to Gibbs.

"Why don't you do a hit and run on him?" suggested Kyle.

"That's how Alison's husband was killed," said Green.

"Oh," said Kyle as he looked at Alison, "I'm sorry."

"It's alright," said Alison waving him off.

"What if you had one of Perozzi's men in the car," said Stormy.

Green considered this. "Be no question as to who it was then, but how would we orchestrate it?"

"A shoot out would be easier to stage than an accident," said Gibbs. "We could kill one or two of Perozzi's guys and throw them in the car."

Green's spirit started to lift hearing the seeds of a good plan. Something like this could work and be quite convincing. He just needed to figure out which of Perozzi's men would be ideal. "These guys would have to be people Reed knows."

"Actually, I know just the guys," said Kyle. "I've noticed Perozzi has a few that Reed would know right off the bat."

"Are they shooters?" asked Green.

"Absolutely."

"Okay, now all we have to do is kidnap them," said Green.

"I can help with that," said Stormy.

Everyone turned their heads toward her.

"I'll make them an offer they can't refuse," smiled Stormy.

"It could be dangerous," said Green.

"I can handle myself," she responded.

Green had no doubt she could. Gibbs had informed him of her martial arts background, but he didn't think she'd need it. She only needed to bat an eyelash at a guy before he fell at her feet. He gave it some more consideration and decided she would be quite useful in leading a couple Perozzi's men to them. Everyone in the room was onboard with the plan.

"Question is, where do we do it?" asked Osborne, who had not said anything yet. "If you want it done quickly, you don't have a lot of time to research Reed's schedule."

Green looked over at the older man. He'd been in the State Department for many years traveling the world to represent the United States and with his foreign contacts would be instrumental in ending the war. He brought up a good point because they didn't know Reed's schedule. Green rubbed his forehead for a second and then stopped when he came up with an idea. It was perfect.

CHAPTER 23

SABINE IOWA

After killing three sleeping bad guys in the same neighborhood, Winters had entered the fourth house while Finley and Laney waited in the car. He could hear voices as he reached the top of the stairs. They grew louder as he crept to the bedroom door and peeked inside. A girl was on top of his next target and there were several candles lit, which would make it more difficult to come in unnoticed. Winters scrunched his face knowing this task would be difficult to accomplish without risking her safety because the target would probably have a weapon nearby, and she might get in the way. He was in too big a hurry to wait for them to finish.

Winters shook his head knowing he didn't have many options so he began to enter the bedroom. He had taken only a couple of strides before a car horn broke the silence. Winters stopped dead in his tracks. Sweat formed on his forehead knowing Finley and Laney were in trouble.

"Who the hell are you?"

A glint of nickel plating alerted Winters of a weapon and he dropped to his knees. A shot rang out. The flash lit up the room and Winters rolled to his left as he pulled up his pistol. "Damn it," thought Winters. He had been correct in assuming a weapon was probably nearby. He crawled to the other side of the bed and heard movement.

"Whoever you are, put your gun down," yelled the man.

Winters peeked up. The man had gotten out of the bed and dragged the girl along to shield him as they stood against a closet door. She let out a sob and began to cry. Winters cursed to himself. This was a worst-case scenario. He wouldn't let this scumbag leave the room alive. The only question was; would this girl have to die?

The man held a gun to her temple. Tears were streaming down the frightened girl's face. Winters reached for the Ruger .22 Sadie gave him and palmed it in his right hand. He then grabbed the Colt .45 with his left and rose up pointing it at him.

"I'll friggin kill her if you don't put that weapon down."

"Okay, okay. Just don't hurt her, okay?" said Winters, lowering the Colt.

"Are you her dad or something?"

"No, I'm not," said Winters, wanting him to point his weapon at him.

"Then who are you?"

Winters laid the weapon on the bed and said. "Does the name Cole Winters mean anything to you?"

The man's eyes grew as he realized who was standing in front of him. He then moved his pistol away from the girl's temple and aimed it at Winters who had anticipated the move. The man was no more than four yards away and was a much bigger target than the girl he held onto. Not a tough shot, but he still needed to be careful. He swung the Ruger up and squeezed the trigger in one swift motion. The round hit his target in the forehead and Winters fired another one. The man fell backwards against a closet door as the girl jerked away from the dead body.

Winters rushed around the bed to check on him before looking up at the girl. "You alright?"

She didn't respond.

"Do you know Finley and Laney?"

She stared at him with blank eyes.

"Hey, it's okay. I'm not gonna to hurt ya, alright? But, I need to get out of here and help Finley and Laney. Do you know them?"

She gave a slight nod.

"They just honked that horn, and I need to go to them, so grab your clothes and let's go."

Winters raced to the window and couldn't make out who was at the car, but it was at least one man. He turned back to the girl, who was still too frightened to move.

"Hey, what's your name?" asked Winters, trying to calm his voice down.

"Collette," she finally answered.

"Collette, well how do you like that, my name is Cole. Now, do you want to stay here while I go help Finley and Laney?"

She didn't answer and Winters decided to leave her. "I'll be back."

He scooped the dead man's pistol up off the carpet and turned to leave. He got out in the hallway and heard Collette call out to wait. She left the bedroom with her clothes bunched up in her arms. Winters didn't have the time for this and started down the steps. He needed to get to Finley and Laney who he prayed weren't in too much danger, but since the gunfire had gone off in the house, he didn't hold out much hope.

He pulled down the goggles as he rushed through the kitchen to leave out the back door. He didn't have to look to know Collette was right behind him. He'd have to evaluate the situation before deciding what to do with her.

He rounded the back of the house and looked across the lawn. A man who was a foot taller than Laney held a gun to her head. He had his arm wrapped around her and seemed to be waiting for help. Winters scanned the area looking for Finley and was frustrated when he couldn't find her.

Winters felt Collette move around him to look down the street. She stared for a few moments before moving back.

"Do you know who that is?" asked Winters, knowing it was difficult to see through the darkness.

Collette nodded. "It's probably Jasper. Mickey said he wanted to come over."

"To see you?"

She nodded.

"Anyone else?

"I don't think so, but maybe."

"Are you really Cole Winters?"

"I am."

"You killed that Sherman guy?"

"Him and a few more tonight."

"Why?" she asked perplexed.

"Because someone has to."

She looked for his eyes behind the goggles. "Thank you. I...I didn't like doing this, but I was hungry."

"I know, honey, It's okay, but it ends tonight."

"Finley and Laney are helping then?"

"Yes, and I'm afraid I've put them in danger."

She looked towards the street and then back at Winters. "Can I help?"

Winters observed that she appeared to have calmed down. She wasn't much taller than Laney and her black short spiky hair was matted down in some places. She had both ears pierced in several different places and a piercing on the side of her nose finished off the look. And, like the other girls, she had a few butterflies tattooed on the side of her left leg and another on the bottom of her wrist.

"How old are you?"

"I'm eighteen."

Winters considered her offer and what she could do to help. He didn't have many options and not knowing where Finley was made them even less so. Did another man hold her as a hostage? Even if he came up from behind, there was no guarantee he could find Finley before being spotted. The best thing he could hope for was to draw them out and then an idea struck him.

"Would you be willing to do a little acting?"

Collette let out a loud scoff. "It's what I've been doing."

Winters told her what he wanted her to do before they both hustled back inside the house. She dropped her clothes and ran upstairs to gather her props for the show. She opened the front door, took in several deep breaths and ran outside screaming in her a high-pitched shrill voice.

CHAPTER 24

Winters moved to the big picture window to watch Collette act in the role of her life. The eighteen-year-old spiky haired girl had freaked out at first but had calmed down upon learning who Winters was and what her friends were doing.

"Help, me! Help! He's dying, I need help! Someone help!"

Winters watched the girl stumble across the lawn crying and then falling to the ground in hysterics. "She's pretty darn good," thought Winters. He looked back toward Jasper who had Laney in his clutches. He hesitated a few moments before looking behind him. Winters looked in that direction figuring someone was waiting in the weeds holding onto Finley. Collette kept up the charade screaming at the top of her lungs.

A flashlight flicked on and a beam of light streamed on Collette, who had smeared blood on her arms to finish off the deception.

Jasper started pushing Laney toward the house, and Winters had to step away from the window when the beam flashed across it. Jasper let go of Laney as he reached the screaming Collette keeping the light pointed at her.

"What's going on?" yelled Jasper.

"He's…" said Collette choking on her words. "He's dead."

"Whose dead. Mickey?"

"No, but he's shot and he's bleeding."

"Who, damn it, who shot him."

"Some guy named Winters."

"Are you sure?"

Collette nodded. "Hurry, Mickey's bleeding."

"But that guy's dead though, right?"

"Yes...yes, Mickey shot him dead."

Jasper turned around and switched the flashlight off and on three times. From across the street, a man started dragging Finley out of the bushes. Winters let out a breath of relief knowing his instincts had served him well.

"You both stay here," ordered Jasper.

Laney fell to the ground and wrapped her arms around Collette. Winters rushed over and hid behind the door where he pulled out his knife. His heart began to race as the door squeaked open. He gripped his knife tighter as Jasper walked in. "Just one more foot," thought Winters as he angled the blade of his knife. Jasper had just put his foot on the first step of the staircase when Winters wrapped his arm around the taller man's mouth and shoved the knife into the side of his gut. Jasper's knees buckled and Winters slid the blade across his throat. Air hissed out as he dragged him into the living room behind a couch. He then looked back out of the picture window. The second man was just now reaching the girls with Finley in tow.

Winters took a couple of deep breaths to slow down his rapid heart rate as he waited for the other man to come inside. Finley dropped to the grass and the three girls wrapped their arms around each other. Winters began to lose patience when his prey hesitated to enter the house. The man had a pistol in his right hand and still seemed to be on edge.

"Lyle, get in there," yelled Finley.

"Shut up, Wannabe."

"Can't you see Mickey's hurt?"

"I said shut up."

Winters decided not to wait any longer and dashed through the backdoor. This guy was nervous and the last thing Winters needed was for him to grab one of the girls again. With the night-vision goggles on he had the advantage, so he snuck around the side of the house. He took a quick look around before turning the corner holding his pistol. The man didn't notice Winters as he lined up a shot and squeezed the trigger. The man's head exploded in chunks and the girls screamed in unison before crawling away from the fallen body.

"You girls okay?"

"Cole!" screamed Finley, who jumped up and wrapped her arms around him. Laney immediately followed her.

Winters gave them both a tight squeeze.

"We thought you were dead," said Finley.

"Thank God you're alright," said Laney.

Winters looked at Collette. "Nice acting job."

"I poured my heart into it," said Collette.

"Listen, girls, we need to get going."

Collette hustled inside while Finley ran to get the car. Winters bent down to grab the dead man's Springfield 1911 TRP pistol. "Nice gun."

"Jasper's got my gun," said Laney.

"Want this one?" asked Winters handing her the pistol.

Laney grabbed it. "It's too big for me."

Winters took it back. "I'll get that other one."

He sprinted inside and yelled for Collette while retrieving the Sig .380 pistol. He bent down and found it inside Jasper's pocket.

"Collette, where are you?"

"I'm in here."

Winters entered the kitchen where Collette was using a wet towel to wipe the blood off her arms. She wore a black t-shirt that had the word "Princess" across it making Winters laugh.

"What?" asked Collette.

"Your shirt."

"But, I am a Princess."

"I won't argue with you, but can this princess hurry."

"Almost done," she said, wiping the final smear of blood off her arm.

Winters tapped his watch with the Sig and Collette responded with a curt nod before throwing the wet towel on the floor. Winters followed her outside to find Finley in the driver's seat and decided to let her drive. Collette hopped in the back with Laney, and Winters got in up front and handed Laney the Sig.

"Get us out of here."

Finley couldn't contain her glee and spun the car around on the front lawn bouncing the car off the curb onto the street. She put the headlights on and zipped down the road out of the neighborhood.

"Where to?" she asked.

"Somewhere empty."

"Know just the place."

Winters turned around in his seat. "So, what happened?"

"Man, they came out of nowhere," said Finley. "They were walking here and saw Derek's car. Then the gunshot went off just as they were asking us, like, why we were in his car."

"Yeah, they freaked out," said Laney.

"I tried telling them that Derek was, like, next door picking up some weed," said Finley, "but man, when that gun went off, they dragged us out of the car. I kept telling them Derek was next door."

"But then two more shots went off, and that's when they really freaked out," said Laney. "They were, like, expecting Derek to come out and help, but when he didn't they separated us."

"Yeah, to use us as protection, the big babies," said Finley.

"Oh, but when you came out, Collette," laughed Laney. "You were, like, all screaming your head off, and Jasper, like, didn't know what was up. But when he saw your naked butt, man he couldn't get to you fast enough." Laney continued laughing for a few moments before catching her breath. "That pervert kept his flashlight right on ya though."

"Man, you were so good, even I thought Cole was dead," said Finley.

"My school plays finally came in handy," said Collette.

"Your first starring role," laughed Finley.

Winters turned back around and was starting to get a headache listening to these three girls chatter non-stop. It was bad before, but now there were three of them, and they talked in high-pitched excited tones. Of course, they deserved to celebrate having done what they just did. It wasn't every day that teenagers, or anyone else for that matter, put themselves in danger as they had done. But then, these weren't ordinary times either. These girls and their families have been toughing it out under extreme conditions. They endured a long winter while most of the men were away. They've had to put up with a gang of thugs taking control of their town and stealing all the food. It left them with little choice but to prostitute themselves to keep their families from dying of starvation. Why more of them hadn't left town was beyond him, but he was certain they all had their own reasons. It was home after all, and if the government wasn't able to force them out, why would they let a bunch of criminals do it.

The one thing Winters did discover was none of them liked what they were doing and had jumped at the chance to help put an end to it. What amazed him was how much the human spirit was capable of enduring in order to survive. He'd seen different levels of it among the Shadow Patriots, but these girls were beyond anything he had seen before. They were kids and still had a pureness that allowed them to remain upbeat despite their ordeal. He liked the way they used the butterfly tattoos as a way to show hope and unity. It was a great symbol to remind each other of their resolve to endure their ordeal.

He leaned his head back thinking about what had led him here. The more he thought about it, the more convinced he became that somehow Cara had brought him here. He remembered that she liked butterflies as a kid and would catch them with her net. She'd put them in a jar to observe them for only a little while before letting them go free. The memory sent a shiver up Winters' spine. Until today, he'd been struggling with her death and was on the verge of giving up. Coming home to Sabine and discovering what was going on here had strengthened his own resolve, and now he knew what he was supposed to do. The weight on his shoulders was becoming lighter and that was easing his sorrow.

CHAPTER 25

ON THE ROAD TO SARNIA

The black SUV, with a full tank of gas, plowed through the dark night as Bassett drove Scar, Burns, Nordell, and Hadley to Port Huron, Michigan. On top of the large Suburban was strapped a canoe. After much discussion, they decided to drive north and paddle across the St. Clair River into Sarnia, Ontario. It was a longer distance to travel, but it was ideal for what they wanted to do. They would have liked to sneak into Dearborn and cross the Detroit River, but the Canadians patrolled the area. There was bad blood between the Americans and the folks in Windsor because gangs from Detroit had been raiding the Canadian side of the river and blood had been spilled. Because of that, Windsor was no longer friendly to Americans. There hadn't been as much trouble, further north and the environment was still friendly, which made their decision easier. They needed to cross into a densely populated area since they would be without transportation, and Sarnia was the closest city that fit the bill. With the short distance across the river, they'd be able to make several trips to load the Suburban.

Scar had put considerable thought into whom to take, and despite Nordell's mea culpa; he still didn't trust him enough to leave him alone with the remaining personnel. Hadley, the young Texan, would stay with the Suburban to make sure they didn't lose their ride back, or if anything did happen, he would be able to go get help. Scar had left Meeks and Badger in charge of organizing groups to replenish their fuel reserves. They would raid the Jiji's vehicles for gas, which was fresher than the gas found in other abandoned vehicles.

The whole trip would take a couple of days because they could only cross at night, and there wouldn't be any stores open until the morning. Once they had supplies, they would have to wait for darkness to transport them back across the river. Scar was a little nervous about their ability to purchase the amount of supplies they needed, but consoled himself with the thought that everything they did get would put them in better shape than they were now.

Scar found himself dozing off during the two-hour trip. The last 48 hours had been long and arduous. Between trying to stop a lynch mob, participating in a firefight, and dealing with stressed out personnel, he hadn't gotten much sleep. In his former life, as a business owner, he was used to being stressed and his new role was similar because he still had a lot of different personalities to deal with and problems to solve.

Bassett pulled into the outskirts of Port Huron, and Burns directed him down to Griswold and Third Street. It was the location of an abandoned YMCA, and the building sat right by the river. The area was desolate enough to conceal the SUV and stealthily launch the canoe after crossing a field.

Keeping the headlights off, they drove slowly through the streets looking for any signs of life. They weren't sure of the presence of patrols or if there were any cops stationed there. Before leaving Jackson, they had talked to some of their men who were familiar with the area and were told most of the people had moved south or across the river into Canada as refugees.

Basset spotted a garage on Griswold adjacent to the Y and stopped the SUV.

"This looks good," Bassett said, putting the car in park.

Both he and Burns stepped out and scanned the area before approaching the small building. Burns jimmied the passage door and vanished inside to open the garage door.

Scar got out and stretched his legs. He looked around with a pair of night-vision goggles on and then heard the door opening. He watched as Bassett backed the Suburban inside and closed the door.

"Let's recon the area," ordered Scar. "Hadley, stay here and watch."

They took off in pairs and for the next thirty minutes, scouted the area looking for any sign of trouble. Not finding any, they unloaded the canoe and headed down to the river. Upon reaching the shore, they admired the lights from across the river flickering on the horizon.

"I'll bet there's a hotel over there," said Burns.

"A hot shower would be nice," said Bassett.

Scar looked at his watch to see it was only midnight. They had hours to kill before they could go grocery shopping. It would also give them a place to stay until it got dark. "I'd be up for a hot shower."

Bassett shook Hadley's hand and told him to keep his head down.

They hopped into the canoe and started paddling across the river. The closer they got to Canada the more at ease Scar felt with the idea. They'd have access to a phone and could call General Standish or Colonel Brocket. They had plenty of cash, as Mayor Simpson had been able to pool a large amount of American and Canadian money. Scar also carried a couple of Canadian Maple Leaf gold pieces just in case.

Because weapons weren't allowed in Canada, they had to leave their M-4's and most of their gear back in the Suburban, however, they decided to carry pistols just in case trouble found them once again.

They reached the other side in good time, and Burns jumped out to tie off the canoe. Scar looked around and noticed they had landed in a sand and gravel quarry. He didn't know if it was still in business but figured it wouldn't be a busy place either way.

They headed north into the business district figuring they would run into a hotel. Keeping to the riverfront and ducking whenever a car came into the vicinity; Scar had to remind himself they weren't in a war zone. It was a difficult thing to overcome, but as soon as they came upon an open grill and pub, all reservations disappeared.

"A cold one sure would hit the spot," said Bassett.

"Yes, it would," agreed Nordell.

"Bet they got big juicy hamburgers," said Burns.

It had been a long time since any of them had a cold beer or any beer for that matter. The idea was appealing, and perhaps they could make a sympathetic friend to direct them around the city.

Scar smiled and said, "I'm buying."

CHAPTER 26

SABINE IOWA

Winters kept listening to the non-stop talking of the three girls who were now helping him put a stop to the madness in his hometown of Sabine. Listening to the loud chatter of two of them had been tough, but now with a third one added to the mix, it was a challenge. He hadn't been around teen aged girls in some time and forgot how chatty they could be. He remembered when Cara would have a sleepover and how they had gabbed half the night before going to sleep. Because they lived in a small three-bedroom, their high-pitched had voices carried throughout the house preventing him from falling asleep.

Finley drove them to a parking lot in back of a school, which was located away from any housing. This would ensure no one would find them there. Before he continued with the mission, he needed to regroup and find where the rest of the scum he sought lived.

Finley put the car in park and asked, "What's next?"

"Where's that list?"

"Right here," said Laney.

"Can you update it with our latest kills."

"Kills, I love it," said Laney.

The comment made Winters twitch. What had he created, or at the very least, unleashed? The way she had attacked Randy with the vodka bottle, indicated there was a lot of pent-up rage for sure.

"Okay, those first four were mine," she said, as she ran down the list crossing out the names."

"Mine too," said Collette.

"Not anymore," laughed Laney giving Collette a high-five. She then looked up at Winters. "Cole, you've killed ten so far."

Collette's mouth dropped open "Damn."

"No, it's eleven," said Finley. "He killed Jimmy Boyd's wife."

"Really?" asked Laney.

"That bitch was coming at me, and besides, she liked to do threesomes."

"Oh, that's just nasty," said Collette. "She's as white trash as they come."

"Yeah, tell me about it," said Finley. "I swear they never brushed their teeth. I mean, c'mon, even if you, like, don't have any more toothpaste, at least use some baking soda. I mean everyone's got baking soda."

"It's what I use," said Laney.

"Me too," said Collette.

Winters shook his head wanting to get the girls refocused. "So, where do the rest of these guys live?"

The girls looked over the list and after some debating came up with the street names. Winters decided to take out the furthest one first. He figured he could just go in and shoot him. He glanced at the girls debating on whether he should bring them back to his hideout now. They'd been through a lot, even been taken as hostages. He looked at their excited expressions and figured they would refuse. It wasn't worth the headache they'd give him, besides they may be young, but they were quick learners and quite brave.

"Okay, let's go over to Grayson's place," said Winters.

"Oh, that ole boy," said Laney.

"You mean, old man," interrupted Collette. "He's, like, forty-five."

Winters rolled his eyes at the comment and ordered Finley to go.

She started the car and drove away as Laney and Collette continued to talk about Grayson's age.

Laney placed her hand on Winters' shoulder. "No offense about the old man thing, but that guy just creeps us out.

"Thank goodness he's not on my list," said Collette.

"Oh, me too," said Laney. "I mean it'd be creepy just being naked around someone that old."

Finley started laughing. "Cole's seen me naked."

"Oh my God, that's right, me too, and you Collette," laughed Laney uncontrollably again.

"All three of us?" asked Collette in disbelief. "I thought I was the only one."

"Cole Winters, you've been getting a show tonight," shouted Finley above the high-pitched laughter.

Winters' face burned red and was thankful it was dark out so they couldn't see his embarrassment. He was never comfortable around girls and even less so when he was their age.

"I can assure you I didn't enjoy it."

"Wha…whatever," Laney said, choking on her laughter.

"Hell, he's even seen why they call me, Wannabe."

Winters buried his head while they busted out laughing and continued to razz him. He wasn't expecting this, but in a way was glad they were in good spirits. The girls he had rescued from the party house were the exact opposite of these three. Even stranger was their response to watching and helping kill people. It must be such a relief that the killing didn't have the same effect on them as it would others.

Finley slowed down as they approached Grayson's place. He lived in a farmhouse his family had passed on to him. The family was no longer in the area. The parents died years ago and both his sisters had moved to St. Louis. Stephen Grayson had gone through a couple of wives while drinking himself into poverty. He'd sold off all the land but managed to hang onto the house.

"Stop here," said Winters.

"You need help?" asked Laney.

"No. You girls stay here and stay alert. I won't be but a minute."

Winters exited the car carrying his M-4 and dashed across the street. He didn't want to take a lot of time with this one and decided to just shoot him. There were no neighbors anywhere near who might hear the gunfire.

He crept up on the porch and found the door unlocked. He twisted the handle and pushed the door open. He stared through the goggles to find the place with little to no furniture. He took a moment to listen for any movement before heading upstairs to the master bedroom. The door was open, and he heard the snoring before reaching the doorway. He walked in and found Grayson sleeping alone. He looked around the room before taking aim and squeezing the trigger. A three shot burst found its mark and the snoring ceased.

Winters got back to the car and found the girls quiet, which was odd for them. Perhaps they were having reservations about what they were doing so he asked them.

"No, not at all," said Finley.

"Me neither," said Collette, who looked at Laney who shook her head.

"Okay, just wanted to make sure. I haven't seen you guys this quiet before."

"We don't want to do anything wrong is all," said Finley. "We know we talk a lot, I mean, we're all friends and we love each other, but we know this is, like, serious stuff so, you know, you can count on us."

"Yeah, like when Jasper grabbed me," said Laney, "I saw how it can go wrong, like, really fast."

"Good, I'm glad to hear this, cuz tomorrow things are going to heat up, which is why I want to take out as many as I can tonight."

"Then let's go," Finley said while starting the car.

Winters leaned back satisfied they were still in good spirits. His leg started to bounce when he realized he'd have to get these girls and their families to the hideout before the night was over. He looked at his watch and saw he had only a few hours until sunrise.

.

CHAPTER 27

Finley slowed the Impala and pulled it into the driveway of a house she knew was empty. She told Winters most of the people from this neighborhood had left the area. She had driven to this particular neighborhood because there were three targets living next to each other. Killing these three would enable them to cross off most of the names on the list, which would be a hell of a night.

He still needed to get these girls' families rounded up and taken to safety. It wouldn't take too long for the remaining men on the list to figure out who had been helping him tonight. All they had to do was to see who had been killed and which girl he had seen last. A little arm-twisting would be all that was needed before one of them coughed up the other names and then they'd kill them all. He couldn't risk getting even one of these girls killed like that. It was already bad enough that they were here helping him, but at least with him, they stood a better chance than if they were alone.

"Do you need help?" asked Finley.

Winters gave it some thought. "Why don't you guys help me recon the area."

"Recon, uh, I love it," said Laney.

"Just keep quiet and stay with me. Okay?"

They all nodded their heads and then exited the car. The girls gathered behind Winters who led them across an overgrown lawn to the next one.

Winters slowly moved his head from side to side. He wasn't too familiar with the neighborhood, having been through but a few times in the past. He didn't know anyone who had lived there and wasn't familiar with the next three targets.

They trekked through the wet overgrown grass for another block before Laney grabbed him by the arm and pointed up the street.

"That one, and the one next to it," she whispered.

"What about the third?" asked Winters.

Laney shrugged her shoulders and looked at her friends.

"It's right behind those two," said Collette.

Winters liked that the targets were grouped together. He decided to do the two up ahead first then sneak through the back for the third. Not wanting to leave the girls at the car again, he decided to have them wait across the road for him.

"Let's go," Winters whispered to the girls.

As they continued to get closer, a pair of headlights lit up the street. A car was coming. "Get down, get down."

They fell to the ground as a car approached. Its headlights lit up the pitch-black neighborhood as the car slowed to pull into the driveway of Winters' next target.

He motioned the girls into some overgrown bushes. They crawled on their hands and knees while breathing in quick breaths and hunching close to him. Their eyes were as big as saucers as they peered across the street at the car. Suddenly the car's horn blasted through the stillness of the night and made them jump.

Two men holding shotguns got out of the car yelling. Something was up because these two were fidgeting around the driveway. The front door opened up and out walked a man wearing nothing but boxer shorts. Winters couldn't quite make out what they were saying but figured it had something to do with him. He scanned the area deciding what he wanted to do. It was no longer feasible to sneak in on them because his targets now knew he was somewhere about and intent on killing them. The other front door opened and out stepped another man. He was taller than the others were but just as young, maybe mid-twenties. He didn't look happy about being dragged out of bed.

Collette moved up to Winters' ear. "Those two at the car are Mickey's cousins."

Winters nodded figuring they had gone to his house and discovered the dead bodies.

The loud voices continued to echo through the quiet neighborhood. They were agitated and appeared to be drunk.

He put his hand on Collette's shoulder and whispered into her ear. "Are they drinkers?"

She gave him an affirming nod.

Winters watched and determined the cousins were drunk. The one wearing the boxer shorts disappeared behind the house, and Winters figured he was going after the third target, which gave him an idea.

"Girls, I need for you to trust me."

"What are you gonna do?" asked Finley.

"You've heard of a drive-by?"

They all nodded.

"Well, I'm gonna do a walk-by."

They all looked at each other trying to figure out what he meant.

"You're gonna attack them?" asked Collette.

Winters nodded.

"That is so badass," said Laney.

"What do you want us to do?" asked Finley wide-eyed.

"Stay here and don't move. No matter what happens, stay out of sight until I come for you."

"What if you don't or can't?" asked Finley putting her hand on his arm.

"Stay quiet and leave."

"No, don't go," begged Finley.

"I'll be alright. You girls just be ready to leave in a hurry, okay?"

Small hands tugged at his jacket as he got up and scurried away. He headed across another lawn to get directly across from the driveway. He studied the cousins who hadn't settled down yet. The one with the shotgun had laid it down on the hood of his car while they waited for Boxer-boy to return.

Their attention was directed toward the backyard as Winters slipped out from his hiding place. The night-vision optics lit up his way as he glided across the street to a big oak tree. He peeked around the tree. Boxer-boy came back with another man who held a gun. Winters liked his chances as the five men began arguing on what to do. He heard the cousins telling the man with the gun what happened at Mickey's house.

Winters flipped the safety off the M-4 and switched it to fire a three shot burst. He peeked around the tree again deciding to first eliminate the one who had joined the party last. He seemed more alert and carried a pistol. The cousins would be next and then the other two.

Winters' heart began to race as he slipped away from the protection of the big oak tree. He raised his weapon to his shoulder and focused on his first target as he eased toward them. The car's headlights blinded them and concealed his presence. He aimed at the first target and began to apply pressure to the trigger when suddenly another set of headlights projected a bright beam of light through the dark neighborhood.

CHAPTER 28

SARNIA ONTARIO

After crossing the Saint Clair River into Canada, Scar agreed to go into a grill and pub they just happened upon while walking toward the business district of Sarnia, Ontario. A cold beer and hamburger seemed like a delicious way to kill a couple of hours before finding a hotel. It had been ten days since they left the base in Winnipeg and they hadn't had a hot meal since.

Bassett reached the door and opened it for the rest of the crew. Delicious aromas of charbroiled hamburgers and a faint suggestion of garlic hit their senses. Scar breathed it all in before approaching the smiling hostess.

"Welcome, a table for four?" asked a young hostess.

"Yes, please," said Scar.

The place looked like any American style sports bar restaurant. A small bar off to the side had a couple of TV screens playing soccer games. The hostess led them to the dining area, which was one big room full of tables.

"Your waitress will be right with you gentlemen."

They had trouble containing their excitement as they sat down and looked around. No one gave them a second look, which relieved Scar's anxiety. He needed to relax and this was just the place to do it. He didn't need to pick up the menu to know exactly what he was going to order.

"I don't know about you guys, but I'm getting a burger, fries, and a beer," said Scar.

"Same here," said Burns.

Nordell looked at the menu and then put it down. "Make it three."

"Well, I hate to be different, but I'm making mine a cheeseburger," said Bassett.

"Corporal Bassett," said Scar, "cheese goes without saying."

A waitress appeared out of nowhere and took their order.

"Notice she was smiling," said Burns. "I haven't seen a genuine smile on a girl in a long time."

The waitress came back with their beers and all four took a moment to just stare at them. Frost began melting off the sides of the frozen glass mugs. They picked them up and clanked the glasses together.

"To the Shadow Patriots," said Scar.

"And America," said Nordell.

"And the Captain," said Burns.

"Here, here," finished off Bassett.

They each began with a small sip before taking another larger one. Smiles spread across their faces as they put the glasses down.

"Forgot how good this tasted," said Burns.

"Can't remember the last time I had a beer," said Nordell.

"I do," said Bassett. "When I came back from the Middle East, I went to visit with my parents back in Yoder, Indiana. They put together a welcome home barbecue with friends and neighbors. Best damn food I thought I'd ever tasted."

"It's always the best food when you come home from war," said Nordell.

They all nodded their heads in agreement, as everyone at the table had fought in one conflict or another while serving in their youth. Now that they fought at each other's sides, they would be bonded together forever.

After the second round showed up, the cheeseburgers followed and they were big and stacked tall. The guys dug in without fanfare, and no one talked as they devoured the burgers along with the fries. As the guys finished off the last of their fries, a couple of strangers stared at them as they left the restaurant. This got Scar's attention and pointed it out to Bassett who sat beside him.

"You saw that too?" asked Bassett.

Scar nodded.

"What's up?" asked Nordell.

"Not sure. Got a couple of gentlemen taking notice of us as they left," said Scar.

"If it's anything, we'll know soon enough," said Nordell.

"They're coming back in," said Bassett.

Scar picked up his mug and took a sip while watching the guy sit back down and say something to his friend while looking at them.

"Something's definitely up," said Bassett.

"Should we leave?" asked Burns.

"Let's get our check," said Scar motioning to their waitress.

"We still need to find a hotel," said Burns.

"I'll ask her," said Scar.

She came over and dropped off the check. Scar had already produced five twenty-dollar bills and told her to keep the change.

"Thank you very much," she said.

Scar was about to ask her where the hotels were when four men approached their table.

The waitress backed away from the table as they pulled out badges.

"Excuse us, gentlemen, I'm Sergeant Major Wilson with the Sarnia Police."

Scar looked at his friends. "What can we do you for?"

"Americans?"

"Yes, we're Americans."

"What is your business here?"

Scar remained calm knowing this could go either way. "Besides getting some amazing cheeseburgers, we're refugees."

"Do you gentlemen have your papers?"

Scar wasn't aware refugees were issued papers. Perhaps they did things differently here.

"That's the thing, we're fairly new refugees."

"How new?" asked Wilson.

"Couple of hours, actually."

"You just crossed?"

"We did indeed."

"You gentlemen are in violation of the American Refugee Act and will need to come with us."

"Sergeant Major, isn't there something we could work out here."

"I'm afraid not. All refugees have to file for status as soon as they arrive."

"But we just arrived and when we saw this place, and well, the cheeseburgers were calling out to us."

"I understand the hardships you Americans have been going through, but still, we need to get you sized up and make sure you're not going to cause any trouble."

Scar let out a disappointing sight. They weren't going to get out of this and would be going with them. He was afraid they were going to frisk them. Each of them carried a sidearm, which he was sure would get them thrown in the slammer. This wasn't how he pictured the evening going. He had made a mistake coming in here and now they were going to pay for it.

Scar looked at his men. "It would appear we have a change of plans."

They all nodded in agreement and began to get up from the table.

"One at a time, gentlemen," said Sergeant Major Wilson.

Sweat formed on Scar's forehead knowing the cops were going to frisk them. He got up first, and one of the other officers approached him and asked him to put his hands on the table.

Everyone in the restaurant watched in silence at the scene unfolding in front of them. The officer grabbed Scar's right arm first and slapped cuffs on him. He then searched him and yelled out when he found Scar's Kimber .45 pistol.

"Gun!" said the officer in an elevated voice.

The rest of the officers drew out their weapons and pointed them at the table while screaming at them.

"Hey, take it easy guys," yelled Nordell. "We're all armed, but we're

118

not here for a gunfight."

"Everyone! Put their hands on the table," ordered Wilson.

They all complied while a policeman pulled Scar away from the table. The remaining cops moved in and cuffed the men one at a time.

"The burgers were worth it, sir," said Bassett.

"And the beers," said Burns.

Scar grew angry with himself as the police escorted them outside. The gun charges weren't going to help them talk their way out of this. He thought about the angle he would use and decided to just come clean and hope they were aware of and knew the truth about the Shadow Patriots. His only ace in the hole was their friends in Winnipeg. They would vouch for them, but what he didn't know was if they had enough juice to get them out of this mess, and, if so, how long it was going to take.

CHAPTER 29

SABINE IOWA

After sneaking up on the five targets, Winters had the element of surprise, but as he was about to squeeze the trigger, headlights broke through the darkness alerting the men of his presence. It took a second for Winters to recover from the surprise before he pulled the trigger on the first man carrying the pistol. Three rounds punctured his chest and threw him to the ground. He had only seconds before the car behind him figured out what was going on. He jerked the M-4 toward the cousins whose reactions were slowed by alcohol. Winters discharged a volley into the one who had placed his shotgun on the hood of the car. He collapsed to the ground as his brother raised his shotgun and fired at Winters. Pellets flew by Winters as he moved out of the way while pulling the trigger. The second cousin fell down screaming in pain, which meant he merely wounded him.

The car squealed to a stop. A door opened and a gunshot rang out.

Winters hustled around the cousins' car for cover and found the tall man huddled on the ground quacking in fear. Winters took no pity on him. At such close range, the man's head exploded in different directions. He finished off the second cousin who was bleeding on the pavement, and then looked around for Boxer-boy whom he soon discovered behind another car taking a shot at him. Winters shook his head knowing they got him in a box. If he went to either side, he'd expose himself, which meant he was staying put for the moment. He took the butt of his gun and smashed the headlights of the car he was using for cover.

He needed to know how good a shot this guy was, so he rose up a little and heard a shot hit the side view mirror. "Not bad." Winters then got on his stomach and looked for Boxer-boy. He spotted bare feet hiding behind the back end of the car. He aimed and took a shot. It missed, forcing him to hide behind the tire.

"I don't have time for this," thought Winters, as he looked toward the road. Tall grass moving up on a lawn across the street got his attention. "What the hell?"

Laney had pulled away from the clutches of Collette and Finley. She tightened her grip on the Sig Sauer .380 as she scampered across the overgrown lawns. The wet grass slapped against her bare legs making her wish she hadn't worn shorts. The petite girl crouched down right behind the driver, who she knew was Mike Furrier.

She hated him because he tried to get with her little sister when they were home alone. It was against the very rules he had helped create being one of those in charge. She fought him off her sister but ended up having to give in to him in front of her. He promised never to come around again as long as she promised never to tell Billy Gamble, who kept a tight rein on things.

Winters' fired a shot and Laney realized she was in the line of fire. She moved down a little bit and waited for the right moment. She had gone hunting with her dad many times, and he always told her to be patient, and wait for a clear shot. She had taken several deer over the years and loved the experience. "Was this any different?" she asked herself. Not really. Her newfound hero was in trouble, and she had a strong desire to help him. She never could ignore someone in trouble and always jumped into the fray without thinking things through. She did it for her sister and again, a couple of hours ago, when she jumped on Owen to help Finley.

She looked across the street and needed to get closer to her quarry. The .380 wasn't as accurate as the old Winchester .30-30 her grandpa had given her. She watched Mike take another shot and miss. He cussed up a storm as he tried to line up another shot. Cole fire three rounds that hit the car in quick succession. Then another three hit the same area. Why were they hitting the front of the car? Surely Cole was a better shot than this. Three more hit the same area. Then it dawned on her, he was signaling her. She shook her head when Mike started making fun of Winters' wild shots.

This was it. Laney sucked in a deep breath before hitting the pavement with her wet sneakers squeaking as she approached Mike who was still chuckling. He fired a shot and lined up another as Laney slinked ever closer to him. She was only fifteen feet away, and her heart was pounding like a trip hammer as she aimed at his back. She let out a breath and took in another. She squeezed the trigger and the gun went off.

Mike screamed out and started to turn around. Laney took a step backward and fired again hitting him in the chest. The round forced him to drop his weapon. Blood oozed from his wound as he put a hand on it. His eyes grew in recognition.

"Laney? Whatcha go and do that for?"

"That's for my sister," she yelled, as she fired again. "And for me."

Mike struggled for air as Winters came running around the car. Laney took aim at him but realized it was Cole.

"Laney!"

"Cole, you alright?"

Winters nodded as she wrapped her arms around him. Her body started shaking from the adrenaline. "You did good girl. You did real good."

When Winters saw what Laney was going to do, he stormed after Boxer-boy, but couldn't find him behind the car. He wasn't sure if he was still around and figured he might have run off for help. He then ran to Laney after she shot Mike.

Winters pulled away from Laney who was still shaking and leaned down to her five-foot-two level. "You sure you're okay?"

She nodded.

Mike was still struggling for air, so Winters pulled Laney away from him. He pointed his M-4 at his chest and finished him off. He was glad he was the one to have actually killed him. It would be easier for Laney to get over it if she needed to, which Winters hoped was the case. He didn't need another Reese on his hands.

CHAPTER 30

Winters grabbed Laney's hand and they ran back to where Finley and Collette waited for them. Neither of the other two girls knew what to say when they got there. The only thing they did was give Laney a big hug.

"C'mon girls, we need to go."

They reached the car, and Winters decided it was better for him to drive. He didn't think they would have a lot of time before Boxer-boy alerted the rest of the gang. He wanted to get the girls and their families out of there as soon as possible.

Winters peeled out of the driveway and was surprised the girls were still quiet. This was unusual for them, so Winters decided to break the ice.

"Laney, that was pretty bad ass what you just did. You got my butt out of a jam, so thank you."

"I just can't help myself sometimes," said Laney. "It was probably pretty stupid."

"No, what I did was stupid. I shouldn't have gone in there and left you girls behind like that. What you did was pure bravery. Isn't that right girls?"

"Laney, you are a badass," said Finley. "I mean, c'mon, I thought you were, like, brave to help me with Owen, but this, I mean, my God Laney, you is craaazy."

"Crazy doesn't even come close," shouted Collette. "The way you snuck up on him! I mean, Finley and I were watching and squeezing the crap out of each other's hands."

"Yeah, and the sweat was just pouring out of me," laughed Finley.

"Girls, all of you," said Winters. "All of you are badasses. Each of you has proven that tonight. Just trust me on this, okay? However, we still have much to do so I need you guys to focus. We need to get your families out of town, so who lives the closest?"

"I do," said Collette."

"And then who?"

"That'd be me," said Laney.

"Okay, Collette, how many are there?"

"It's just my mom and little brother."

"Perfect. What about you Laney?"

"My mom and little sister."

Winters already knew Finley had her mom and sister at home. There wasn't enough room in the Impala, so he planned to go to Collette's place first. He'd drive them to the police van he left on the outskirts of town. He'd have her mom drive the Impala back to their hideout.

Winters pulled into Collette's driveway and turned his head to the back. "How do you want to handle this?"

"Let's just all go in. I think that would more dramatic."

"Huh, an actress tried and true," said Winters.

"Big entrances," smiled Collette.

Collette opened the front door and they all followed her inside. She began lighting candles in the living room and kitchen. The room was soon bright enough to see the place was neat and well kept with little furniture.

Collette disappeared down the hall and reappeared a few minutes later with her mom in tow.

"Mom, this is Cole Winters, Cole this is my mom, Stacey."

Winters came forward and shook the hand of a woman who looked like she was in her late thirties. She looked worn down and the hard living was stealing what youth she had left.

"It's a pleasure to meet you, Stacey."

She shook his hand with a limp-wrist. "I heard you were in town." She turned to Collette. "What have you gotten yourself into?"

She gave her mom a short version of the night and pleaded with her to grab some things. Stacey shook her head angrily and muttered to herself while she went back down the hallway to gather up her sleeping son, Seth, who was nine years old.

Winters was surprised at her reaction. Shouldn't she be happy her daughter wouldn't have to prostitute herself anymore? Perhaps they didn't get along very well or maybe she herself had been involved with it. She had the looks for it, but he couldn't be sure. It was a delicate thing to ask and it didn't really matter. He had hoped to ask her to drive, but because of her poor response to what they were doing, he decided against it.

After a few minutes of waiting in silence, they exited Collette's house and hopped into the Impala. The smaller Laney sat up front on Finley's lap while Collette and her family squeezed into the back seat. The silence continued for a few minutes until Stacey broke the ice and asked where they were going.

"There's a place west of town where I'm staying. It's big enough to be comfortable."

"How long will we be there?"

Winters wasn't sure. "A day, maybe two?"

"Do you have food? Because this one is supposed to be working to get us some today?"

Collette turned to her with a frustrated look. "Mom, why can't you be happy about this?"

"Because come morning your little brother is going to be hungry and I've got nothing to give him."

"But I won't have to work anymore," pleaded Collette.

Winters could not believe what he was hearing and realized there was something wrong with this family. "You don't need to worry. I have food there."

"Worry is what we do, Mister Winters. When you've gone days without food, worry is what you do."

"I understand," Winters said, with more than a tinge of irritation in his voice.

"Do you?" she asked in a harsh tone.

Winters gripped the steering wheel tighter deciding to give Stacey some perspective.

"I do. You see Stacy, I've been all over the Midwest and I've seen old people, women, and children executed for no other reason than the killers didn't want to feed them. I've rescued young girls taken into slavery and raped repeatedly all day. I've seen the bodies of close to a thousand people murdered inside churches all at once. I've seen people begging and scrounging for their next meal."

The dead silence in the car was eerie as Winters continued.

"But I've also seen amazing things. Men and women rising up to fight evil, forfeiting their lives to save the person next to them. I've seen young girls like these three here, muster up incredible courage and do things they never would have thought possible. I know an eleven-year-old girl who fought with everything she had and never gave up on me. You don't get to see that kind of human spirit every day, but when you see people fight when they had nothing to go on but faith, that is something quite special."

Winters could almost hear everyone breathing it was so quiet.

"You should be proud of Collette. She helped save her friends' lives tonight. She did it willingly and bravely. All three of them have been nothing but courageous."

The rest of the drive to the hideout was in awkward silence. Winters hadn't meant to be quite so blunt, but he couldn't take her negativity any longer. He thought he'd seen it all before he had come back to his hometown. However, if the other parents were anything like Stacey, it would be even more unimaginable than the prostitution itself. She seemed to have completely given up and had adopted a level of acceptance that Winters hoped wasn't prevalent.

CHAPTER 31

Winters ushered everyone inside and introduced them to Ashley who looked like she had been dozing off and on. He checked on Blair, the girl from Jarvis's house who had passed out and found her still sleeping. He thanked Ashley for the help and told Finley and Laney to get ready to go.

Winters stepped outside to wait for them when Collette joined him. He turned around to her and said, "Hey, you alright?"

"Yeah, thanks for sticking up for me."

"You deserved it."

"I'm really sorry about my mom."

"Don't be."

"She's always been, like, a negative person."

"Some people are just like that."

"Well, it makes it hard to live with her. I was supposed to be going away to college this last year and was really looking forward to it."

"What about your dad?"

"Off to war like everyone else's."

Finley and Laney stepped outside ready to go.

"Can I come?" asked Collette.

Winters was expecting the question and had already decided to let her come. He didn't think it'd be a good idea to let her stay there with her mom. "Of course you can."

"Yes," said an excited Collette.

"C'mon girls, the sun's gonna be up pretty soon."

Winters floored the car and headed toward the police van having decided to have Finley drive the Impala to her house. There was no sense in not utilizing both vehicles to save time. Besides, he needed to finish up so he could get some sleep.

He pulled into the field and found the van untouched.

"Listen, girls, we need to save some time. Finley can you take the car and pick up your mom and sister."

"I can do that," said Finley who then turned to Collette. "You want to come with me?"

"Sure."

"Okay, now don't take any chances. In fact, you might want to park the next street over and sneak in. I'm sure that one guy in the boxer shorts went for help."

"Oh, you mean, Bobby."

"Bobby? That's his name, really?" asked a surprised Winters.

"Yep," said Finley.

"Well, it's Bobby Boxers now," quipped Winters.

"Ha, Bobby Boxers, I love it," laughed Laney."

Winters watched Finley pull away and then got into the van.

"I hope your mom isn't like Collette's mom," said Winters as he started the van.

"Oh, gosh no. That poor girl, I don't know how she puts up with it."

"She's still her mom."

"Yeah, I know. My mom hates that I work, but there's no other choice."

"You don't need to justify that to me."

"I just don't want you to think I'm, like, a whore or something, or that I enjoy it."

Winters stopped the van before pulling out of the field. He looked at

Laney through the goggles. "Laney, you're a brave girl, that's what I think of you, nothing more."

"Thanks, that means a lot."

"Though you are a bit impulsive."

"I know, right? I, like, can't help myself. I mean, I react without thinking, like, all the time."

"Well, it saved my bacon tonight, so it's not so bad."

"It was pretty stupid. I don't know what the heck I was thinking. I mean, I guess I didn't want to see you get hurt."

"Like not wanting to see Finley get hurt?"

"Yep."

Winters looked back toward her and wanted to know how she was processing her shooting. "You okay with what you did though?"

Laney paused before answering. "It's a little weird, but yeah I guess. I mean, like, I've killed deer before and this was, well, it was different for sure, but yeah, I am."

Winters sensed she was having trouble with it. "Killing someone isn't an easy thing for anyone. My first time I ended up getting sick and throwing up."

"Really?" she asked wide-eyed.

"Yep. That's just between you and me though, alright? I've got a reputation to uphold now."

"I promise I won't say anything, but seriously, you threw up."

"Oh yeah. Not only that, but I shook uncontrollably for, like ten minutes."

Laney put a hand to her mouth to muffle her laugh.

Winters' confession helped relieve her mind. It wasn't easy for someone that age to do what she did, but then she had been doing things no one should have had to do. It made you grow up and leave your childhood behind.

Winters pulled into an abandoned house one street over from where Laney lived. He cautioned her that they needed to be careful since Bobby Boxers had escaped and was out there somewhere.

Laney led him through the backyards to the side of a house that sat across the street from where she lived. They crouched down on the ground at the corner of the house and Winters took off the goggles and helped her put them on. She let out a gasp when she saw everything light up green.

"Look carefully for anything out of place."

She nodded her head and looked across the street. "Everything looks good."

"You sure?" whispered Winters.

"Yep."

They stood up and started across the lawn. Just as soon they approached the sidewalk, she grabbed Winters' arm.

They both froze.

She started pulling him backward.

Winters bent down to her ear. "What is it?"

"Over there. That car, it doesn't belong here."

Winters looked up the street. A parked car sat on the side of the road and was pointed toward them.

"Whose is it?"

"I don't know, but it doesn't belong here."

They turned around and rushed toward the backyards.

"What are we gonna do?"

"Take out whoever it is," said Winters, as he helped Laney take the goggles off. He didn't want to tell her just yet, but someone was probably already inside her house.

The hairs on his arms raised as he realized Finley and Collette were in danger as well. They needed to hurry. He grabbed Laney's hand to make sure she stayed out of sight as they ran across the backyards toward the car. They reached the corner of the house and he motioned her to get down. They crawled to the end of the house, and Winters stared at the occupant in the car. He wished he had a silencer for his weapon. The last thing he needed was to alert whoever was inside the house.

"You up for doing another stupid thing?"

"You know me."

He gave her instructions before she streaked across the yard to hit the pavement and began to casually walk toward home. Winters then crawled on all fours across the lawn and got into position behind the car. He reached the back of the car just as Laney was also approaching it from the rear, but she walking in the middle of the street. She didn't dare glance at him as she sauntered past the car.

It took a second before the car door opened. Winters crept around the back end before leaping up. He wrapped his arm around the man's mouth just as he got out. The blade cut cleanly across his throat.

Laney raced over and watched Winters drag the man behind the car.

He gave her a nod while shutting the car door. Then he let Laney lead the way to the back of her house. Winters grimaced and readied himself for what was about to happen. Without a doubt, he knew someone was inside waiting for her. He just hoped they hadn't done anything to her mom and sister. They reached the patio where there was a big sliding glass door. Inside, several candles burned on the coffee table giving out enough light to show her mom and little sister sitting on the couch. The heavy-set mom held onto the frightened child as an older man, who was holding a rifle, watched over them.

CHAPTER 32

Winters recognized the man to be Ed Sherman Jr. Earlier that day he'd killed his parents and his son, Tim. He slowly let out a breath because he was about to kill another Sherman. This one was as useless as the others and it wasn't a surprise to find he was involved. Sherman's state of mind would be out of control and would shoot Laney on sight so Winters decided against sending her in there.

"Any suggestions?" asked Winters in a whisper.

"I could just walk in and distract him."

"Now that would be the impulsive thing. This one will take something better."

"I know. My bedroom window is cracked open for air."

"Where is it?"

She pointed to the other end of the house.

"Anything in the way?"

"No."

"Any creaking floors I should know about?"

"Wow, you really do think ahead."

"Learn this, okay?"

She nodded.

"Watch him while I crawl in. If he moves, come and tap on me."

Winters moved to her window and pushed it open. He looked inside before placing his M-4 on the carpeted floor. He then jumped up on the frame and shimmied inside. The room reminded him of Cara's. Posters of her favorite bands and pretty boys covered the walls. He let out a small laugh realizing that Laney was still just a young innocent girl at heart. She seemed to be holding onto whatever teen years she had left. He didn't blame her. This room was her sanctuary where she could still be herself and forget about her obligations.

He moved to the door and tiptoed down the carpeted hallway. He now had an open view of the living room and peeked around the corner. Sherman moved to the picture window and pushed aside the heavy drape. He then flicked on a penlight and flashed it toward the car outside. He waited a moment before trying again.

"He better not be sleeping," muttered Sherman.

Winters let out a smirk before stepping out into the living room. The movement alerted Sherman, whose eyes grew wide when he recognized Winters. He tried in vain to raise his rifle. Winters pulled the trigger and fired a three round burst into his chest throwing him into the drapers before he crashed onto the floor.

Laney's mom and daughter screamed.

"It's okay, Laney's outside," Winters said while moving to the entrance and unlocking the sliding glass door.

Laney rushed inside and ran to her mother and sister both of whom started crying.

"It's okay, Mom. Everything's okay."

"Honey, what's happened? He said he wanted to kill you?"

"I know Mom, but it's okay now."

"Who is this?" she asked looking at Winters.

"This is Cole Winters and he's here to help."

"Cole Winters?" She looked at Laney. "Oh honey, what have you done?"

"You mean besides never having to work again?"

"What?"

"Look, I'll explain everything later, okay, but right now we have to get out of here."

"But honey, this man," she said looking at Winters.

"He's here to help and has been. He's stopping Billy Gamble and everyone else."

A light seemed to go on making her realize the significance of that statement. She grabbed Laney and gave her a big hug.

"I'm sorry, Mister Winters," she said getting up to shake his hand.

"It's okay, I get that a lot."

"I'm Jamie and this is my daughter Riley."

"It's nice to meet you. Laney has been a big help tonight and very brave."

"Yes, she's always been rambunctious. Little impulsive, too."

Winters cracked a smile. "You don't say?"

Jamie gave him a puzzled look.

"Look, mom, we have to go, okay. So, get Riley some clothes and let's go."

Winters laughed to himself watching Laney taking charge. She might be impulsive, but she was also a quick thinker and seemed to easily take charge of situations. Her mother dutifully took Riley down the hall to get dressed.

"I'm gonna get out of these wet clothes," said Laney.

She disappeared before getting an answer, and Winters began to grow impatient. If they were here waiting on Laney, then it made sense they were at Finley's place as well. He didn't have time to get Jamie and little Riley to safety and decided to have them drive the car Sherman and his partner conveniently left out front.

"See, only took a second," said Laney, who put on another pair of jean shorts, a black cami top and a dry pair of sneakers. "My feet were totally wet from the grass."

"Think your mother could drive that car out front?"

She nodded. "Mom! C'mon, chop, chop."

Winters shook his head and let out a chuckle.

135

"I'm coming, honey," said Jamie as she entered the living room. Riley, now out of her pajamas, followed close behind her.

They exited through the front door and walked up the street toward the car.

"Mom, we need you to drive to our hide out."

"Where?"

Laney gave her directions and told her who was already there.

"But where are you going, honey?"

"I still need to help Cole."

Jamie seemed hesitant, so Winters assured her that she was going to be perfectly safe. It took a few more seconds of convincing from Laney before she got in the car. They watched her drive off before running back to the van.

"Your mom seems nice," said Winters, putting the van in gear.

"She is, but she's always been a little unsure of herself."

"She's just careful is all."

"Yeah, I suppose, I'm just more like my dad."

Winters didn't bother asking about her dad because he had gone to the Patriot Center just like everyone else in town. They were all dead now and there was no sense in bringing it up.

"How far to Finley's?"

"Not far. Make a right up ahead."

"We need to come in stealth like again."

"Stealth like, I love it," said Laney.

Winters gave her a curious glance. This little one was intrigued with the operations.

It only took a few minutes before Laney had Winters pull into the driveway of another abandoned house. He pulled it into the backyard to hide the police van since it stuck out like a sore thumb.

They hopped out and threaded their way through backyards and over a chain link fence before coming to Finley's house. They sat across the street hiding behind overgrown hedges. Winters noticed the front door was wide open. Sweat dripped from his temples knowing something was wrong.

"Front door's open," whispered Winters.

"They might have left it open when they took off."

It was a possibility and gave Winters pause. "Let's check the streets."

They moved back behind the house and traveled across more back yards.

Winters had a knot in his stomach, and it was getting tighter as they trampled through more wet grass to the street behind Finley's to find the Impala.

He shot his arm out, stopping Laney. "The Impala is up there." They climbed over another chain link fence and crossed the yard. They were across from the Impala and could see no one in it. Winters' pulse quickened as he looked up and down the street expecting the worst. It was becoming obvious that someone had scooped up Finley and Collette. Why else would the front door be open and the Impala still be sitting here?

"Let me look through those," ordered Laney.

Winters took the goggles off and helped her put them on. He watched her bob her head around looking for anything out of place.

"I don't see anyone."

Winters decided to let her keep them on while he approached the car. He rose up and started across the yard. He kept his M-4 at the ready as he reached the car to find it empty. Laney followed close behind him darting her head around, keeping watch.

A kicked stone bounced on the pavement up ahead and Winters jerked around pointing his weapon. He began to pull the trigger when Laney called out.

CHAPTER 33

Winters strained his eyes as he looked through the darkness trying to figure out who was approaching when he heard Laney speak up and rush past him.

"It's Collette."

"What?" asked Winters, wishing he was wearing the goggles.

"Collette, you're okay?"

Winters saw Laney wrap her arms around her friend. He found himself doing the same thing, happy she was unharmed.

"Where's Finley?" asked Winters.

"They got her and her mom and sister."

"What happened?" asked Laney.

"We came in through the back like you said and didn't see anything wrong, but Finley told me to wait while she went inside because she didn't want to, like, freak out her mom, who always slept on the couch. I heard her scream so I knew they had her. I backed away then moved around the house and watched them take her."

"Who's them?"

"Billy Gamble and Bobby."

Winters mind began to spin trying to figure out his next move. The sun would start to rise in the next half hour, which would negate his biggest advantage. He needed to know where they had taken her and how long ago. He also needed to know how many were left.

Laney grabbed onto Winters' arm. "Oh my God, they'll torture Finley and she'll tell them about the hideout."

"Girls, I need you to focus."

They both nodded.

"Laney, you got the list?

"Yes," she replied pulling it out of her pocket.

"Update it and tell me how many are left."

"Collette, how long ago was this?"

"About thirty minutes. I stuck around hoping you'd come here."

"You were right to do so. Now, where do you think they took her?"

"Billy's place. I heard him yell to Bobby to meet him there."

"You've killed eighteen," said Laney. "Wow, eighteen. You've got four left."

"Very doable," said Winters wanting to give these two a confidence boost.

"Where does Billy live?"

"Over on Pine Street. At the end of the street."

The street was a cul-de-sac, so there was only one way in or out. Winters needed to get over there as soon as possible. If they tortured Finley, which he had no doubt they would, then they would send someone to go fetch the rest of them.

"Girls, c'mon. We need to get to the van."

Rather than running through more wet grass, Winters led them up the block and took a right on the next street. They were out of breath as Winters fired up the van. Laney sat on Collette's lap while still wearing the goggles.

Winters turned on the interior lights, reached back, and grabbed some water bottles and power bars.

"Oh, just what I needed, I'm starving," said Laney, flipping the goggles up.

"Me too," said Collette, tearing open the wrapper.

Winters took a few moments to gulp down some water and start munching on a power bar. He had spent a lot of energy tonight and needed to recharge. Sleep was what he needed, but that wasn't an option. He turned to the girls who were devouring the energy bars as if they had never eaten one before, or at the very least, not in a long time. Looking at how underfed Laney appeared this was probably a luxury for her.

Winters finished off the bottle of water and tossed it in the back. He put the van in gear and pulled out onto the road. He figured the last four targets would all be at Billy Gamble's place, so he turned on the headlights. It would be light soon enough anyway and they would be exposed.

His heartbeat slowed down in relief as he turned onto Pine Street. He stopped past the last street that intersected Pine. He parked the van right in the middle of the street and leaned back in his seat. He figured it had been forty-five minutes since they took Finley. They wouldn't know exactly what happened and she would lie as best she could. She would feign ignorance and they wouldn't be sure if she was lying or not. All of that would take a minimum of thirty minutes. If they got anything out of her, they would argue amongst themselves, which would take up more time. They would then need to go check it out. Who would go? It wouldn't be Billy Gamble. No, he would send someone else, but that person wouldn't want to go alone. Winters straightened his back certain that two people would be leaving the house.

"What are we doing, Cole?" asked Laney.

He turned to her. "Something stupid."

"Oh, right up my alley then."

"Yep," said Winters, noticing the darkness was beginning to disappear.

"Are you gonna think about it?" asked Laney as she took off the goggles.

"Would you?"

"C'mon now, you know I wouldn't."

"So, what are we gonna do?" asked Collette.

Winters told them what he suspected was going to happen.

"You sure?" asked Collette.

"Nothing's for sure, but I've got a gut feeling and sometimes that's all you can go on."

"So, what do you want us to do?" asked Laney.

"Well, why don't you get in the back and pick out a bigger weapon than that Sig," said Winters, as he turned on the interior lights.

Laney slid off Collette's lap and looked in the back. "Oh my God, look at 'em all. Is that an AR?"

"It is?"

"I want that one, I love that gun."

Winters looked at Collette. "Ever fire a gun before?"

"A few times with my Dad."

"Take a look."

Collette climbed in the back, and the two girls started talking in excited tones. Laney was the more experienced one and suggested Collette grab the Glock 17 that Winters absconded earlier tonight. The 9mm was a good size for her, and she had some practice with a similar gun.

Winters hopped out of the van and scanned the neighborhood. He wasn't sure how many people still lived here, and didn't really care. They'd see the police van and stay inside. He spotted a couple of old oak trees standing tall next to each other on the left and decided that was where he would place the girls. It was a good place to hide and big enough for protection should someone try to run them over.

The girls stepped out of the van, each holding their weapon of choice. Winters gave them both instructions with the weapons until he was satisfied they wouldn't shoot anyone by accident. He then told them what he wanted them to do and that it was a waiting game. They walked over to the oak trees but decided to sit down on the street not wanting to sit in the wet grass.

Winters's eyelids began to close and he had to stand back up. He walked toward the van and leaned back against it. The sun was peeking over the horizon and the neighborhood was starting to come alive. Squirrels began jumping through the branches and birds were chirping away. The chirping became mesmerizing, and he started to fall into a trance when Laney yelled out. "Here they come."

CHAPTER 34

SARNIA ONTARIO

The back of the paddy wagon was not a comfortable ride, and worse yet when you were wearing handcuffs. The steel bench seat was not cushioned and the men bounced up in the air whenever they hit a pothole. Thankfully, the ride was a short one, but long enough for Scar to tell the guys it was best to just come clean. He had no doubt they would separate them once they got to the station. They had no time to come up with some BS story so he decided to throw the dice and cast their fate.

The wagon pulled into a garage and the back door opened. The station was like any other police station with fluorescent lights, steel doors and cameras watching your every move.

They led Scar to a small room that had a narrow table and two chairs on either side. Scar sat down and waited alone a few minutes before Sergeant Major Wilson came in.

"Scott Scarborough, this is your real name?" asked Wilson.

"It is indeed."

"Why are you here?"

"I beg your pardon?"

"I've dealt with a lot of American refugees over the past year, hundreds in fact. They come here desperate for shelter and food. Some are trying to escape criminals that seem to be running the show over there. The one common thing they all have is a certain look of desperation on their faces and the way they act. My problem with you and your friends is that you don't have that look. In fact, you have the exact opposite look. Besides not coming through our official border crossing, you're bold, confident, and you were armed, which tells me you are a criminal and you guys came here to cause us trouble."

Scar fought to control the outburst that boiled inside him. He needed to hear the man out before he responded. He took a deep breath and pretended the man was a past customer of his who had a problem with the work his company had completed for him.

"Add to the fact that we found you with a pocket full of money, both Canadian and American, and a couple of gold Maple Leaf coins, which leads me to believe you didn't just cross the river. In fact, I believe you've been busy at work robbing the good citizens of Sarnia."

Scar tightened his fists listening to this cop who seemed to have already made up his mind as to what it was they were doing. He was going to have to remain calm and try to explain to him who they were and hoped they didn't believe the American media who had painted them as raping, murdering, anarchists.

"So tell me, am I wrong? And before you try to lie your way out of this, I know when someone is lying to me."

Scar cleared his throat. "Sergeant Major, you couldn't be more off base. You're correct in assuming we're not refugees. We came here not to steal, but to buy supplies and bring them back to a town that is starving."

Wilson's left eyebrow hiked at this information. "Then why didn't you come through the border entrance up the road?"

"If we had we would have been arrested by the National Police, who are trying to kill us."

"Oh?"

"They're corrupt as they come and would like nothing more than to take us in."

Wilson looked doubtful. "Why do they want to take you in?"

Scar paused before answering knowing he was about to roll those dice. "Have you heard of the Shadow Patriots?"

Wilson nodded his head.

"I'm one of them."

"You're sure about this?"

Scar cocked his head in confusion. "Why would I lie about that?"

"Not sure that you would, but I wanted to make sure."

"Why? Are you gonna let us go?"

Wilson choked back a laugh. "I'm afraid not."

"Listen, it's extremely important that we get back to Michigan. We've got a town that is surrounded by bad guys and they've already killed over a thousand innocent people. For the last week, we've been defending that town while sneaking the citizens out of there. They're down to their last few days of food and we still have over a thousand people to remove. We need to get back."

Wilson looked apologetic. "That's not going to happen."

"Don't we get a phone call or something?"

"Things are run a little differently over here and especially with so many Americans. I'm sorry, but you'll need to see the judge first."

Scar wasn't giving up. "Then can you do me a big favor?"

"Depends on the favor."

"Can you make a phone call for me?"

"I don't know about that," said Wilson in a hesitant tone.

"Please, it's important."

"Who is it you want me to call?"

"General Standish at his base in Winnipeg."

"Winnipeg? A general? What does he have to do with you?"

Scar wasn't sure if he should tell this man. He wasn't sure if Standish's help was something he'd get in trouble for. "He's a friend of mine is all."

"I'll see what I can do," said Wilson.

Scar wasn't convinced the man would keep his word, but could only hope for the best. They made a tactical error going into the restaurant. However, the more thought he put into it, the more convinced he became they would have been eventually arrested. With all the trouble the Canadians had been going through with refugees, it would have only been a matter of time before some cop stopped them for questioning.

CHAPTER 35

SABINE IOWA

Winters had been waiting on Pine Street for the thugs who were holding Finley and her family. After giving instructions to the girls, he was standing in the middle of the street to block any escape. It didn't take too long before Laney yelled that they were coming. He pulled the slide back on his Colt M-4 and flipped the switch to full auto. He had four magazines ready to go. He looked down the road and watched the car as it moved toward them.

"Girls, get into position, and fire when they pass that house I pointed out."

Winters stepped away from the van but stayed in the middle of the road. His heart began to quicken as the car got closer. He took in several controlled breaths and rolled his shoulder before pressing the rifle in place. The car began to slow down as it came within three hundred feet and the driver didn't seem to know what to do.

"C'mon, just a tad bit closer," said Winters, knowing he was well within the effective range of the gun. He just wanted maximum exposure before he opened fire.

The car came to a stop, and Winters wasn't sure if they would begin to back up, so he pulled the trigger. The quiet neighborhood exploded in thundering echoes as rounds ripped through the still air and into the car. He emptied the magazine in seconds and slammed in a fresh one. The car's engine roared as it shot forward. It closed in fast as he squeezed the trigger again. The car began to swerve left as it passed by the designated house. Laney stepped away from the tree and unloaded her rifle into the side of the car. Collette flipped around and began taking pot shots as the car zipped past her.

Winters slammed in a third magazine as the car drew within a hundred feet. Both occupants were bleeding, and Winters shot at the windshield peppering the glass with holes. The car careened off to the left and headed toward a house. It crashed into the foundation, and the engine began to rev high as the dead man's foot pressed on the pedal.

Winters charged in keeping his weapon pointed at the car. He pulled open the driver's door and found the man slumped over the wheel with the air bag draped over his head. He peered over him and found the passenger to be bleeding out of multiple wounds. Winters grabbed the driver's left arm and pulled on it. He fell over and the engine settled down. He reached in and turned the key off just as Laney and Collette raced over.

"Oh man," said Laney. "Look at this."

"You know these guys?" asked Winters.

Collette and Laney looked at the bloodied bodies and nodded. Laney pulled out the list and checked off two more.

"That was Brian Holiday and his buddy Smitty."

"Wow, you called that one right," said Collette.

"That leaves two," said Laney.

"Yes, and these will be the toughest to get at."

"Do you think they heard the gunfire?" asked Laney.

"More than likely. It's only a couple of blocks and that gunfire would have echoed off these houses, so yes, they heard."

"What are we gonna do?" asked Laney.

"I'm hoping to flush 'em out. Let's grab some more ammo and get down there."

Winters helped the girls reload and gather some extra magazines before running through backyards toward Billy Gamble's house. Winters wasn't sure what he wanted to do and wouldn't be able to make a decision until he set eyes on the place. He had only two more people to go, but now there were hostages involved.

"There it is," said Laney as they came around a house.

The house was a single-story and sat at the very end of the cul-de-sac. A quad cab pickup was parked in the driveway. White curtains, which were shut tight like all the other windows, covered the picture window. The houses on either side appeared to be empty and one even had a few broken windows.

Winters kept staring while trying to come up with a plan. He could try to enter through a back window, but he had no idea where anybody was. He couldn't storm the place without risking getting someone killed. He shook his head remembering all the hostage movies and shows where they had high-tech gadgets to help.

"Any ideas?" asked Laney.

"Well, we can't see inside, which limits our options."

"We could ring the door bell," smirked Laney.

"Or, I could do my naked act again," said Collette.

"I'd like to see that, again," quipped Laney.

"Girls, can we get serious?"

"I am being serious," said Collette. "I don't mean get naked, but I could, like, yell out from the driveway and distract them."

Winters looked at her as he gave it some thought, but knew it was too dangerous. While he needed for them to come outside, he wasn't sure of just how agitated they might be. Perhaps she was onto something when she offered to distract them. He wouldn't let her be the distraction, so they needed something else. Then an idea struck him.

"Either one of you ever been inside?"

"Well, yeah, we both have," said Laney.

"Is there a room where you know for certain he wouldn't have them in?"

Laney looked at Collette. "What about the laundry room?"

"Or his office," suggested Collette.

"Where are those located?" asked Winters.

"Office is in the back corner," said Collette. "Give me that list of names and a pen."

Laney pulled out the paper and handed it to Collette, who then drew a layout of the house. Winters stared at it and came up with an idea. He told them it and they both nodded their heads.

Winters ran back to the van and grabbed a couple of empty water bottles out of the back. He then hustled over to the car that had crashed into the house, got down on his knees and drew out his knife. He punctured the gas tank and waited patiently for the bottles to fill with gasoline. It reminded him of when he was on the run with Elliott and Reese out on Robinson Road. They had set an SUV filled with weapons on fire so they wouldn't fall into the hands of their enemies.

The last bottle overflowed with gas, and Winters put the cap on before racing back to the girls. The three of them snuck over to the corner of the house where Collette had indicated there was a small office. Staying behind overgrown bushes, he studied the vinyl-covered house, which would melt and create a deadly smoke. The occupants would have no choice but to exit from the front door or the sliding glass door in the back. Winters kept the girls next to him where they could keep an eye on both exits and would be able to draw down on either of them.

He left the safety of the overgrown bushes and rushed to the house to splash the corner of the house spreading gasoline up and down the house. He stepped back and flicked a lit match into the flammable liquid. The fire huffed as it instantly lit, and within seconds, the back corner was in flames.

CHAPTER 36

DETROIT MICHIGAN

Coffee spilled on his desk as Vatter sat down in his office. The thirty-year old station commander cursed at himself because he had filled the cup to the brim and hadn't taken a couple of sips before moving it. He leaned over to grab a couple of napkins out of the trashcan to blot the liquid up before it damaged his papers.

As he lifted the cup to take a sip, the steam from the hot liquid floated up into the bandage on the side of his face, which was still sensitive from the knife wound he'd received from his cousin. This reminded him of the decision he'd made to kill her and sell the twin girls to Mordulfah. At first, he was ecstatic to have come up with such a brilliant plan to save his own head. There was no way he'd be here today had he not done so, which was an easy way to rationalize the decision. However, he then had to deal with his mother, who unfortunately was the one who had found her bloody corpse. He didn't want to put her through that but figured it was the only way to divert the attention from himself. He tried to act shocked about the whole thing, but his mother knew right away that he had killed her. The wounds he had received were a giveaway and besides, he never could keep a secret from her.

He hoped it wouldn't take her too long to forgive him for not cleaning up his mess. Surprisingly, having to see the mess, rather than the actual killing, was what she angriest about. She grieved for the twins but shrugged her shoulders because their lives were not as important as her son's was.

He took another sip of coffee and thought about the disaster that took place the other night in Grosse Pointe. Once again, the Shadow Patriots got away, but this time, Mordulfah couldn't blame him. He and his men had stayed right where he had ordered them to be. Somehow, Winters knew what was really going on and staged quite a rescue of his daughter and the twin girls. Satisfaction spread across Vatter's face because the twins were no longer with Mordulfah. He was surprised at how happy this information made him. Even though sacrificing the twins had saved his life, it hadn't been an easy thing to live with and he actually lost sleep over it. When he heard what had happened, he found himself silently thanking the Shadow Patriots for easing his conscience.

He hoped the girls were doing well now that they were safe in Jackson. He let out a laugh because they had the town surrounded and would eventually lay siege on it. He hoped they'd keep their heads down when it happened, which would probably be sooner than later. After what happened the other night, the men were making bets on the timeline. There was no way Mordulfah wouldn't want revenge and strike back.

Vatter stayed away from Grosse Pointe yesterday, figuring nothing good could come from it. He wasn't asked to come out and he sure as hell wasn't going to voluntarily go, especially with what happened the last time. His guys were also taking bets on how many men Mordulfah would execute if any. It wasn't as if he had an endless supply of M and M's, a term the cops used for Mordulfah's men. Some of these guys had to be regretting their decision to sign up with the Saudi Prince. They were losing vast numbers of men with little to show for it. He knew how disheartening it was from his own loses, and he had not lost anywhere near what Mordulfah had. Besides, it wasn't anyone's fault but his own for having Cara Winters there, to begin with. It was ridiculous to think the Shadow Patriots would believe she was in Detroit. These guys didn't get this far for being a bunch of idiots. He'd learned that the hard way over the past week and had to hand it to them for their tactical ability. It was a daring rescue to sneak into the mansion, again and had it not been for Charlie Chivers screaming out, they'd have gotten away with a clean break. Vatter shook his head at the stupidity of that girl getting herself killed. She'd be alive today if she had just waited a couple of minutes. Stupid girl.

The holes in Mordulfah's plan were obvious to begin with, but Vatter didn't dare tell him because he was too arrogant to be told anything. He had tried in the past but learned a valuable lesson when Mordulfah gave him a long cold stare. Those black eyes of his freaked the hell out of him. It was as if you were in some sort of horror movie. They penetrated deep into your soul making you quiver in fear. He remembered he was so nervous that beads of sweat had formed on his forehead. You never knew what this man was capable of doing. Vatter choked on his coffee laughing. "Beheading his own people is what he's capable of doing." How could he forget?

A knock on the door brought Vatter back to reality. Without permission, in walked Tannenbaum, a twenty-five-year-old cop who sported a splotchy beard on his baby face. He was Vatter's right-hand man but didn't always know his place.

"Oh, just come right on in," said Vatter in an annoying tone.

"Sorry, but you're not going to believe who I have on the phone."

Vatter raised his eyebrows waiting in anticipation.

"Some cop over in Sarnia has some Shadow Patriots in custody."

Vatter had to think for a moment where Sarnia was and then remembered it was in Canada. "And?"

"Wants to know if the reward offer is still good."

Vatter leaned forward excitedly. "Hell ya it is. Is he on the line?"

"Yeah man, let me transfer him to ya."

Vatter waited for the button to light up. His heart began to beat faster hoping it was Winters. He couldn't believe this was happening and had to control himself when the line lit up. His finger shook as he pressed the button.

CHAPTER 37

SABINE IOWA

After setting fire to the house where Billy Gamble was keeping Finley and her family hostage, Winters rushed back to the hiding place where the girls waited for him. They were alert and breathing rapidly as they stared wide-eyed at the exits. The knuckles on Laney's left hand were white as she tightened her grip on the AR-15. The girls' hearts were pounding as fast as Winters' was. This was a risky move with little leeway for error. Too many things could go wrong, starting with Billy Gamble or Bobby Boxers not even being in there. If that was the case, and Finley was tied up, then she'd die of smoke inhalation. He kept that in the back of his mind as he watched the flames start to engulf the back of the house. The fire crackled and snapped as the flames ate through the wood. Putrid black smoke filled the morning air, which had started to seep all around the area and was blocking his view. If the occupants heard this and still didn't come out to investigate, then they might know who was waiting outside for them. Would they come out to investigate what was happening first, or would they just drag their hostages out with guns held to their heads? With the fire raging, he wouldn't have to wait too long before finding out.

Movement at the sliding glass door caught his attention and Winters watched as Bobby Boxers crept out holding onto Finley's twelve-year-old sister, Kayley, who was crying in his arms. He kept her close to him while holding a gun to her head. Winters then heard a muffled scream on the other side of the house. Billy Gamble staggered out with his arm wrapped around Finley and a pistol to her head. He kept spinning around looking for any shooters.

The fire began to envelop the whole house when Winters realized Finley's mom was still inside. He had to make a choice who to go after first. He looked back and forth to both men and decided.

Without looking at the girls, he ordered them to stay put. He pulled out his knife with his left hand and crept down low using the black smoke as cover. He pointed the blade up as he came out of the smoke and charged Bobby Boxers, who had just turned toward him. He looked confused as Winters reached up with his right hand to push on the pistol while shoving the blade into his armpit. Bobby let out a yelp as Kayley squirmed out of his clutches. Bobby threw a punch at Winters, which landed on his right cheek but didn't deter him from pushing Bobby backward. The force tipped them both over and Winters fell on top, which gave him the advantage. He took the blade and thrust it into his throat finishing him off.

Kayley stared at Winters in shock while Collette rushed over and took her into her arms.

"Where's her mom?" asked Winters.

Collette brushed the girl's hair off her face and got the answer Winters had expected. She was tied up inside.

Winters raced into the burning house. The smoke hung low in the air and Winters dropped on all fours trying to take in short breaths. It took a few seconds before finding her in the living room tied to a chair. He scooted over to her and grabbed his knife to cut her free. He led her outside where she coughed a few times trying to suck in clean air. Her daughter rushed over and wrapped her arms around her while continuing to sob.

Winters turned back to where Laney was supposed to be. "Where's Laney?"

Collette looked and shook her head.

"Oh, hells bells," said Winters, knowing she was jumping into the fray without thinking, "Better go do your naked thing and help her."

Collette's eyes grew big and then took off around to the front.

Winters dashed around the other side of the house and hid behind bushes to look at the situation. Sure enough, Laney was screaming at Billy to let her friend go. He was holding onto Finley and a .380 pistol, small but still deadly.

"I started the fire you Jackass."

"What the hell, Laney? Where's Winters?"

"I don't know where he is. You let go of her."

Gamble jerked his head around like a lizard, not sure what to do next, while Finley looked surprisingly calm despite the redness on her cheeks from being smacked around. Seeing Laney, she must have known her rescue was imminent. Collette ran up to Laney and joined in the yelling at Gamble. The man still had the gun on Finley, but he was discombobulated as the two girls continued to yell at him. Winters noticed Laney had dropped the AR-15, which was smart on her part. It allowed Gamble to not be afraid of them and let his guard down a notch. If he was going to shoot them he would have already done so, or maybe he thought pointing the gun at them would get him shot.

Winters waited for the right moment before dashing across the driveway to hide behind the pickup truck. Gamble was on the walkway and backed up toward the driveway when Finley's mom and sister came around the corner. Now, Gamble, had four girls screaming at him. He was frustrated and tried to shut them up as he kept moving towards the truck.

"She's coming with me," yelled Gamble.

Winters crawled around the back of the truck and kept low behind the bumper. Gamble fumbled for the door handle while holding onto Finley by her ponytail. He started to pull it open but his hand slipped.

This was Winters' best chance. He put the rifle in single-shot mode, sprung up and came around the back of the truck with the M-4 to his shoulder. Gamble reacted by trying to shove Finley in front of him. Winters squeezed the trigger. The round hit him in the shoulder twisting his body around. The motion pulled Finley with him as he lost his balance. Winters tried lining up another shot but didn't have one. Gamble fell to the ground and Finley bounced off his chest and onto the cement. The .380 pistol fired and Finley screamed out in pain just as Winters put another round into Gamble's head.

CHAPTER 38

DETROIT MICHIGAN

After getting word from his right-hand man, Vatter pushed the speaker option on his desk phone and said hello.

"This is Sergeant Major Wilson with the Sarnia Police."

"What can I do for you?"

"I have four members of the Shadow Patriots in custody and wanted to inquire about the reward."

Vatter found the question curious. "Are you representing your government?"

There was a long silence.

"No. This would be a private transaction."

A smirk broke across Vatter's face and he said to himself, "My kind of people."

"Are you interested?" asked Wilson.

"Sergeant Major, I am most interested and yes, this can be kept private. Tell me, who do you have there?" asked Vatter as he grabbed a pencil.

"Scott Scarborough, David Burns, Joshua Bassett, and Nick Nordell."

Vatter's eyebrows rose when he heard Bassett's name and didn't have to look to know who he was. He was currently listed as AWOL and a traitor. Vatter reached over and pulled open a desk drawer to get the sheets on the other three. He found Scarborough and Burns but had nothing on Nordell.

"Well?" asked an impatient Wilson.

"So, you don't have Winters, huh?" asked a disappointed Vatter.

"No, but from what I can gather, Scarborough is in charge."

This was an interesting bit of news making Vatter think perhaps Winters was dead, that he might have caught a bullet the other night. "Why do you have them?"

"They were here to get supplies."

Vatter put his hands behind his head as he leaned back in his chair learning Jackson was desperate for food. If Mordulfah was smart he'd just starve them out, but the man was impatient and wouldn't wait that long. He'd rather waste more of his men in a big battle. Regardless, these four would be a nice present to offer Mordulfah. He determined the reward amounts to be thirty thousand for the three. He didn't know who this Nordell was but figured he could get another ten grand for him.

"From what I can see, you've got twenty-five thousand coming to you."

"Shouldn't it be forty? I've got four of them and they are supposedly worth ten each."

"I'm paying you out of my own pocket, so I need a cut. Besides, I've no idea who this Nordell guy is, for all I know he's just along for the ride."

"No, not this guy. He's a thirty-year retired Marine. Hell, he's a Gunnery Sergeant, so he's not just along for the ride."

Vatter let out a chuckle. He liked this guy and admired his tenacity. "Look, I'm taking a chance on him. I'll raise it to thirty-thousand total."

After a few moments of silence, Wilson agreed.

Vatter smiled because he just made ten grand. Even better was he had enough to pay for it with his own money. He wouldn't have to go to

Mordulfah and beg for the cash or wait for Washington to send it. He'd get his money back plus the additional ten grand and get credit for it. No one would be the wiser that some cop in Canada did the actual work.

Vatter got the particulars from Wilson as to the time and place to pick up the prisoners. They'd have to make a trip into Canada, which wouldn't be too much of a problem. His station wasn't on the best of terms with the border guards in Detroit so they'd have to drive up to Port Huron and cross there. Wilson guaranteed he'd have the border guards bribed so they could cross over unabated. Vatter liked the sound of this and hoped there might be more business they could conduct in the future. They were always in need of liquor and it wasn't always easy to come by. The big crash affected liquor supplies even in Canada, where you could only buy so much of the stuff unless you were a bar or restaurant. Everyone else had to wait in line with ration coupons, which of course, was the perfect recipe for the black market.

Detroit still had plenty of money floating around to those who had the right product to sell. Since he was the station commander, not only did he know the right people, but he controlled the market. His guys hired the gangs to row across the river to rob the good citizens of Canada. They didn't always succeed, which is why he was always on the lookout for other opportunities.

He looked at the reward sheets again and was extremely pleased that he was about to get his hands on Corporal Bassett. This idiot was a traitor, and Major Green would love to get him back. He should be able to negotiate a better deal than the ten grand they were offering. After all, he was an active member of the United States Army and an embarrassment to that fine institution. He couldn't wait to have them in his custody. He'd torture them all before turning them over. He wanted to know what was going on in Jackson and just how desperate the food situation was. He'd also find out what the hell had happened to Nick Posey. He hadn't heard anything from him since Sunday. His last transmission was that the rebels were going to storm the police station. Vatter let out a scoff, "That was obviously a decoy." They either forced him to do it, or fed him the lie first, and then busted him out afterward. A shiver shot through Vatter thinking about what they would do to him if he were caught. After all, he was the one who ordered the raid on the hospital.

Vatter started to put the reward sheets away but paused on the sheet for Cole Winters.

"One hundred thousand dollars alive or seventy-five thousand dead." Vatter wanted nothing more than to put a bullet in his head, but a hundred was better than seventy-five. That'd go a long way toward his retirement fund, and it would be a personal victory to put him in the ground. With all the trouble he's caused with his men, he was more than an annoyance. Somehow, he kept the party house from being reopened, which was a promise to the men he had yet to fulfill.

Vatter leaned back in his chair thinking about the conversation he'd just had. The man said Scarborough was in charge. Was Winters dead? Or, was this just some bluster from Wilson? Either way, he'd find out once he had these men in custody. It would be a shame if the man was dead and there wasn't a body. Need a body to collect a reward.

Vatter got up and walked out of the office. He gathered his men together to tell them the good news.

CHAPTER 39

SABINE IOWA

Finley cried out in pain as blood leaked from her thigh and soaked her jeans. Winters turned her over and found blood oozing from the exit wound.

Everyone rushed over just as Winters pulled out his knife to tear open the jeans.

"Finley, Finley, you okay?" cried her mom.

Winters thought it was a strange question to ask a wounded person, but then, what else would you say.

"Mommy, I've been shot, am I, am I gonna die?"

"No, honey, you're going to be okay," answered her mom in an unconvincing tone.

Winters turned to Finley. "Hey, hey, you're gonna be okay, alright? Just hang in there."

"You sure?" she asked through watery eyes.

"Yes, you're going be fine. Although, you're gonna have a couple of badass scars."

"I am?"

Winters nodded as he tore open her jeans. He looked at the bleeding and was thankful it was a full metal jacket bullet rather than a hollow point; otherwise, he'd be dealing with something much worse. He tore off his jacket and removed his shirt leaving him in a black t-shirt. He then ripped the shirt in half and pressed it against the exit wound.

"Can you keep pressure on this?" Winters asked the mom.

"Yes, I can do that."

"What's your name?"

"Debbie."

"Okay, Debbie, just keep pressing down on it."

He placed the other half of the shirt on the back wound and instructed Debbie to press them together.

Winters stood up. "Laney, there's a first aid kit in the van behind the driver's seat. Can you get that?"

She nodded and took off running.

Winters turned toward the house, which was now engulfed in flames. He needed to move Finley away from the smoke, which was starting to come toward them. He stepped over Finley and fished through Gamble's pockets finding the keys to the truck. He needed to get Finley some medical attention to make sure there were no nicked veins. Thoughts of Cara blazed through his mind as the scene was very reminiscent of the other night and it gave him pause. He had watched his daughter being stabbed and wasn't able to do anything to save her life. He shook his head and yelled at himself. "Damned if he was going to lose another one."

"Collette, any doctors or nurses around?"

"Yeah, my mom."

Winters jerked his head back in surprise.

"I know, I know, but she used to be a paramedic."

"But, she'll help though, right?"

"Yes, of course, I mean, we're never gonna hear the end of it."

Winters put his arm around her shoulders. "It'll be worth the price."

Laney came running back, out of breath and handed Winters the first aid kit. He applied fresh bandages and taped the leg up best he could before picking her up and placing her in the bed of the truck. He had

Collette drive the truck while Debbie sat in back with her daughter.

Winters hustled back to the police van, and they were at the hideout within fifteen minutes. Collette beeped the horn as she pulled into the driveway and then ran inside yelling for her mom.

Winters carried Finley inside where Stacy waited.

"What happened?" asked Stacy.

"She caught a bullet."

"You let this little thing get shot?"

Winters fought to remain calm. "Couldn't be helped."

Stacy ordered Collette to go get her medical bag from home. She then ordered Winters to carry Finley into the bedroom and then to leave the room.

Finley grabbed Winters around the neck as he carried her. "Thank you, Cole. Thank you for everything."

"Your welcome, Wannabe," smiled Winters.

"Hey, you…"

"Just kidding. You did good tonight," said Winters, laying her down on the bed.

"Really?"

"Yep, all three of you did."

"Out you go," ordered Stacy, waving her hand.

Winters left the room and walked into the kitchen where Ashley had begun boiling hot water for Finley and the freeze-dried food she pulled out for breakfast.

"What happened?" asked Ashley, who shuffled her daughter, Kaitlyn, out of the room.

Winters briefed her on the night's events.

"So, they're really all dead?"

"Every one of 'em."

"I can't believe it, I mean, I just can't believe you did it."

"Yeah, well, neither can I, at least not in one night."

"So, what now?"

"What do you mean?"

"What are you gonna do now?"

Winters leaned back in the kitchen chair thinking about the question.

He hadn't had time to give it much thought. He came here to bury Cara and wasn't sure what he was gonna do then. Now that he had taken care of this bad element, it gave him a different perspective on things. He let out a yawn and realized this wasn't the time to come up with an answer. He was too tired and needed sleep before he did anything else.

"I need to sleep."

"You'll have to take the bedroom down the hall. Blair is still passed out in the other and Finley has the master bedroom."

"Where did they store all the food?"

"At the Community Bank," answered Ashley.

"Really? The bank? Is it in the vault?"

"Yeah, but it's not locked. It had the best security doors though."

"Okay, well, we'll need to get in there and pass it all out."

Ashley placed a bowl of oatmeal on the table, and Winters devoured it before getting up and retiring to the bedroom. Two single beds sat on either side of the room. His friend, Paul, had twin boys who had shared this room until they finished high school. The room still had multiple trophies and medals sitting on the dressers. Both boys competed in track and field through high school and now served in the Army. He remembered Paul was excited about joining them in the war effort. Winters shook his head in disgust because Paul was not with them, but lying dead in a mass grave.

He sat down on the bed and took off his boots. He was about to stretch out when he heard a knock on the door.

"Come in."

Laney opened the door. "Hey, can I take the other bed?"

"Of course."

"Thanks. Mom's staying to help with Finley and I don't wanna, like, go home alone."

"I don't blame ya."

Laney took her sneakers off and slipped between the sheets. "Will Finley be okay?"

"She'll be fine," said Winters not knowing for sure.

"You're not, like, mad at me are you?"

"Why would I be mad at you?

164

"Uhm, you know, for doing what I did with Billy."

"Not at all."

"Well, I mean, it got her shot."

"Laney, that's not your fault. If anything you saved her life, there's no telling where he would have taken her."

"Seriously?"

"Oh, absolutely. Laney, you were amazing tonight."

She leaned up and rested her head on her fist. "Thanks. It's just, uh, you know, like, a lot happened tonight and, um, I mean, it's just so much, like, I just don't know what to think about all of it."

"I know how you feel and it's perfectly natural to feel that way, but Laney, just know that they all deserved it. There was no other way of stopping them, okay? You did nothing wrong. Again, you were amazing. All of you girls were. I couldn't have stopped those animals without your help."

Laney smiled and nodded her head. "Thanks, I just needed to hear it."

"Sweet dreams kiddo and remember, you no longer have to work."

She let out a loud "YES!" as she flopped on her back while moving her limbs back and forth like she was making a snow angel on the sheets before curling up on her side.

Winters heard her fall asleep within minutes as she started to snore in a low tone. He couldn't help but be impressed by what she and the others had done tonight. He just hoped they'd be able to come to terms with their involvement.

CHAPTER 40

SARNIA ONTARIO

Sergeant Major Thomas Wilson put the phone back in its cradle. The phone call to Detroit had gone as well as he had expected. He'd been a cop for seventeen years, which had resulted in a failed marriage, child support for two teenagers, high blood pressure, and a stomach ulcer. He had just celebrated his fortieth birthday and he looked more like fifty. His receding hairline kept growing, as did the bags under his eyes.

The last year had been an especially hectic one for the town of Sarnia as it was just across the river from Port Huron, Michigan. A bridge connected the two towns and kept them busy with refugees. The Canadian government's policy was one of compassion and all who were in need were welcomed. They erected temporary housing and supplied the extra food needed to feed all the additional mouths. For the most part, things ran smoothly, but with so many refugees, there was bound to be trouble. Justifiably, as America fell into ruin and the trouble moved north, the department decided everyone needed everyone to work overtime. He wasn't thrilled with having to work the extra hours as it robbed him of the little personal time he had left.

While he didn't necessarily agree with his government's policy of compassion, it was his job to deal with it and the ungrateful refugees who were included in the package. It ran from theft to fighting, raping, and an occasional homicide. The troublemakers were mostly younger individuals and some were not necessarily refugees. They would come across the river to do their thing before skipping back across. For the most part, this was happening down in the Detroit area, but Sarnia had its fair share. Now he had an opportunity to be paid for all his additional efforts.

*　　*　　*　　*

Scar stretched his legs before getting up from the jailhouse bed. It wasn't his best sleep, but then it wasn't his worst either. He'd gotten used to sleeping in some rough conditions over the past few months. However, in the last week or so, sleeping on the hospital beds had spoiled him. The beds were quite comfortable, and before that, they were up in Canada sleeping on even better beds.

He looked over at Bassett and Burns, who were in the next cell over. Nordell was in the bunk above him. He got up and walked around the cell hoping the Sergeant Major had made the call to Winnipeg. The man must have thought I was crazy making such a request. Scar didn't know the procedures in Canada and thought they might even be different from the norm for American refugees. They were happy to help, but they had to modify their rules and systems to accommodate their guest.

Scar turned on the faucet and splashed water on his face. The cool liquid woke him up and now wished he had a cup of coffee. His main concern was; would the Canadians notify the Americans that they held some of the Shadow Patriots. He wasn't sure of what their standing was or if they were in jeopardy of extradition.

He sat back down wishing he hadn't decided to bring in firearms. This one thing was going to get them in the most trouble. It wasn't even something he gave even a second thought to because of what they'd been through. He never considered not being armed.

"Hey," said Nordell.

Scar looked up as Nordell came down from his perch. "Morning."

"You get any sleep?"

"Not much, too many beers."

"We had two," said Scar.

Nordell stretched out his back. "I know, but then I haven't had one in forever."

"Yeah, me neither."

"I don't regret going to that bar."

"No?"

"For once, even if it was for only a short time, it was like everything was normal. You know, just out with some friends having a beer. Nothing else going on in the world."

Scar stood up. "Yeah, it was kinda nice."

"Don't worry about anything, we'll get out of this."

"I appreciate your optimism, but I have my doubts."

"Look, if that Sergeant doesn't call your general friend, we'll get our attorney to do it."

"If we get one."

Nordell gave him a puzzled look.

"I don't know how things work around here, but Wilson's demeanor changed when I told him who we were."

"Oh?"

"Yep. Questioned me several different ways just to make sure I wasn't lying."

"Funny, he came in to talk to me about it as well. I thought maybe because they were on our side or something."

This gave Scar pause, "were things not as they seemed?" He then realized that they hadn't even gone through a booking process. They didn't take mug shots or fingerprint them. This was odd.

"Don't worry, Scar, we'll get an attorney."

"Yeah, I suppose you're right."

"Of course, it might be a few days before we get released," said Nordell.

Scar grimaced. "Don't know if I can take a few days in here."

"Hell, we're like prisoners in Jackson anyway."

"It does seem that way."

"When we get with that general of yours, you think we can get more weapons?"

"They've been extremely gracious. I don't see why not."

"Good, cause I've some particular weapons in mind I want us to have."

"Oh?"

"Yes. Look, you guys stumbled into our little town not knowing what you were going to run into, so you didn't come prepared."

"We didn't?"

"No, not with what we have to do. Scar, I want to defeat these bastards and I want to do it with a big offensive. I'm sick of my town starving to death because of this. We need to go to Detroit and take them out."

"I hear ya and I'm with ya."

"Good."

It was another hour before the guards brought them something to eat, and after they finished eating they came back holding handcuffs. They ordered them to face the wall where they cuffed them before escorting them to the windowless paddy wagon.

"Where are you taking us?" demanded Scar.

"Don't worry about it," said one of the cops.

"You think they're letting us go?" asked Bassett.

"I couldn't say," said Scar.

The cop shut the door and hopped into the driver's seat. The drive took only ten minutes and the van stopped before they heard a garage door open up. Everyone sported confused looks as the van pulled in and stopped. A cop came around and opened the door. An empty feeling grew in the pit of Scar's stomach when he stepped out of the van into a large empty warehouse. The ceiling was at least twenty-five high, and the open area was approximately five thousand square feet with a couple of rooms in the very back. The concrete floors were clean, and the air smelled of fiberglass as if the place had been used to manufacture boats at one time or another. This all made Scar figure they were still near the river. He turned to his friends, and they all had the same look on their faces. "What was going on?"

Scar tried again to ask where they were and why were they here. The cop in charge didn't answer and ushered them into one of the back rooms. He took their cuffs off and told them they would find out soon enough what was going to happen.

CHAPTER 41

ALEXANDRIA VIRGINIA

The morning rays were breaking over the horizon as Green, finishing a quick thirty-minute run, turned the corner toward home. The early morning jog gave him the solitude he needed to think over their audacious plan. They planned on kidnapping two of Perozzi's men today and holding them hostage. With any luck, they'd be able to put together a shoot-out with Reed today as well.

The plan had come together in Manassas at Senator Seeley's place where their group met last night. The whole thing relied on their newest member, Stormy, who would lure the two men in. Her good looks should do the trick on their own, but would she be able to apply brute force if needed? How far was she willing to go? She'd already put herself in danger by mouthing off to Reed. The insecure fat man had ordered her arrest, which she was able to avoid thanks to Perozzi. That little stunt inadvertently helped them to drive the wedge between Perozzi and Reed even further.

Perhaps Stormy could take it to the end of the road and kill if necessary. Green didn't think she could do it without provocation though. Nothing against her, but she wasn't a trained soldier. It was not something that came naturally unless you were well trained or a psychopath.

Thankfully, Kyle Gibbs was a trained operator and had ten years of experience. The only reason he wasn't out west aiding in the war effort was because of his father, Jacob, told him something wasn't right with China attacking California. He had heard too many rumors from respectable people that the whole thing was just plain fishy. Before resigning from the FBI, he was able to pull some strings to keep his son's name out of the hopper.

After a shower, and then a quick breakfast with his mother, Green drove to work and parked his car in the underground parking lot. He parked further away from the entrance than usual, as he wanted to scope out the lot. He began walking down the slope and took note of spaces, which would be ideal for what he had in mind. He reached the door and turned around for one last look. He now had a good idea of what he needed to do to prepare, and that included disabling the camera pointed at the entrance.

The mission to induce fear into Reed would take place here. It was a place he came through and where they could control the situation. Reed was typically one of the last people to leave each day, so the garage should be empty.

Green grabbed a cup of coffee entering his office where Grace, his secretary, reminded him of a meeting he needed to attend at nine. He'd forgotten all about it and wanted to duck it, but he couldn't. These meetings were nothing more than ego driven drivel his colleagues needed to get through their week. The group was formed to capture Winters and the Shadow Patriots but had morphed into something entirely different. It had quickly become a way to root out anyone who opposed the government in any form. It was eye opening to watch good intentioned people go from catching a small group of rebels, to spying, and arresting, all kinds of different groups. Power definitely corrupts.

It was ten o'clock before Green could escape the meeting and get out of the building. He needed to meet with Stormy, who was waiting for a phone call from Kyle. He had left early in the morning to monitor Perozzi's men. Kyle had a general idea where they would be and didn't want to chance missing them so he left before Stormy was ready.

Green headed to one of his storage units and swapped his car for a white work van he had picked up. It was the perfect way to transport and keep their captive hidden until they needed them. He started the van and couldn't help laughing at the irony of using the money he stole from Reed's man, Pruitt, to use against Reed.

Green arrived at the three-bedroom house that Stormy was renting. It sat on a quiet, tree-lined street, which appeared to be even quieter since everyone was at work. He pulled into her driveway and got out just as the front door opened.

"Good morning, John," said Stormy, who was wearing an above the knee, light blue sundress with lace trimming the bottom of it. Her black hair flowed over her shoulders hiding the spaghetti straps. She wore white, low top sneakers to finish off the look.

Green's heart skipped a beat. "Hey, Stormy."

"Come on in."

Unpacked boxes were stacked against the wall, and for furniture, she used a couple of collapsible beach chairs for furniture. They sat in front of a television, which was sitting on top of a box.

"Sorry about the mess, haven't really had a chance to go through all of this and don't own any furniture. My place in New York was furnished, so I never bought any."

"Oh, please, it's fine. Not only do I not own a single piece of furniture, but I'm living back at home with my mom."

"Well, then I'm one up on ya. You want coffee?"

"You have some?" asked a surprised Green.

"I can go without a lot of things, but coffee's not one of them."

They entered the kitchen where a patio styled glass table substituted for a kitchen table.

"Who ever lived here before left the table out back, so I thought it'd be perfect in here," said Stormy.

"Whatever works," said an amused Green.

"Cream or sugar?" she asked, as she poured the coffee.

"None for me."

"Do all soldiers drink it black?"

"Not all, but it does make it easier when you're on the go."

"I drink it black because it's no calories."

"But, of course, you do."

"Need to keep my girlish figure, don't cha know," smiled Stormy as she handed him the cup.

Green blew on it before taking a sip and noticed how strong it was. He raised the cup and acknowledged it. He watched her take a sip and hoped she was up for the mission. She certainly was dressed to grab any man's attention. She looked cute and innocent, but she could handle herself. They hoped to not have to take these men off the street, but instead have her lure them in close enough to the van where Green and Kyle would knock them unconscious.

The phone rang and Stormy hustled into the living room to find the buried phone. It was Kyle and he had the first hostage picked out. Stormy set the phone back on the floor and then went her hall mirror. She stared into it took a couple of deep breaths to psych herself up. She was nervous and Green couldn't blame her. It was going to be a tough operation.

CHAPTER 42

PORT HURON MICHIGAN

Hadley, the young Texan, and former National Police officer, sat on the ground and rested his elbows on his knees as he held the big 10x42 binoculars to his eyes. Any slight movement made it difficult to focus the big glasses, especially something that was twenty-five hundred feet away. He took slow breaths as he looked across the Saint Clair River into Sarnia, Ontario. His nerves jumped into high gear when a police car pulled up to where his friends had tied off the canoe. Two cops got out of their cruiser and walked across a set of railroad tracks to the small dock by the sandpit. This wasn't good as there wasn't anyone else around who could have spotted the canoe. It took only a few seconds before the cops found the canoe and Hadley swallowed a gulp of air as he watched one of the cops pull out his pistol and fire three times. It took a few minutes for the boat to disappear under the water. Hadley cursed the cops as he watched them go back to their vehicle and take off.

He began tapping his fingers on the binoculars. His friends were in trouble. Why else would they have sunk the canoe? But why the cops? If the cops had them, then they should be able to get lawyers and make a phone call to their friends in Winnipeg. They'd get them out of there. Hadley's mind kept stirring around trying to come up with an answer when it finally hit him. "The reward," he said aloud. Goosebumps formed on his arm as he realized this was the only explanation. Hadley began pacing the riverbank, wondering if someone was watching him. If they were in trouble, then maybe he was too. He started back to the SUV realizing he was on his own. He took one last look around before entering the garage where they had hidden their ride.

He got in and tore open a power bar while contemplating his next move. "Should I stay or should I go," he said to himself and then began singing the words. Scar told him to take off if he thought he was in danger. He looked at his watch. It was too early in the morning for the cops to be roaming the roads. If Scar and the others made it here, they could always find another ride. The thought brought him some comfort, so he turned the key and started pulling out of the garage when he remembered they'd left their big weapons in the Suburban. He got out and looked around trying to decide where best to leave their guns and which ones they would need.

Hadley scanned the area for prying eyes before shutting the garage door. He jumped back into the Suburban and started on the return trip to Jackson. The further he got out of Port Huron, the more satisfied he was of his decision. He didn't know what kind of help they'd be able to bring to them, but Meeks needed to know the situation.

The two-hour drive back to Jackson took three hours as Hadley stayed off the interstates as much as possible, at least around the larger cities. There were contingents of cops still patrolling their nearly empty streets. Most of the people from places like Flint or Lansing left long ago when the trouble had begun in those areas from either the gangs or the cops themselves. Because of the close proximity, most of the residents had migrated into Canada. There were still pockets of people here and there, but for the most part, the cities were abandoned. Of course, the National Police were also forcing people out of their homes, which is where they had found most of the girls who were enslaved at the party house. For reasons Hadley didn't understand, folks in smaller Michigan towns further south decided to stay put, while the folks up north fled. He reasoned they hadn't wanted to leave their homes and banded together to help each other make a go of it. It was fascinating how folks in different locals handled the decisions that affected their personal well being. Some moved south, some left for Canada, but some just stayed put. The people in Jackson reminded him of his people back in Texas. You couldn't tell them what to do if your life depended on it. They were as independently minded as you could get. Everywhere was different and everyone sure did things differently.

Hadley was north of Jackson when he drove past the town and then drove south to a new area Bassett had found to cross enemy lines during the day. It was located down on Reynolds Road, which was off McCain Road. The road ran under the power lines that ran through the woods. It was an ideal place to drive through and keep hidden. It led you right to Highway 60 and the Jiji border, but instead of a four-lane road, it was two lanes. He'd still have a five-mile hike, which he didn't look forward to with his gimpy leg, but he was in too big of a hurry to wait until it got dark to cross.

The Suburban rocked back and forth, as he drove through the tall grass under the power lines. The thousand-foot path turned right, but he drove straight into the trees to hide the big truck. He grabbed his weapon and silently thanked Bassett for finding a place closer than what originally would have been a ten-mile hike from Michigan 52. These long hikes were never a stroll in the park for him. His old soccer injury would flare up and his knee wouldn't work properly because it was a prosthetic replacement. It was the reason the Army wouldn't take him and why he joined the National Police, which had a lower standard for enlistment.

He dashed through the woods to Highway 60, or Spring Arbor Road, as they called it in this area. This was the Jiji border. He dropped down on his stomach, crawled to the edge of the wood, and looked both ways. A car sat in the middle of the intersection of Spring Arbor Road and Reynolds Road, with another fifty yards or so to the left. Hadley strained his eyes and could barely make out that someone was in the car, but he didn't think they'd spot him if he stayed low. So, rather than put pressure on his knees by crouching down, he decided to do a low crawl across the road. The asphalt was rough as he crossed the road. He was only halfway across when he heard the distinct sound of a car approaching.

CHAPTER 43

Green flashed his headlights across the street to get Kyle's attention. He nodded to acknowledge him before looking both ways and then running over to the vehicle. He pulled on the handle and slid the side door open; then hopped into the cargo van which had no seats in the back.

"He's in there," said Kyle as he sat down on a milk crate Green had thought to bring. Green looked at the convenience store across the street and didn't like it. "Too many people here."

"I've got a better place to grab him anyway."

"Oh?"

"Our guy is dressed for the gym, oh, there he is."

A man with a medium build was wearing shorts and a white t-shirt. He carried two cups of coffee to his red Mustang.

"You see that?" asked Green.

"Looks like he's meeting someone. With any luck he'll meet up with target number two," said Kyle.

"You sure this guy is known to Reed?"

"Absolutely, and he's for sure a hired gun. I know the type."

Green put the van in drive and started to follow target number one. His mind started thinking about all the different scenarios they might encounter and not all of them ended well. This was an "on the fly" operation and each of them needed to think quickly and not hesitate. He only knew about Kyle's talents and experience from talking to his father, Jacob, who couldn't stress his son's qualifications enough. He trusted the former FBI man and took his word for it. What he didn't know was how well Stormy could handle herself. Granted she had martial arts experience, but you can't quantify something like that when you've never been out in the field. Did she understand they were going to have to kill these two people? It wasn't even an easy thing for him to swallow since it wouldn't be on a battlefield. He had to keep reminding himself that he was fighting on a different type of battlefield now and there were different rules. There was no honor in what they were doing and some might call it murder. Green took in a deep breath thinking about that. He was up against people who were responsible for killing hundreds of thousands of innocent Americans. In this battle, the ends actually did justify the means.

After a few miles, the red Mustang pulled into a plaza where a gym sat in the middle with an empty store beside it. Green slowed down and took the next entrance to the complex. He watched as the Mustang parked in the back where there were no other cars.

"Doesn't want any scratches on that baby," said Kyle.

"Can't say I blame him," said Stormy, "it is a pretty one."

Green parked four lanes over from the red Mustang and they sat there watching their target. A few minutes later, another car pulled in behind him.

"That's target number two," said Kyle. "I was hoping it was gonna be him. They always work out together."

The two chatted together while drinking their coffee, before grabbing their gear and heading to the gym.

Green turned around in his seat. "This is an ideal situation. We can park with the side-door right at his driver's side."

"What do you want me to do?" asked Stormy.

Green looked at Kyle. "Dead battery?"

"You got cables in here?"

"In the back."

Kyle looked at Stormy. "My dear, you just need to look pretty and ask for a jump."

"I can handle that."

"You bring the stun gun?" asked Green.

Kyle reached into his bag and pulled out a handheld stun gun. It was a close quarters weapon and not one that fired pronged probes. You had to physically make contact to disable the attacker, or in this case, the victim.

Kyle pressed the button and the stun gun crackled in the van. The loud arcing sound got your attention.

Stormy jerked back as the sound echoed in the empty van.

"Twenty million volts," boasted Kyle.

Green nodded in approval and thought he should get one for his mother, but then remembered she was now packing a pistol. He placed his hand in his jacket to give his M9 a reassuring pat.

"Also brought a baton," said Kyle pulling out a collapsible black baton. He flicked his wrist and ejected the baton with a snap. He then handed it to Green.

"Don't I get a toy?" asked Stormy.

Kyle laughed. "You've got your feet."

"In this dress?"

"Well, it certainly won't restrict your movements."

"I'm more modest than that."

Kyle leaned forward. "Ah, excuse me Miss Lingerie model."

"Yeah, okay, touché."

Green laughed to himself at their jovial mood. It was always better to joke around rather than start worrying over an impending mission. Of course, that would change as soon as their targets came out of the building.

Green put the van in drive and drove it over to the Mustang, parking it right alongside it. The van now blocked the view from the building and high hedges bordered the parking lot, blocking any view from the road. He looked at his watch and figured they had at least another thirty minutes before they would come back out.

"Grab those jumper cables in the back, would cha?" asked Green.

Green pulled on the hood latch and then gave Stormy instructions on what to do. She gave him a terse nod and Green exited the van. Kyle would remain hidden in the back, while he would wait somewhere in the lot. It would be better if he approached them offering his assistance. They had two targets to deal with and both would want to help a damsel in distress, especially one that looked like Stormy.

CHAPTER 44

SARNIA ONTARIO

Knowing something was not right, Scar paced the floor of the small room the cops had put them in. Hours had passed and it had begun to dawn on him that they were not going to go before a judge or get an attorney. He hadn't seen Sergeant Wilson yet and had no idea if the sergeant had called General Standish. He was growing impatient and wanted answers.

"Guys, something is off," Scar said, "if they were going to let us go, they'd have done so by now."

Bassett rose from his chair. "It's strange they didn't even take our mug shots or fingerprint us."

"They kept us out of the system on purpose," said Burns.

Scar scoffed, "So, no record of us."

"Good thing or bad?" asked Bassett.

"It's a crap sandwich, that's what it is," Nordell quickly added. "Don't forget, there's a reward on your heads."

"But not yours," chided Bassett.

"I'm as clean as the driven snow, Corporal," said Nordell.

"You're just lacking a good headline," Burns shot back.

"A good headline would make me famous."

Burns waved his hand in the air. "Retired Marine goes postal on cops."

"I like it," said Nordell, nodding approvingly.

Scar crossed his arms over his chest. "Guys, can we focus?"

"Yes, of course," said Bassett, in a contrite tone. "I think we should assume we're being sold off."

"Like cattle," said Nordell sarcastically.

"Then we need to think about escaping," said Scar. "Any ideas?"

They shot each other questioning glances before Nordell spoke up. "Before we try anything, we need to set these guards at ease. Give them no reason to suspect we're worried about anything. That we're cooperating and just waiting to be released."

"Get friendly with them," agreed Burns.

"When we strike, we'll strike fast," said Nordell, pounding his fist into his hand. "Look where they've got us, we're in a friggin warehouse. A half-ass, make-do solution they came up with on the fly. We're not in a jail cell guys, so we've got a damn good chance of getting out of here."

Burns nodded. "We only need to overpower one cop and get his gun."

"Chances are we're right by the river so we might need to swim across, everyone a good swimmer?"

Everyone nodded.

"What about Hadley?" asked Nordell.

"He'll stay until he's sure something is wrong," said Bassett.

Scar pondered all of this for a bit. They still didn't have a plan, but everyone was on board to try an escape, which was always an important first step. He was glad they agreed that they were being held for the reward and they couldn't allow themselves to be surrendered to the National Police.

Nordell had brought up a good point about getting the guards to relax a little bit. This couldn't be a normal situation for them, so they wouldn't have procedures to rely on. He thought about the layout of the warehouse and how the room they were in was at the end of the building. Bathrooms were off to the side in the only other room in the big wide-open building. He needed to know how many guards they had posted and just how alert they were. He decided to send Bassett out to recon the situation.

"Bassett, can you ask to go to the bathroom?"

"You got it."

"See if you can get friendly with him."

"No problem."

Scar sent Bassett because he was about the same age as the cop outside the door. Bassett had an easy manner about him and was able to get along with anyone. His youth and good looks also helped put people at ease. He looked less grumpy than the rest of them. Scar knew the stressful life he was now living had been aging him. He had noticed new lines forming on his face and spotted it on some of the others as well. He hoped his wife, Tera, wouldn't be too surprised whenever they reunited again.

Scar had everyone sit down at the table and look bored as Bassett went to the door and gave it a few knocks asking to use the restroom. It took a few seconds before the door opened up.

Bassett back away from the door as the cop pulled it opened.

"Hey, Officer, I need to use the bathroom, would you mind?"

The cop looked inside the room for a moment and then motioned Bassett out the door. He was about the same build as Bassett and had short blond hair, which was combed over neatly. His flack vest had "POLICE" across it in big yellow letters. It was the only color on his dark blue uniform. His deep-set eyes gave him a serious appearance, and Bassett noticed he was hesitant.

"Thanks, man, I've been holding on since breakfast."

The cop walked several paces behind him with his hand on his holster ready to pull his pistol out. Bassett chuckled to himself because they made a big mistake in not handcuffing him. If they only knew how quick he could take him down, they would cuff him.

He walked across the empty warehouse floor in a casual way and nodded to another cop sitting at a card table that they must have been brought in since their arrival. This cop didn't look like he pulled guard duty very often and only looked up from the newspaper to see if his colleague needed any assistance.

This second cop would be the biggest obstacle to their escape attempt. Everything would depend on how alert they were and how fast he was. So far, from what he could discern, the guard didn't look too worried. Not paying attention was their second big mistake. If the cop was a good shot, he might be able to get one shot off, maybe two before Bassett had a gun. Even then, bulletproof vest or not, the second cop wouldn't take the chance hitting his friend. This would slow him down giving Bassett the advantage.

The cop was smart to not allow him to shut the door to the bathroom, which, so far, was their only smart move. He flushed the toilet and walked out of the bathroom.

"Hey, thanks again, man."

"No problem," said the first cop.

Bassett noticed neither cop had stripes, which meant they hadn't been on the force too long. "So, how the hell did you guys draw this assignment? You guys have got to be as bored as we are?"

"Tell me about it."

"Any idea how long we're gonna be here?"

The cop shrugged his shoulders.

"It's just that we're all bored, but at least you got something to read. You think maybe we could get some reading material, maybe even a deck of cards?"

The first cop looked over at the second cop. "Listen, ahh..."

"I'm Bassett, Corporal Bassett."

"Army?"

Bassett nodded.

"Were you over there?"

"Got back about six months ago."

"You?"

"Calgary Highlanders."

Bassett knew they were a reserve regiment that had been in Afghanistan in years past, but nothing as of late. He figured the Canadians were using them on the border in case the Chinese decided to keep heading north.

Bassett looked at his name badge. "You're from Calgary. What are you doing way over this way, Officer Johnson?"

"It's Quinn and my girlfriend's family lives here."

"Yep, that'll do it every time, Quinn," laughed Bassett.

"Hey, I'll see about getting you guys something. We'll be bringing in some chow pretty soon anyway, so hang tight."

"Thanks, Quinn, really appreciate it," said Bassett, as he walked back inside the room. He hated the fact that in all likelihood, he was going to have to kill this man, but Quinn was in the wrong place watching the wrong people.

CHAPTER 45

WASHINGTON D.C.

Green looked at his watch again wishing time would speed up. Running out of things to do in the parking lot, he decided to walk into the gym. The place wasn't too busy and it was easy to spot his targets on their treadmills. They were doing a slow walk and cooling down, which meant they were finishing up. Their energy wasn't going to be the same as it would have been if they had taken them at another place. After waving off a girl at the counter, he walked back outside and killed time by looking through the window of the empty store space next door. He started pacing again wondering what was taking so long when they finally emerged wearing suits.

Green's heart sunk when he realized they were more than likely armed. He had hoped they'd come back out wearing their gym clothes. He waited a few seconds before heading toward the van. He picked up his pace when he saw Stormy was already talking to them. Target number 1 disappeared around the corner of the van to open the hood of his car.

Goosebumps exploded on Green's skin when he heard the stun gun crackle to life. Kyle was too early. He started to run toward them while pulling out the baton. Target number 2 had reached inside his jacket to pull out a gun. As he pulled the weapon out, Stormy grabbed the hand and punched him in the face. The blow didn't deter him and he swung his left hand at her. Stormy ducked down and punched him in the groin while still holding onto his wrist. He hunched over and tried to pull his gun hand away, but Stormy twisted around and jumped up on his back. She put him in a chokehold while leaning back to bring him down to the pavement.

Green finally reached them and swung the baton across Target number 2's face. He then buried it in his gut a couple of times before grabbing his gun. He looked up at Stormy and noticed the excitement on her face as she seemed to be enjoying herself.

"I had him all the way," she said while catching her breath.

"I saw that," said Green, as he turned around to Kyle who was manhandling Target number 1 into the van.

Green looked around the parking lot for any unwanted attention. Relief swept over him when no one had taken notice.

Green looked at Stormy. "C'mon, grab his legs."

They picked up Target 2 and carried him inside.

Kyle handcuffed them both and bound them together with duct tape.

"You were early," said Green.

"Couldn't be helped. Son-of-a-bitch saw the door cracked open so he pulled on it. I mean what the hell. I had to jump him, but he fell back on his car."

"Well, it worked out," said Green, as he shut the hood of the van. He then hopped into the driver's seat. After starting the vehicle, he took a couple of deep breaths before driving out of the parking lot.

"Damn, that was a friggin rush," said Stormy in an excited tone. "Did you see me take him down?"

Kyle finished tying them up and moved in between the two seats. "Hell, I was too busy getting my boy in the van. Damn if it didn't take a couple of jolts before he went limp. Nice job bringing the storm on yours."

"That was so much better than being in the ring. Man, the adrenaline, I mean, I am as high as a kite."

Kyle let out a laugh. "Don't worry, it'll last awhile."

"Dude didn't stand a chance after I punched him in the sack. He didn't give up though, so I jump on him and put him in the death hold."

"And, you did it all in a dress," laughed Kyle.

"Right," said Stormy, as she looked at Green. "Was my dress just flying all about?"

Green couldn't believe how cavalier and excited she was. She thoroughly enjoyed the mission and impressed the hell out of him. The way she practically flew up around him and took him down was something he'd never seen anybody but Corporal Bassett do.

"It was like you were wearing a superhero cape," said Green grateful he had something witty to say.

"Ah, did you hear that?"

"Captain Storm," yelled Kyle.

She beamed at the name, but Green thought of a better one. "Lady Storm."

"Oh I like that. Lady Storm," she said with flair twirling her finger in the air.

Green drove the speed limit not wanting to be pulled over for speeding with a couple of hostages. He looked at his watch and grew anxious wanting to get back to the office. They still needed to set up the next part of their plan, but he would have to rely on Kyle and Stormy to help get things ready and in place. It was important that he be seen at the office today.

He pulled up to a garage door and honked his horn. The door began to raise and Green drove into the darkened building. He shut off the engine and opened the door as Jacob Gibbs approached him.

"Everything go alright?" asked Gibbs.

"It did, we actually got two."

"Perfect."

"Hey Dad, went off without a hitch. And Stormy was brilliant."

Gibbs turned to face her. "Glad to hear it."

He turned back to Green. "Your car is out back. We'll handle it from here."

"You sure?"

Gibbs nodded. "Just get those cameras disconnected and be ready when the shooting starts."

"I'll be ready."

Green turned to Kyle and shook his hand. Stormy came around the van and put her arms around Green.

"You were great," said Green.

"Thanks and thanks for trusting me."

"We'll talk soon."

"I hope so."

Green liked hearing that and wondered if she would date him. She seemed to like him, but he wasn't too sure if it was him or the excitement of what they had just done. Their experience was completely out of the ordinary and he couldn't assume her high level of excitement was a valid gauge of her intent. He shook his head wondering if they would ever be together during normal circumstances. He let out a laugh thinking that wasn't going to happen anytime soon.

He got in his car, thankful the first part of their mission was over but knew the second part was going to be the toughest. Staging a shootout with real bodyguards was going to be dangerous, and if it didn't work as planned, they could be killed. It wasn't going to be easy but it was worth the risk. Success would ensure Reed would be at war with Perozzi.

CHAPTER 46

JACKSON MICHIGAN

Having left Port Huron and while making his way back to Jackson, Hadley was half way across the road on his stomach when he heard the roar of a car engine approaching. A small car with a loud muffler was coming down Spring Arbor Road. It could only mean a Jiji was coming his way. He hurried to the grass, rolled into the culvert and swung the M-4 off his back before clicking the safety off. He then froze waiting for the car to pass. A bead of sweat ran down the side of his head and dropped onto the grass as the loud car screamed by him.

Keeping an eye on the enemy Hadley crawled into the safety of the trees and then got up to begin the long hike. He crossed a golf course and filled his water bottle from a pond before hitting the streets. The pavement was easier to walk on, and now that he was across the border, he was able to relax his tense muscles. He hoped to run into some of the guys guarding the border and get a ride.

He stopped on the corner of Denton and Kirby to take a drink of water. The sun was out in full force on this cloudless day. The water began cooling him down as he splashed it on his face. He put the cap back on and was putting it back into his pack when he heard another engine up

Kirby Road. He pulled out the binoculars and zeroed in on the approaching vehicle. It was a pickup truck traveling at high speed. He let go of the binoculars and stepped to the side knowing this thing would fly by him in mere seconds.

Hadley made eye contact with the driver as it sped by him in excess of seventy miles per hour. The driver recognized him and jammed on the brakes. Smoke rose from the tires as the back of the truck swerved and bounced making the brakes squeal in the quiet neighborhood.

Hadley waited as the driver shoved it in reverse and smoked the tires. It came to a dead stop in front of him. He smiled at Reese, who wore a wild expression.

She ran her hand through her tousled hair, pulling it away from her big brown eyes, before asking, "Don, what are you doing here?"

Hadley opened the door and hopped up on the bench seat. "I think the guys got busted by the cops."

Reese shot him a concerned look.

"I was waiting for them across the river when I saw a Canadian cop pull out a pistol and shoot holes in the canoe."

Reese didn't wait for him to finish before backing the truck onto Denton Road and fishtailing it back onto Kirby. Hadley buckled his seatbelt as she floored the pedal. After a turn on Greenwood Avenue, the speedometer climbed to eighty miles per hour.

Reese laughed at Hadley's frightful appearance. "Don't worry, Don, I won't kill you."

"You do this often?"

"Whenever I need to let off some steam. You should try it; it does wonders for the soul."

Reese wore a serious expression as she took a tight turn. The expression changed to a wicked one after the turn and she floored the gas pedal. The faster she drove the more steam she blew off.

Gripping the door handle tight Hadley said, "I'm sorry about what happened with Cole."

Reese looked at him through flying strands of blonde hair and gave him a small smile as she took a left on Jackson Street.

Back a few months ago, when Captain Cox arrested Hadley for

suspicion of helping Corporal Bassett escape, he had tossed him in a jail cell right next to Reese and Sadie. Both looked like they were out of hope. Hadley took great satisfaction telling them that help was on the way. It was then that Reese reached through the bars of the cell, pulled his face toward hers, and gave him a big wet kiss. The memory of that kiss still made him weak in the knees. He hadn't kissed a girl in a long time and never someone so beautiful. He looked over at her and liked the way the strands of hair flew about her face. He couldn't soak in enough of her beauty and wished he could have a girl like her in his life. He had been making friends with some of the girls around town and flirted with a couple of them who'd showed interest, but it was difficult because everyone wanted to leave.

Reese made quick work getting them back to the hospital, and she pulled right into the emergency room entrance. The quick stop pressed Hadley up against his seatbelt.

"See, you're safe," she said, hopping out of the truck and grabbing her red crutch out of the bed of the truck.

Hadley followed her inside and down to the cafeteria where Meeks was getting something to eat.

Meeks put his cup down when they approached. "What the hell happened?"

Hadley told him all he knew.

"Damn. This isn't good," said Meeks.

"What are we gonna do?" asked Hadley.

"Need to get everyone together first," said Meeks, as he looked at Reese, "you been out driving?"

Reese gave him a puzzled look.

"Your hair's a bit messy. Think you can scoot over to city hall. Badger's there with the mayor."

"Done."

"As a matter of fact, get up to Lansing Road and grab Eddie. Meet us in Elliott's room; he'll want to be in on this. Hadley, let's get upstairs and round up whoever we can."

CHAPTER 47

As she climbed the hospital stairs, Reese felt the surge of adrenaline she had gotten from receiving her orders. She was feeding off the rush it offered and would top it off with another crazy drive. It helped stave off the depression that threatened to creep back in and overwhelm her. She didn't want it and did whatever she could to fight it. Nate had helped her recognize the symptoms and made her realize what would happen if she didn't fight it. No way did she want to mope around all day feeling sorry for herself. That wasn't why she was rescued from hell and it certainly wasn't the way to act around these incredible people she now called family. She took a deep breath at the thought. Scar had told her everyone here was family, and her heart had melted hearing those words as she had no one else.

She hopped into the old truck, started it up, and stomped on the gas pedal causing the engine to roar. The covered entrance to the emergency wing ensured the right acoustics to shout out her departure. She jerked the steering wheel back and forth out of the parking lot and onto Michigan Avenue. A tingling charge shot through her reminding her of making-out with Cole. That day burned into her memory as it was the most meaningful relationship she'd had in a long time. It was the day she finally got what she had desired for so long, but never had the courage to go after. She let out a laugh at the silliness of that thought, but it was a real thing.

Over the past couple of days, with the help of her new family, she had decided to remain optimistic and believe Cole would come back to her. It gave her the motivation to fight off the depression that camped out on the outer edges of her mind. It also made her aware of the ever-present Mister Hyde. The one thing Cole stressed was to always be cognizant of him. She saw how it had overpowered him with the death of his daughter being the final straw. Mister Hyde swallowed him whole and took him to the deep end of despair. Her stomach turned into knots witnessing that kind of power. To leave the Shadow Patriots, the group he had started, in the middle of the night, without saying a word to anyone wasn't something done by a sane person. She let out a sigh and prayed he would somehow find his way back to her. Even if it didn't work out between them, she still hoped he'd come back.

Needing to get her head out of the clouds, she took a hard left on Frances Street and slid the back end around as she over steered the turn. The squealing tires on the short S curve of the street induced another shot of adrenaline and got her heart racing again. It took only a few more seconds to reach City Hall where she parked out front. Reaching inside herself, she let out a scoff at the tall staircase before gimping up the steps.

Gasping for air, she reached the mayor's office where he was talking to Bill Taylor, who turned in his chair when she walked inside.

"What's happened?"

"Meeks needs ya. Something's happened to Scar."

Taylor stood up. "Mayor, we'll finish this up later."

Reese put up a finger to hold on a second to catch her breath.

"Yeah, these stairs will kill anyone. C'mon, jump on my back."

Taylor leaned down as Reese jumped up. She handed him the red crutch and wrapped her arms around his neck.

"You sure you can handle this?" she asked, in a humorous tone.

"Are you poking fun at me?" asked Taylor, as he started down the stairs bouncing them on each step.

"Well, ya never know," quipped Reese.

"Girl, I swear, I'm gonna tan your hide one of these days."

"Oh Badger, you know you love me."

"Ahhggg…and that's the problem. I never could punish my own daughters either."

"Daughters? How many kids do you have?"

"I got three daughters, thank you, and five granddaughters. All of them, the apples of my eye."

Reese started laughing. "Eight girls! Oh my God! And you pretend to be such a grouch, but really, you're just a big squishy marshmallow."

"Only with the girls, honey, I can't seem to help myself."

"You poor man. It's because you never had any boys."

"Just don't tell anyone my little secret."

"I swear I won't say a word. Besides, I think it's cute when you're grouchy."

Taylor shook his head in disgust as he reached the last step. "Cute huh?"

Reese slid off and grabbed her crutch. "Yep."

He opened the front door for her. "What the hell kind of father did you have?"

She stopped and looked at him. "He was a drunk and walked out on us."

Taylor frowned. "I'm sorry, sweetie, I didn't know."

"Don't worry about it."

They hopped in the truck and Reese backed up, peeling the tires again before throwing it in drive.

"How old were ya?"

"I was nine and glad he left."

"Oh?"

Reese turned onto Jackson and headed north. "Yeah, he was beating the hell out of my mom, so when he left that all ended. So, in a way, he did us a big favor."

"Too bad for him, because he missed out on a raising a great kid."

Reese flashed him a smile.

"I thought we were headed to the hospital?"

"Meeks wants me to grab Eddie, too."

"Yeah, good thinking, something tells me we're gonna be taking a trip."

"Probably so."

Reese noticed Badger was at ease with her aggressive driving and seemed to enjoy how fast she was going. He would have been a great dad and she was thankful to have him in her life as well. Each of these guys played a big role in her life now. She could see how he would be naturally good at raising daughters. She was always at ease around him, even when he was being grouchy with everyone else.

They reached Lansing Road in good time and Taylor climbed out to find Eddie at the overpass. Fifteen minutes later, the three of them entered Elliott's room where the meeting was ready to begin.

CHAPTER 48

SABINE IOWA

Winters woke up in a sweat and opened his eyes. The air in the bedroom was hot and stagnate making it difficult to breathe. He rolled over on his side and looked at the other bed. Collette had lain down next to Laney and he was surprised he had not heard her come in, but then realized just how tired he was. He had only slept sporadically over the past few days and was exhausted. He put his feet on the carpet and looked at his watch to see it was three in the afternoon, which meant he'd gotten a solid seven hours of sleep. He glanced over at the sleeping girls and noticed how innocent they looked. He let out a scoff because these girls had been dealt a bad hand. No longer were they innocent kids. They had been forced to grow up and leave behind whatever remaining childhood they should have had.

Winters nodded his head thinking about their willingness to help and how they handled themselves. They were quick thinkers and acted fast, which was a good combination.

Their explanation of the butterfly tattoos spoke volumes about who they were and how they viewed their situation. They never gave up the hope that it would eventually pass and they could be reborn and hold their heads high. They had done what was necessary to survive and save their families, and now these trials were over.

The big question was how they would handle what happened last night? Laney already had some doubts and was confused over the matter. Winters hoped he had told her the right things. He thought maybe he had by the way she reacted when he mentioned she no longer had to work. That reality would help get them over any lingering doubts that might creep up on them over the coming days. Taking a life is never an easy thing, but perhaps experiencing what they had gone through would make it easier.

He continued to stare at the girls and found himself drumming his hands on his knees as his favorite song popped into his head. He hadn't done that in a long time and then it dawned on him why. Last night's operation had a different meaning than his previous killings. These had nothing to do with revenge, but with helping a bunch of girls in need. A damsel in distress was always a worthy cause. Looking back on it, after meeting Finley, he realized he never thought about Mister Hyde or noticed his presence again. Her talkative spirit penetrated deep into his core and gave him a renewed purpose, which began to flush away all his anger. He helped a young girl out of a bad situation and there was a pureness to it. He took a deep breath and held it for a second before slowly releasing it.

He then assumed a one-sided smile, wondering, if in some strange way Cara had led him here. Had she not died, last night never would have happened. These girls would still be living in their own hell. A warm sensation shot through him because not only had he done a good thing here, but it also gave Cara's death a meaningful purpose. He decided to take this notion and hold onto to it for everything it was worth.

He grabbed his boots and laced them up. He tiptoed out of the room leaving the door open for fresh air. He entered the living room where Ashley played cards with her daughter Kaitlyn. The scene reminded him of playing cards with Cara when she was younger. She learned to play Go Fish before moving to Crazy Eights and then Gin Rummy. Those were the good years before she became a teenager and for the most part, they were a happy family. Winters brushed the thoughts away, scared they would lead him back into melancholy.

"Hey," said Winters.

"Well, hey yourself, how'd ya sleep?"

Winters sat down in a kitchen chair. "Soundly." Winters turned to Kaitlyn, "you letting your mom win?"

"Just a little," replied Kaitlyn, "she isn't very good."

"Hey, now, I'm just unlucky," said Ashley.

Winters winked at Ashley before turning back to Kaitlyn, "sounds like you're pretty darn good."

"I am. Do you want to play?"

"Geez, I don't know, I'm not sure I want to get shown up by a kid."

"I'll go easy on ya," giggled Kaitlyn.

Winters laughed. "Maybe later, I've got lots to do." He turned back to Ashley and asked where everybody was.

"Finley's mom and sister are resting with her, and Stacy left a little while ago with Laney's mom. That passed out girl, Blair, woke up and took off."

"How's Finley doing?"

"Stacy says she needs to see a doctor, she's running a fever."

"Is there one around here?"

"No."

Winters leaned back in the chair. If Finley needed a doctor, then he had little choice but to get her up to Winnipeg. It was an eleven-hour drive if all went well. He would need to take along as much gas as possible. He remembered the girls telling him Billy Gamble had fuel stashed somewhere.

Ashley got up and prepared Winters something to eat. While she did that, he peeked in on Finley. Her mom and sister were on the bed with her sound asleep. He closed the door deciding to wait to discuss the trip to Canada.

CHAPTER 49

JACKSON MICHIGAN

Meeks had never been in charge of a Shadow Patriots meeting before, but here he was with eight of them waiting for him to begin. As a high school football coach, he had a lot of experience holding meetings with his players and other coaches. It could be as many as a hundred people, so he had no problem speaking in front of large numbers of people. He decided to treat this as he would any other meeting. The only difference was, these people would talk back and offer him suggestions. This was a good thing because he needed suggestions as to what they might do. Everyone in this room would offer sound advice because they cared about Scar and the others.

He looked into the faces of his friends and was about to begin when it dawned on him that if it was the reward the cops were after, then Americans would have to be involved for the payout. Since cops sank the canoe, this meant they wanted to deal with Americans on the sly and nothing official. At first, Meeks thought this was bad until he realized it was too good to be true. It was a good thing because that meant the cops from Detroit would be involved and Meeks had no problem shooting any cop from Detroit.

He started the meeting by telling everyone his thoughts.

"Meeks, my boy," said Taylor, "I got to hand it to ya, that's a brilliant analysis."

"Thanks, Badger."

"You're gonna need to think about an ambush site then," said Nate.

Meeks gave him a firm nod and then dug into his satchel full of maps and found one of Port Huron. Amber took some medical tape and hung it up on the wall.

Meeks turned to Hadley. "Don, point out where Scar launched and landed."

Hadley took a red marker and made two circles.

Nate moved to the map. "Question is though, which way will the cops cross into Canada, Detroit or Port Huron?"

The room remained silent for a few moments before Amber spoke up. "Port Huron."

Everyone turned to her.

"The Sarnia cops would be able to control things on their home turf, maybe even bribe the border guards. They can't just be letting American cops come and go without proper authorization."

Meeks stared at her for a second. "Amber, you're no longer just a hot looking chick."

"Finally," said Amber, throwing her palms up in the air. "I've been waiting forever."

Meeks shot her a kudos nod.

"You need to set up a position right here," said Nate pointing to the last exit before the bridge. "Get Nordell's friend, Hollis, to man a sharpshooter position."

"He's a hell of a shot," said Hadley. "The way he took out those spot lights from the lake was amazing."

"You'll need look outs along the route," said Nate.

"Meeks," said Elliott trying to get his attention from his bed.

Everyone quieted down to hear Elliott speak.

"You also need to get back to that garage and wait for them in case they escape. And check the river downstream as well in case they swim across."

Meeks nodded. "Okay, how many guys are we gonna need?"

"At least twenty," suggested Nate. "Eight at the ambush site, four more for backup and then you got the lookouts to spread around. Another waiting at the garage and some along the river bank."

"Whew, that's a lot of vehicles to take and a lot of gas," said Meeks.

Nate put his hand on Meeks' shoulder. "Yeah, well, it's what you need."

"I wanna go," said Reese.

Everyone turned to Reese as Meeks scrunched his face.

"Don't deny me this. My leg's better, and besides, I can at least baby-sit the garage. You might as well let me cause if you don't I'm gonna be burning through more fuel around here anyway."

No one had said anything to her about using the precious fuel because everyone saw how it had improved her overall attitude.

Meeks gave it some thought. "Okay, but the garage is yours."

Amber put her hand out and gave Reese a fist-bump.

"Alright, it's done. We need to leave right away, so let's meet in the parking lot in one hour. Badger, can you get five vehicles fueled? Oh, and we need to monitor the cops' communications, so make sure one of them is a squad car. And we'll need supplies, no telling how long we'll be out there."

"I'm on it."

"Eddie, round up some guys," said Meeks, counting the bodies in the room. "We need fourteen more. Hadley, go find Hollis."

Meeks waited for everyone to leave the room and turned to Nate and Elliott, who would be staying behind. It was never easy to go on an operation without these two because they were original members and an important part of the group.

"Good meeting, Meeks, you did good," said Elliott.

"Thanks, I just hope we can find them."

"You'll find 'em. Just trust your gut," said Nate, "and keep your six clear. Always have an exit."

"I hear ya. You guys gonna be alright?"

"Well, I don't know," sighed Elliott, "you're taking the two prettiest girls away from nursing me back to health."

"I could order them to stay," offered Meeks.

Nate let out a scoff. "Yeah, that'd be like telling them not to go shopping."

Meeks burst out laughing. "Damn, Nate, you are sexist."

"Yeah, well, I'm sexy too."

"Sexy enough to tend to your friend while we're gone?"

"Please, he's just milking it for all it's worth, aren't cha buddy?" asked Nate, with a sly smile.

"I won't deny I like having Amber hovering over me."

"I'll be sure to tell your wife next we see her," kidded Nate.

"Oh, I don't think Amy would be too worried about me getting some TLC, you know, being in the shape I'm in and all."

"Don't worry, buddy, I won't tell her."

"Yeah, it's probably best you didn't."

Meeks let the two lifelong friends continue to pull each other's legs as he left the room hoping he'd be able to find his friend. He and Scar had been through thick and thin over the years and even more so over the past few months. It would suck not having him around even more so than Winters.

CHAPTER 50

WASHINGTON D.C.

Green tried to stay busy and keep his mind off what was coming next. His skin was crawling as he tried to get through his paperwork and make a few phone calls. He looked at his watch and saw he had only had another hour before most everyone went home, and then an hour after that when Reed would leave for the day. He still needed to turn the security cameras off, but couldn't do that until the building was vacated enough to minimize the chance of being detected.

He thought about the two guys they had kidnapped earlier. It was a spectacular operation and he was pleasantly surprised by how well Stormy had performed. He had to admit he wasn't expecting much from her. She seemed too beautiful to be anything but a china doll. Green let out a laugh at how wrong he'd been about her. Her biggest asset was her looks and how she was underestimated because of them. You wouldn't even imagine someone like her could kick your butt? He rolled his eyes because he'd never think that about her again.

His thoughts moved back to the two guys and how they were going to die for them. It was brutal but this was war and war was hell. He'd begun to accept the idea of this new kind of war in which he was now involved. The battlefields were different and most often were underhanded, but then that was Washington D.C. now and always had been.

He tried to visualize what was going to happen tonight and how he could most effectively contribute to their success. He would enter the underground parking garage at the right moment and save Reed from certain death. Besides his looking like a hero, Reed would be convinced Perozzi was targeting him. Green drummed his hands on the desk at the thought of Reed having complete trust in him. No telling what he'd be able to accomplish with that trust.

Green looked at his watch again and decided to grab his stuff as he was going to head to the room where the security cameras recorded all movement at the entrances. He offered his secretary, Grace, an early time off, of which she took advantage and shut down her computer before grabbing her purse.

After she left, he shut the office door and started down the stairs where he noticed some of the staff in the offices below had begun to leave. The bankers typically left when the markets closed, which cleared out the majority of the offices. The building didn't have any other form of security staff, but then it wasn't an important target. This place paled in comparison to the many highly desirable targets in the district.

The security closet was just ahead and no one was in the area, so Green approached the door and slipped on a glove before opening it. He rolled his eyes having expected to force the door open. A good shove would have done the trick, but it was unlocked. He entered the small room and shut the door. The room was dark with the monitors providing the only light. He sat down in the chair to observe all the entrances and watch the people leave. He looked over at the power strips and figured out which buttons to switch off per Jacob Gibbs' instructions. He started flipping switches until the green lights turned red. The cameras continued to run, which he needed to monitor the garage, which weren't too far away. At a quick pace, he could be there in seconds.

Thirty minutes later, the parking lot was empty with the exception of a vehicle here or there. Then he noticed his van come in and park by the entrance to the building. Blood rushed to his head knowing that inside the van, bound and gagged, were the two men they had kidnapped. He rocked back and forth in the swivel chair while staring at the monitors waiting for Reed to leave. He looked at his watch again to see that time was fast approaching. He grabbed his Beretta M9 and pulled out the magazine again to make sure it was full. He then pulled the spare mags out of his jacket and gave them the once over.

His pulse skipped a beat when Reed's bodyguards came into view on the monitors. They were escorting him down the hall toward the exit. Neither man looked too concerned as they approached the double glass doors. Both figuring it was just another day of getting the paranoid Lawrence Reed home.

Green got up and left the security room just as popping sounds echoed in the background. He bolted down the hall to the glass doors. Both guards were bleeding on the concrete floor. "Nice shooting," thought Green. He found Reed cowering behind a car. He rushed over to him just as a shot hit the gray painted concrete wall just above his head.

"Stay down, Mister Reed," yelled Green, as he fired his pistol.

"Major, please help me," Reed cried out in a shrill voice.

"Just stay down! I'll get you out of here!"

Green raised his head as Jacob Gibbs slid open the van door. He manhandled one of the unconscious men out and stood him up. Green took careful aim and pulled the trigger twice. Both rounds exploded into the man's chest. Kyle then pushed the other one out onto the garage floor. He and his dad, Jacob, picked him up and leaned him on the front of the van. Green took careful aim before shooting him. The body crumpled to the ground.

Gibbs gave him a thumbs up before they both fired the dead man's pistols a few more times and then dropped the guns by the corpses. They both then ran out of the garage where Stormy was waiting out on the street.

Green looked at Reed. "I got 'em both, sir."

Sweat poured down Reed's face to his double chin. "Are, are you sure?"

"I'm sure, sir. We should get you out of here."

"They're dead?"

"Yes, sir."

Green rose up and helped Reed up off the concrete floor. Reed's hands trembled and his pale complexion turned back to red as he looked at the scene. "I want to see them."

Green bit his lip to contain his satisfaction with the operation. He needed to keep focus and get Reed out of there to follow through with their charade. He kept his gun at the ready as Reed regained his composure and moved to the carnage. He bent down and took a good look at the first one he killed. Reed then went over to the other and pushed him over with his foot. Reed shook his head a couple of times but stayed silent. This didn't surprise Green because Reed always kept his cards close to the vest.

"Get me home," ordered Reed.

"Yes, sir."

"You'll find the keys to my car on one of them," said Reed pointing to his two dead guards by the glass doors.

For show, Green continued to hold his gun out as he escorted Reed to his car. He then got in and asked for directions to his house. Of course, he already knew where Reed lived but needed to continue the ruse. He took note on Reed's demeanor as the man called his security team leader and in a calm matter, told him what had just happened. He never once mentioned whom he suspected to have made the attempt. After hanging up on him, he stayed silent all the way home.

Green pulled into Reed's driveway and four of his bodyguards rushed to the car to protect Reed.

"Major, I cannot thank you enough for your bravery."

"Sir, I only wish I could have been there soon to help your security team."

"You've served honorably tonight, Major, and I shall not forget it," said Reed, as he opened the car. "You can take my car home and bring it to the office in the morning."

"Yes, sir."

Green watched the security team hustle him inside and then let out a deep sigh of relief. He didn't dare say anything in the car since he didn't know whether or not it was bugged. However, he couldn't help but pump his fist in the air at the success of their mission. Without a doubt, Reed recognized the two supposed assassins. Reed's world changed in an instant and Green planned to be involved in that new world.

CHAPTER 51

Winters gobbled down the food Ashley had prepared and was on his way to regaining his strength from last night's mission. Now that there were no more bad guys to control the town, they discussed getting everyone back home. Ashley offered to stay until they could move Finley.

Winters left to go into town as he wanted to check on the status of the stores of food sitting in the bank vault. He got into his van and made the short trip. In front of the bank, mothers and children, along with a few elderly people, had formed a line that extended out into the parking lot. Almost everyone had a smile on their face and they chatted amiably with each other. They all turned their heads when Winters pulled into the lot.

A wave of excitement swept through the line and everyone started clapping as he exited the van. His body stiffened as he didn't like accolades and would never get used to having them bestowed upon him. He always tried to shy away from notoriety if he could, but it was too late as a few of the mothers left the line and rushed over to him. He recognized the first as a friend of his late wife, Ellie. She had a couple of sons and a daughter who had been a friend of Cara's.

"Cole, Cole, thank you," said Gail, as she came in to give him a hug. "Cole, you're a life saver."

"Gail, please, there's no need."

"Nonsense. You're our hero."

More came over and began shaking his hand and cheering his presence.

"You saved my little girl," said a mother who Cole thought looked familiar. "Those filthy bastards are all dead now thanks to you."

Not wanting to be rude, Winters spent a few minutes greeting everyone and accepting their gratitude. After about five minutes with everyone outside, he entered the bank where more handshakes and hugs greeted him. Winters' heart began to melt as mothers broke down in tears while expressing their gratitude. He hadn't taken the time to consider the affect it had on them, but he now understood. There had been a darkness in Sabine and it weighed down everyone involved, but now a new found joy was released and it overwhelmed them.

"Okay, everyone, let the man breathe," said a male voice from the back.

Michael Grant was at least in his seventies and had a portly build. He had been the mayor here in Sabine some years ago, and he reminded Winters of Mayor Simpson back in Jackson. His wisps of white hair flew about as he greeted Winters.

"Cole, is it really you?"

"Yes, Mike, it's really me," said Winters, shaking his hand.

"I always knew those media reports about you were bogus. How the hell are ya? Oh, that's a stupid question, hell, look what you've done for us. We can't thank you enough."

"Well, you're welcome, Mike. So, how's it going here? Tell me about the food situation."

"C'mon, I'll show ya," said Grant, who led him to the back.

Winters' eyes grew wide looking at the bounty before him. The vault wasn't big but it was stuffed with all kinds of food, from freeze-dried packages to canned goods. Bags of wheat stood off to one side next to boxes of rice.

"Whoa," said Winters.

"Yes, it's literally all the food in the area and plenty for everyone."

"And then some," said Winters.

"Yes. Listen, Cole, I don't want you to think too badly of us, but we…"

Winters interrupted him. "Mike, you don't need to go there, I understand."

The man frowned and shook his head in a sad manner. "It's just that we tried to stand up to them, but they killed those of us who did. And our poor girls, it's just sickening what they had to go through."

Winters put a hand on his shoulder. "Mike, everyone did what they had to do to survive. Believe me, I've seen much worse over the past few months."

Grant gave him a blank stare and Winters decided the man needed a boost to his morale.

"Mike, I've seen whole towns executed because of a lack of food. Girls put into chains and forced to perform day and night. In some ways, everyone here is very lucky." The fog started to lift from the man's eyes. "And from what I've seen, your daughters and granddaughters are the bravest girls I've ever encountered. As a matter of fact, I couldn't have done what I did last night without their help."

"You mean that?"

"Absolutely, which reminds me, one of those brave girls is sorely in need of medical attention."

"Finley? I heard. How's she doing?"

"Running a fever and needs proper care. Is there anyone around to help her?"

"Everyone left town long ago."

"Okay, well, I'm going to need to take her somewhere and I'm going to need fuel."

"Oh, that won't be a problem. Billy had stores of gasoline stashed away as well, right across the street at the old quickie mart. He put the gas down in the underground tanks and covered the access with a bulldozer."

Winters walked out into the lobby and looked through the big glass window at the bulldozer. "Not a bad way to guard against theft."

"You probably have the keys," said Grant.

"I do?"

"You killed him and took his truck, right?"

Winters nodded.

"They're probably on that key ring."

Winters wasn't sure where the keys were but figured Collette knew since she was the last one to drive it. He said his goodbyes to everyone after getting assurances they were going to divide the food with everyone. He got back in his van and gave one more wave to everyone as he pulled out of the parking lot.

He drove back to the hideout and found Billy Gamble's truck sitting in the driveway. He walked inside the house and began looking around for the keys. Not finding them, he went back to the bedroom to find the air much cooler than before. He looked around and found Collette's jeans crumpled on the floor. He picked them up and felt the keys in the back pocket. They jingled as he pulled them out, which made the girls stir.

"Hey," said Laney, as she opened her eyes.

"Hey," Winters answered quietly.

"I'm awake too," said Collette.

"Sorry about that," said Winters.

"No, I've been awake for a bit," said Collette.

"Me too," said Laney.

Collette sat up and ran her hand through her short black hair. The disheveled hair began to stand back up the more she fussed with it. She stretched her back as Laney sat up as well. Her light brown hair was also in dire need of a brush as she flung it away from her face.

"How's our baby sister," asked Collette.

"In need of a doctor, I'm afraid."

"What are we gonna do?" asked Laney in a concerned tone.

"Take her to Winnipeg."

"Oh? When are we gonna leave?" ask Laney.

"We?" asked Winters.

"Of course, silly," said Collette, putting her arm around Laney. "You're not gonna take our baby sister to Canada without us."

Laney threw out her chest. "Not gonna happen, Mister Winters.

You're not done with us yet."

Winters sat down on the bed and cocked his head. "Thought for sure, I was."

Collette turned her head to Laney. "Isn't he just a silly-boy?"

"The silliest."

Winters laughed to himself at their attitudes. They were acting like the teen girls that they really were and not the jaded adults they had been forced to be. The relief of not having to prostitute themselves lifted a heavy burden from their shoulders. So much so that they didn't seem to be at all bothered by what they had done last night, and in light of all the killings, that was powerful.

He watched them embrace each other and give him pouty looks. Winters, of course, was going to let them come to Canada with him. It would help Finley to have her friends with her.

"I suppose you could come along."

"Yes," they both replied while shaking their shoulders around in a dance.

"We'll leave tonight. It's an eleven-hour trip, so think about what you'll need and tell your families."

"Do we take the guns?" asked Laney.

Winters got up and gave them a serious look. "We go everywhere armed."

"Yes, I love it," said Laney, throwing out a fist.

CHAPTER 52

The guards brought food and a deck of cards to the warehouse hours ago but hadn't given Scar any answers to his questions. He didn't want them to think he was alarmed, but the hours had dragged by and nothing was happening. The more time that flew by, the more obvious it became as to why they were there. He was grateful the cops didn't handcuff them whenever they took a trip to the bathroom. So far, none of them had seen a clear opportunity to overpower the guards whenever they made the trip. Even Bassett commented the two guards left themselves more space than before. They would have to get creative if they were going to have any kind of a chance to escape.

Scar got up and stretched his legs trying to work out the kinks. Staying in this small room didn't bode well for him, and he ached to get outside for some fresh air. He had hoped to see Sergeant Wilson to try to reason with him, but so far, he hadn't shown up. He figured Wilson had made some phone calls on the sly and was probably waiting to hear back or was trying to negotiate a time and place. Scar didn't know who would be in charge of something like this but figured it had to be someone in Washington D.C., which meant it would take a while. This would work in their favor as they had already decided they should try to escape here, figuring they had a better chance than if they were handed over to the National Police. It was going to be dark soon, and it seemed they were staying the night here. These were not the greatest facilities to be holding prisoners, which cemented the fact Wilson was doing this under his superior's noses. There was no other explanation for the relocation and never being booked. The garage door started to open and soon they could hear a truck pulling into the warehouse.

"Hmm, wonder if that's for us?" asked Burns.

"Oh, it's for us alright," sneered Nordell, "Question is, are we going out dead or alive?"

Scar shot him a glance. "So, much for optimism."

Nordell shrugged his shoulders. "Lost that hours ago."

A loud thud hit the cement floor, which echoed throughout the empty warehouse and gave the men pause as they tried to figure out what it was.

Nordell let out a scoff. "I know what that is."

Burns looked doubtful. "Do ya?"

"Cots. We're spending the night in comfort boys."

They let out a collective laugh since they all had experience sleeping on cots.

A key was inserted into the door and unlocked it before a cop pulled it open. A cop brandishing a shotgun ordered them up against the wall. The four prisoners moved toward the wall and watched another officer carry four cots into the room.

Burns gestured at Nordell.

"I know my cots," grinned Nordell.

"Excuse me, but how long are we gonna be here?" asked an impatient Scar.

"One night only," said the shotgun-toting cop.

"And then?" asked Scar.

"Don't worry, you'll be out of here in the morning."

Scar didn't like the sound of that but didn't think he'd get anymore answers from this guy, so instead, he asked for something else to eat.

"How's a pizza sound?" asked the cop.

Everyone's eyes lit up and began arguing over the ingredients.

"Despite all of this," said Bassett, "pizza sounds pretty damn good."

"I'm with ya," said Burns. "I can't remember the last time I had pizza."

Bassett's easy expression hardened. "Besides, we're gonna need to keep our strength up when we escape tonight."

All eyes shifted to Bassett waiting for him to continue.

"These cots have nice metal square bars that we can use to scrape through the drywall."

Scar considered this for a moment. "Nothing on the other side of this wall is there?"

"Just more dead space between it and the outer wall," said Bassett moving to the corner of the room. "Last time I hit the head, I noticed the guard's table was not positioned where they could see the other side of this wall completely. So, if we burrow right about here, we can squeeze between the studs easily enough."

Nordell patted Bassett's back. "Corporal, you'd have made a great Marine."

Bassett accepted the compliment.

"We'll do a recon later tonight and decide on our approach," said Scar.

It took about an hour before the pizza showed up but was well worth the wait. It was a deep dish Chicago style pizza, and they praised the chef. They devoured it in a matter of minutes and couldn't compliment it enough. The cops had been gracious enough to get them brownies and cold sodas as well. Bassett had been right, the pizza was awesome and put everyone in a better mood.

They let their stomachs settle while resting on the cots before they did another recon. After everyone used the bathroom, the one thing they all noticed was the two cops were now busy playing video games on a laptop. The faint sound of explosions and gunfire from the video game traveled through the empty building. The guys stood still and tried to hear it in their makeshift cell, but only Basset was able to.

"Oh, to have such young ears again," said Nordell.

"They do come in handy," said Bassett. "Don't worry, once we bust through this wall, you'll be able to hear 'em."

Nordell rolled his eyes.

"If they keep playing the game then I think we could rush them," said Burns.

"The element of surprise will give us at least two extra seconds if not more," said Nordell. "Bassett, you and Burns should take the lead, you're faster than me or Scar."

Bassett looked at Burns and gave him a fist-bump.

"These metal posts should come in handy as well," said Nordell, picking up a folded cot.

Scar sat back listening to them. He now understood why Winters allowed the men to hash things out before making a final decision. It allowed you to consider everything before locking yourself into a position. He was glad he didn't have to worry too much about these guys planning an operation. Everyone here knew what they were doing especially Nordell, who had the most experience.

After they finished, they all looked at Scar for approval.

Scar nodded. "Let's get to it."

Nordell and Burns began to tear apart one of the cots and then started to scrape through the drywall. It didn't take too long before they tore through the first layer exposing the studs, which were spaced twenty-four inches apart. They had just started on the outer wall when they heard the garage door open and a vehicle drive in. The men froze realizing there was drywall laying all about.

CHAPTER 53

PORT HURON MICHIGAN

The streets of Port Huron looked as eerie as all the other empty streets Meeks traveled through over the past few months. He could never get used to the stark emptiness with overgrown lawns encroaching into every area that wasn't paved. Trash always blew about or was stuck in trees and there was always burned down houses. This town was no different, although he could sense people still lived in the area. It would be easy to cross into Canada via the St. Clair River and bring supplies back home. Of course, if it was so easy, then why was Scar in trouble?

The five-vehicle convoy pulled through the streets and headed to the garage Hadley had used with Scar's team.

"Right here," said Hadley.

Reese hit the brakes on the big Suburban. The rest of the convoy pulled in behind them.

"Alright, let's check it out," said Meeks.

Hadley was the first one to reach the garage and pulled open the door. He walked toward the back and found the weapons. After removing them, Meeks pulled out a map of the city and spread it on the hood of the squad car. During the drive, he had decided who he wanted on which teams. Despite the fact it would take only Reese to watch the garage, he wasn't going to have anyone not partnered with someone else, so he would have Amber stay with her. He gave out the other assignments based on experience and who had typically worked together. Badger would stay with him, while Hadley and Hollis would scout out a sharpshooter position. He dropped Eddie Perlee and Taylor's old friend Harris down the river about a mile to watch the shoreline and a couple more to keep watch up on the interstate. He wanted a heads up on anyone moving in or out of the city.

"Listen, guys, this is going to be a big waiting game, we might not see anything here for quite some time. We just have to be patient and stay out of sight. We can't risk engaging anyone. So, keep your heads down and the radios on."

Everyone began loading up in their assigned vehicles and Meeks gave the girls a pair of night vision binoculars.

"Wait till dark to pull these out," said Meeks.

Reese took the styrene case. "C'mon Meeks, this isn't our first rodeo."

"Don't worry about us," said Amber.

"I normally don't, but damn it's weird being in charge, I can't help myself."

"Makes you appreciate Cole," said Amber.

"Man, does it ever. I don't know how he did it."

"Does it," interrupted Reese. "He'll be back."

"I sure as hell hope so. Being in charge of a football team is one thing but this…"

"Whole new ballgame," smiled Amber.

"Yeah and that's an understatement."

Meeks gave them both a hug before getting into the squad car where Taylor sat in the driver's seat. The older man gave Meeks a curt nod before letting off the brake. They snaked their way toward Interstate 94 and out onto Lapeer Connector, which was the last exit before entering Canada. They were able to get off that road and head through the giant parking lot of an abandoned home improvement store. Behind the store was a large wooded area that bordered the interstate. The area was out of the way of any residential homes, which is what he wanted. He didn't dare take the chance that none of them were occupied. Now was not the time to be making new friends.

Taylor pulled through the empty parking lot and into the woods stopping beside a small creek. Meeks was satisfied this was where they would wait to ambush the cops if they came this way. That they were coming at all was a big assumption he was making. Meeks wouldn't rest easy for the remainder of the day not knowing for sure.

He got out of the squad car and the eight men on his team began trudging through the trees and up on the interstate. They noticed a couple of buildings sitting alongside the side of the interstate and guessed they were for state trucks.

Meeks looked at Taylor. "What ya think?"

"Got a nice high roof, and it's, what, a hundred feet from the road."

Meeks waited for Hadley and Hollis to catch up. "What do ya think, Hollis?"

"Oh, it's perfect."

"Let's go see if there's a ladder inside," said Meeks.

The four of them walked over to the building and looked inside where they found several big dump trucks. Meeks looked at Taylor and flicked his eyebrows.

"Whatcha thinking?" asked Taylor.

"Badger, these big ole snowplow trucks will be just the ticket to jam up the road a bit. Make these two lane roads into one lane."

"I like your thinking," said Taylor, as he took the butt of his M-4 and broke the glass on the door. He reached in and turned the handle. "Shall we?"

"We shall," laughed Meeks.

"Hell, I can drive anything in here," said Hollis a former over the road truck driver.

Meeks stepped into the office and found the keys inside a box attached to the wall. He grabbed the keys and handed them to Hollis who began matching them up. As soon as he started the first one, Meeks and Taylor opened the garage doors. Over the next thirty minutes, they pulled four trucks out onto the interstate and parked them in pairs on each side of the road blocking one lane. Meeks loved the idea so much he ran over and jumped into one of the cabs. He liked how high they sat and how the big side mirrors gave you a great view to the rear. He took another quick glance in the mirror as he thought he had noticed something moving in the distance. He snapped his head back and the blood drained from his face. Four National Police vehicles were coming around the bend.

CHAPTER 54

SARNIA ONTARIO

After pulling down the inner layer of drywall, Burns was beginning to tear at the outer wall when the garage door opened. Sweat formed on Scar's forehead when he realized they had drywall lying on the floor and needed to hide it.

Scar and Bassett fell to the floor to begin scooping up the larger pieces and Bassett stacked them in the opposite corner. He also caught the smaller pieces as Scar flung them over. Nordell opened one of the cots and rushed it over to the stack of drywall. Burns grabbed another cot and sat down on it, almost hiding the hole in the wall.

They heard someone unlocking the door. Scar gave a quick inspection and motioned Bassett to get over by Burns to help him hide the hole. As the door began to open, Scar rushed over to stand in front of it.

He was surprised to find Sergeant Wilson at the door. "Hey perfect timing, I've got to go to the bathroom."

"Mister Scarborough, you think you can hold on for a minute?"

Scar stood six inches over the smaller Wilson and could be intimidating if he wanted to. Right now he wanted to and glared angrily at Wilson. He didn't want him to enter the room and stood his ground.

"I can do that, but only if you explain why we're being held here."

Wilson backed up a little. "I understand how upset you must be, but I can explain it to you and your men."

"Then let's do it out here, I'm sick and tired of this room," said Scar, shifting his big body a few more inches forward.

"Okay, have it your way. What about your men?"

"Trust me, you don't want them out here, they're even more pissed than I am."

"Come over here," said Wilson.

Scar walked toward the table the guards had set up and noticed Wilson had come alone in his personal car. He couldn't wait to hear what the man had to say.

"I'm sorry about all of this, but you must realize that you are wanted men and there are people who want to turn you over to the US National Police for the reward money."

"So, you brought us here?" asked Scar.

"For your own protection."

The man was lying so Scar decided to play along not wanting to raise any alarm. "Our own protection?"

"Yes, you see we weren't the only ones to find you. Last night, in that restaurant you caught the attention of others. I have informants that told me they were lying in wait for you."

"Which is why we're here?" asked Scar in a thankful tone.

"Yes. We've got corrupt cops on the force, hell even some of the judges have been bought. Ever since your country fell, you Americans aren't the only ones having problems. Had I not gotten you out of there, you'd be in some American jail right now. It's why we didn't book you; I didn't want you in the system. As of right now, I've got everyone confused about your whereabouts."

"So, why not just let us go?"

"There are too many people looking for you. They even found your canoe and my informants tell me they're waiting for you on the other side of the river as well."

Scar had to hand it to Wilson for coming up with a convincing story. What he couldn't understand was why he was here telling him this.

"How many know where we are?"

"It's just five of us."

The answer made Scar realize why he was telling him this. He didn't want them to give his guards any trouble because he was sorely lacking in manpower. He wasn't about to bring in more help as he had no intention of splitting the money with more people.

"Did you call my friend, General Standish?"

"That's the good news. He told me to hang onto you guys and that he'd be sending his right-hand man down to get you guys to safety with all the supplies that you'd need."

Scar decided to have a little fun and made up a fake name. "Oh wow! So, Major Peabody will be coming. How soon?"

"He said the good Major should be here by late morning."

Scar fought to control his facial expressions. "That's good news. Sergeant, I can't thank you enough."

"Hey, it's my honor. I love America and want to see her back where she stood before."

Scar wanted to grab him by the throat and give it a good squeeze. Instead, he gave him a big fake smile. "So, by morning then."

"Yep. Just hang out. I know these aren't the greatest accommodations, but we've got you in here for your own protection. My men will keep you safe till morning."

Scar extended his hand and gave him a convincing shake. He continued to play the fool and waved at Wilson as he got back into his car. Scar then headed back to the room.

"Major Peabody," said Burns, in a humorous tone, "nice one."

"The guy thinks I'm an idiot," said Scar shaking his head.

"So, the exchange is in the morning then?" asked Bassett.

"That's what I'm thinking."

"Okay, so nothing changes," said Nordell.

After Wilson drove back out of the warehouse, Burns moved the cot away from the wall and continued to scrape away the outer drywall. As they removed the pieces faint sounds from the video game became louder giving them confidence their so-called protectors had let their guard down. After removing the final pieces, Nordell fashioned four metal clubs out of the torn up cot and handed one to each of them.

Bassett grabbed onto the makeshift weapon wishing it was his tactical tomahawk. He stretched his legs and twisted around to get ready. He then slipped between the studs and waited for the rest to follow. Bassett peeked around the corner. His prey was enthralled in a video game not knowing they were about to become his video game.

CHAPTER 55

Meeks was sitting inside one of the four big snowplow trucks to check out the strategic positioning when he noticed four National Police vehicles coming their way. His heart quickened as he grabbed his radio.

"Everyone hit the deck, hit the deck."

Without questioning the order, everyone fell to the ground just as the vehicles came around the bend. Meeks pulled out his Sig Sauer 9mm and lowered his head just enough to watch the approaching vehicles slow down as they closed in on the two trucks sitting in the fast lane. He waited until they passed before looking up to see how many were in the cars. It looked like the three squad cars were full. He couldn't be sure but suspected the paddy wagon had a passenger, which added up to fourteen cops.

Meeks let out a big sigh of relief because they gotten there just in time. Thank God they got these trucks moved before they came through, otherwise, the cops would be suspicious if they saw something different about the road when they were coming back.

Amber had been right guessing these bastards would come through

Port Huron. He assumed a cunning grin because, now, they knew their numbers. Fourteen cops wouldn't be a problem and the paddy wagon would make it easier because they would know what not to shoot at.

Meeks waited until they were out of sight before hopping out of the truck and running across the road. He began to laugh excitedly as he approached Taylor, who was picking himself up off the ground. "Damn that was close."

"A little too close," grumbled Taylor. "We need better spotters don't cha think?"

"They should have been there by now. But, no matter, now we know they'll be coming this way for sure."

"Did you get a look at their numbers?"

"Yeah, I figure no more than fourteen."

"We better let everyone know," suggested Taylor.

Meeks walked back to the building where Hollis and Hadley had erected a ladder. He swung his rifle onto his back and began to climb up to the roof for a better radio signal. He looked around and liked the wide-open view. He pulled out his radio and keyed the button.

"Listen up, Detroit just passed us. I say again, Detroit just passed us, over."

The various teams began responding back.

"Amber and Reese copy," said Amber into the radio.

"Damn girl, you called that one right," said Reese.

"Well, I had a fifty-fifty shot."

"Oh, c'mon, stop being modest. You were right and the boys know it."

"I suppose they do now, don't they," snickered Amber.

Reese flicked some strands of hair the wind blew across her face. She and Amber sat on a park bench that sat alongside the walkway bordering the river. She looked across the water into Canada. "I wonder what it's like over there."

"Definitely more normal than this side of the border," said Amber.

"Our next-door neighbors had crossed over and we never saw them again. Ever since then, I always wondered. I suppose it can't be much different than being in Winnipeg."

"I couldn't say. I never left the base. Did you?" asked Amber,

"You know, neither did I. I never even thought about it. Hell, we had everything we needed and they kept us pretty busy with all the training."

Amber turned to her. "Yes. They. Did. I thought I was in shape when I played college softball, but man did they wear me out."

Reese laughed. "Right, I mean c'mon, I ran track and field not that long ago and I could barely keep up with that instructor."

Amber sighed. "He was in good shape."

"Ooooh was he ever, hmm hmm."

"He was definitely a hottie."

Reese grabbed Amber's arm. "And he was British...oooh I loved his accent."

"Yeah, even when he was yelling at us."

"Right!" laughed Reese.

"Okay enough of that," said Amber standing up, "c'mon, it's getting dark. We should get our night vision gear on."

Amber swung her Colt M-4 around to her chest while Reese grabbed her red crutch and they began to walk back across the field to the garage and their supplies. They dug into the food and ate while waiting for it to get dark. Reese remarked how different the other side of the river looked with all the lights on. She walked out of the garage and looked around for any lights on their side. Not a single light was on. She rested her hands on the rifle hanging from her shoulders staring at the desolate skyline. It was a depressing sight and a bit on the scary side to see no sign of life. It was the same in Jackson, but there were people still about, which seems like a small thing but it made a big difference.

CHAPTER 56

ON THE ROAD TO WINNIPEG

After telling the girls they go to Canada, Winters was able to get an update from Finley's mom. Debbie stated her daughter was in pain and her fever was still high even after taking the antibiotics that Stacy had. The former paramedic had said the antibiotics were probably too old to be effective and was glad to hear about plans to take her to Canada. She volunteered to go with them and look after her as best as she could. With Stacy and her son, Finley's mom, sister, and the two girls, there would be eight people going, which meant two vehicles.

Both Collette and Laney volunteered to help Winters find a suitable van to accommodate Finley and to find some extra gas cans. They took Billy Gamble's Ford Crew Cab and drove back into town. The first thing they needed to do was get the bulldozer out of the way. Winters had no idea how to operate it and asked Mike Grant to find someone who did.

It took nearly an hour before someone moved the bulldozer so volunteers could begin to fill their vehicles. They had come up with a newer passenger van and a pickup truck that had a tank in the back with a pump handle. It had been used as a farm truck to fuel the tractors out in the fields.

After getting food supplies and water, they headed back to the hideout with Collette driving the van. Winters hurried everyone together, loaded the sleeping patient into the back of the van, and handed the keys to Stacey.

Winters gave Ashley and Kaitlyn a big hug and wished them well before getting into the pickup truck. He started it and they began the long journey to Winnipeg. He was excited with anticipation of seeing Sadie. It had been only a couple of weeks since he'd last seen her, but with everything he'd been through it seemed like months. He looked over at his passengers, Laney and Collette, and was glad they were along. All three of the girls had been a big help in more ways than they knew. Not only did they help last night, but they lifted his spirits as well.

He tapped the steering wheel thinking about Sadie and couldn't help but break out in a grin. This attracted the attention of Laney, who sat next to him on the bench seat.

"Is there something you want to share?"

Winters turned to her. "What?"

"You're smiling and I thought maybe you wanted to share."

"I was?"

"Yes, you were."

"Give it up, Cole," said Collette.

"I'm just excited to be going to Winnipeg is all."

Laney grabbed Winters' arm. "Is there a girl you want to tell us about?"

Winters cocked his head back.

"I knew it," said an excited Laney. "You have a girlfriend. Tell us about her."

"It's not what you think?"

"C'mon Cole, don't hold out on us," said Collette leaning forward.

"I'm telling you, it's not what you think."

"But it is a girl?" asked Laney.

"Yes, it is, but she's not my girlfriend. She's more of an adopted daughter. Her name is Sadie, and she's eleven."

"Oh, darn," said a disappointed Laney. "I thought maybe you had, like, a girlfriend."

"Well, I do actually, but she's not in Canada."

Laney straightened up. "Yes, I love it. Tell us all about her, what's her name?"

"Her name is Reese, and she's a very special person."

"Is she pretty?" asked Laney.

The joy on his face was obvious. "Oh yeah, she's quite pretty."

"You're in love with her!" said Collette. "I can see it written all over ya."

Winters flinched.

"He is," laughed Laney.

"No, it's just that it's complicated," protested Winters.

"Why's that?" asked Laney.

Winters wasn't sure about telling them that Reese was only a couple of years older than they were. It was odd, impractical, and not acceptable to most people in society, but how do you control a mutual attraction, especially in these trying times.

"C'mon Cole, you have to tell us, we're on a road trip and that's the rules of a road," said Collette.

"It's just that she's a little younger than me."

"How much younger?" asked Laney.

Winters hesitated for a moment. "Well, she's twenty."

"Twenty! Cole Winters, you are a stud," shouted Laney, grabbing his arm again and shaking it.

"Wow," said Collette wide eyed, "you are a stud muffin."

"How did you meet her?" asked Laney.

Winters thought this was an interesting question. How do you tell the story of releasing a girl from the chains of slavery and then bond with her over the course of a few months? Winters looked over at the girls. They had gotten over their initial giddiness and showed genuine curiosity. It was a long trip so he decided to tell the story from the beginning. For the next couple of hours, he told them everything from the murders at the train station and the Patriot Centers to finding Sadie, rescuing Reese and the other girls from the party-house. He told them about all the battles and how the National Police were involved. Both girls shed tears hearing their dads were not coming home as they both had gone through the Patriot

Centers. He had considered candy coating it, but they wanted the truth, so he spelled it out for them. It was a tough truth to swallow, but the war casualties were high, and most everyone in town had resigned themselves to the fact they'd never see their loved ones again.

Hearing about Amber, Reese, and Sadie brought their moods back up, and they wanted to know everything about them. They peppered him with all kinds of questions about what the girls did and how they did it. Who and what kind of girls were they and the battles they fought.

Winters was happy to answer their questions and to observe their fascination with the girls. They couldn't wait to meet Sadie, and found a special kinship with Reese, as they had a shared a similar experience with her and could relate to what she endured. They found his relationship with her romantic and advised him to take it slow, but not give her up because of any societal norms.

The last part of the story was about Cara, who Collette knew from school, and asked about her. As he told the story, tears streamed down both the girl's cheeks, which made him react in kind. Winters wiped the tears from his face and paused to regain his composure. When he did, Laney gave him reassuring pats on the arm and asked him to continue. After telling them of all the trials and tribulations, another unexpected release of tension lifted more of the burdensome weight from his shoulders and he let out a deliberate sigh. He finished up by reassuring them it was okay about Cara, because everything happens for a reason.

CHAPTER 57

Bassett turned to Burns and asked him if he was ready. After getting an affirming nod, Bassett took in a few deep breaths and sprang around the corner. With each stride, he picked up his pace and closed in on his prey. Neither of the guards saw him until it was too late and then they panicked and tried to go for their weapons. Bassett jumped over the table with his club raised in the air. He landed between them while striking one over the head and continuing the full motion turn and hitting the other in the forehead. Both had time only to yell out in pain before Bassett had knocked them unconscious.

Burns stopped before even reaching the table and watched Bassett in action. He always admired the way the man moved and should have known better than to even try to help. "Need any help there, buddy?"

Bassett looked up. "Nah, I'm good."

"Hey Gunny, why did you bother with four clubs?" asked Burns.

Nordell shook his head. "Yeah, I can see that was overkill."

"These are new guys," said Bassett. "My buddy Quinn isn't here."

"C'mon guys, let's grab their weapons and get the hell out of here," ordered Scar.

Each cop had a Sig Sauer P229, which was a .40 caliber pistol, and one had a Remington 870 pump-action shotgun, while the other had a Colt C8 carbine with only one full magazine.

Scar handed the pistols to Nordell and Burns, while Bassett took the rifle leaving him the shotgun. It wasn't much, but he hoped they wouldn't need much. If they could sneak out of here and find a boat, they'd be able to make it back to their ride, which was full of weapons.

Scar led the men to the door and pushed it open. He looked outside and a pain bolted through his forehead with the realization Wilson had lied. Several vehicles were driving into the parking lot and Scar recognized some as being from Detroit.

Scar closed the door. "Wilson lied. We're being sold tonight."

"How many?" asked Bassett.

"Can't say for sure but it's a lot more than us."

Burns motioned to the back. "Let's hit the back door."

They ran across the hundred-foot cement floor in seconds and reached the door. Burns opened it and took a quick peek. The coast was clear, and he gave the okay just as the garage door began to open. They scooted out the door into a back parking lot full of shipping containers and a couple of dumpsters.

As they ran toward a shipping container, they could hear yelling inside the makeshift prison they had just escaped. Thankfully, there were no streetlights to give away their position. Voices grew louder as the cops came to the back exit of the warehouse. Burns led the way across the parking lot to a shipping container where they hid as the cops came out with flashlights lighting up the area and pointing their way.

Scar's heart was pounding as he tightened the grip on the shotgun. It was the last weapon he wanted to use as it would give away their position. He looked over at Bassett who nodded knowing what he needed to do. Scar fell to the ground and peeked around the large metal container to take a quick look. A pair of cops charged their way and another pair headed in the opposite direction. Scar raised his hand and signaled there were two cops. Bassett gave him another nod and got down in a squat position.

Scar could make out the cop's conversation as they closed in on their position. He steadied his breathing as he heard their footsteps. The flashlight beam swung back and forth and Scar pushed his big body up against the shipping container as much as he could. The flashlight beam came around in front of him. He raised the shotgun and came around the corner the same time as Bassett. He threw the butt of the gun against the side of the cop's face. The blow made a loud crack and the cop's knees buckled. He delivered another one into the side of his skull knocking him out. Bassett's victim fell on top of his partner. Nordell picked through their pockets grabbing their pistols and ammo before helping Scar hide them between the containers. He also found a knife, which he handed to Bassett who gave him a big smile upon receiving the gift.

Scar wasn't sure which way to go and looked up into the cloudy night sky to find the North Star. It took a few seconds to find it and he then led the men west hoping to run into the river. The only questions remaining were; how far was it from their present position, and what was in their way? They came to a ten-foot wooden fence and Bassett fell to the ground to act as a step. Burns jumped over first, followed by Nordell and Scar. Bassett then backed up, ran toward it, and leaped up grabbing the top.

Scar led the men across the back lot of another large building where there were more shipping containers. They ran between them to find a parking lot that emptied out onto a street. The big railroad containers kept them hidden while Scar stopped to catch his breath and figure out his next move. No doubt, Wilson will try to catch them without alerting the whole police force because then he'd have to explain why there were cops from Detroit lurking around. This would be an advantage, at least while they were on this side of the river. Once they got back across he had no doubt Captain Vatter would have his forces out looking for them. Tires squealed in the night as the cops left the warehouse to begin the manhunt. Up ahead a few cars sat in the parking lot, and Scar wished Nate were here to hotwire one of them. A locomotive horn broke through the night air and the distinctive clacking noises made by the train made became more pronounced. Scar remembered the tracks led to the chemical production area bordering the river. He strained his eyes across the lot and could barely make out that the road became an overpass, which meant it crossed over the railroad tracks. This is where he wanted to go. This would lead them to the river. He turned to tell the men when a cop car came barreling into the parking lot and stopped. Four men, armed with long rifles, exited the squad car and began to approach their position.

CHAPTER 58

SARNIA ONTARIO

Scar, watching the four cops using minimal caution as they approached their position, figured they were on a fishing expedition. The cops didn't know where they were, but were in a hurry to cross the most logical area off their list.

Scar ordered everyone to the other end of the containers hoping to avoid a conflict with these cops or at the very least take them out quietly. A shootout would only alert everyone to their whereabouts.

A beam of light flashed down the center of the containers just as they turned the corner. The light moved around and kept moving, which meant the cops were walking between the containers.

Nordell got closer to Scar and whispered. "We need to take them out."

Scar nodded and motioned Bassett to flank them. If nothing else, they'd have wheels to get to the river faster.

Bassett reached for the knife Scar had just given him. He stole a quick look around the corner. The coast was clear, so he charged down the side of the container with Burns on his heels. He pulled up at the end for another peek to find a lone cop standing guard. He turned to Burns and held up one finger.

Bassett tightened his grip on the knife handle and took in a deep breath before springing up around the corner. The moonless night and his silent approach gave him an edge as he wrapped his hand around the cop's mouth. In one motion, he slit his throat and carried the limp body out of sight.

Bassett then looked down between the containers. The three remaining cops continued toward the other end unaware of the impending danger. Bassett began to slide toward them, as Burns stood in a Weaver Stance with the .40 caliber pistol ready to take them down if necessary. Bassett was waiting for Scar and Nordell to engage them when they reached the end. Then he would strike the third cop at the last second. If he acted too soon, the other two cops would be in play. All three were at the ready with their guns leading the way.

Bassett lowered his body as the cops came to the end. He heard the cracking of skulls before seeing the two cops fall to the ground. He jumped up and was about to thrust his knife into his target when the cop fell to his knees with his hands in the air. Bassett pulled back the knife but jumped on top of him.

"Please don't kill me."

Bassett recognized the voice of Quinn Johnson, the man who served with the Calgary Highlanders. Bassett pulled out a pistol and pointed it at his head.

"Don't move a muscle, Quinn," ordered Bassett.

"I won't, please just don't shoot me."

Bassett kicked the rifle away and then removed the sidearm handing it to Scar as he approached.

Scar looked down at him. "Stand him up."

Bassett helped the cop up.

"Care to tell me what the hell's going on?" asked Scar.

"It's Sergeant Wilson, sir. He's the one that had the bright idea of turning you over for the reward."

"Then why are you helping?"

"If I didn't, he'd make my life miserable."

Nordell came forward. "Oh, so you didn't do it for the money, huh?"

Quinn shook his head. "I didn't even know who you guys were until yesterday."

Scar decided this man could help them. "Look, Quinn is it?"

He nodded.

"Help us get out of here and you can go about your merry way and say whatever you want, I don't really care. Deal?"

"I can do that."

"Good. You got the keys to that car."

He nodded.

Everyone piled into the car with Bassett taking the driver's seat. Quinn sat between Burns and Nordell in the backseat.

"Take a left up on Confederation Street. It'll take you to the river," said Quinn.

Bassett looked both ways before zipping out of the parking lot. He heard the radio chatter come alive on the police radio, but it wasn't about them. So far, Wilson hadn't spilled the beans, which would work in their favor. The only problem was the cops from Detroit. They would make getting back to Jackson a challenge. He wasn't sure how many were in the area or how many they had across the river.

Bassett spun the wheels as he took a left down Confederation. The long straight road had little traffic and he reminded himself that he was driving a police car. No one would give them a second look, as long as it wasn't another policeman. Bassett wanted to ask Scar about Hadley but didn't want to relay any information to Quinn despite how helpful he was being at the moment. Alliances quickly turned in war, especially when you're a prisoner. Bassett looked at Scar in the passenger seat and tapped him on the leg.

"Don?" was the only word he said.

"Yeah, I don't know."

"Are you headed to your canoe?" asked Quinn.

"Why?"

"I heard him say he sank it."

Scar grimaced. "Any suggestions?"

"I can help you get another one."

Scar turned around in his seat to look at Quinn. "You can? Where?"

CHAPTER 59

PORT HURON MICHIGAN

Amber helped Reese adjust the straps on the night vision goggles after she pulled her hair back in a ponytail. She then moved the weapon out of the way so she could loop the case of the big binoculars around her neck. The breeze from across the river cooled the air enough that both were glad they had brought their dark running jackets. It was pitch black on this side of the river, and they disappeared into the night as they moved closer to the water. The walk across the field was fascinating because of all the twinkling lights on the Canadian side. They were everywhere, in homes, office buildings, streetlights, and the cars that drove the streets. Neither Amber or Reese had seen anything like it for so long they couldn't help but be mesmerized.

"Look at it," said Reese, "it's so pretty."

"Isn't it though? I can't remember the last time I saw city lights."

"Oh man, wouldn't you just love to be able to walk those streets," said Reese as she sat down on the park bench. "Can you imagine just walking along and stopping to get some pizza."

"A beer would be better."

"I've never been to a bar," said Reese.

"You haven't?"

"I'm only twenty, remember."

"No fake ID?"

"No, I was never bold enough."

Amber started laughing. "You're bold enough now, aren't cha?"

Reese flipped up the goggles. "It's amazing, isn't it? How one can, like, change themselves completely in a matter of months."

"That much, huh?"

"Amber, I was, like, the biggest wimp-dog around. Didn't get into any kind of trouble because I was always scared I'd get caught."

Amber's laugh continued to build.

"I know...I was a big baby."

Amber held up a finger. "Bu...bu...but you're such a badass now, I mean what the hell girl."

Reese joined in the laughter.

"Can you imagine being at your high school reunion," said Amber between breaths.

"Oh, hell, all them bitches would be all fat and preggers with baby-snot running down their dresses."

Amber smacked Reese on the arm trying to catch her breath. "I can see it now, you'd walk in there dressed to the nines, with your rocking body, swinging Glocks on each hip."

"Not taking crap from anybody," said Reese.

"But giving it, asking what they did to save America."

"Hell ya, asking if their butts were cowering over in Canada like a bunch of little bitches."

"Tell 'em sister."

Reese slowed it down. "Eh...it'll never happen. Hell, they're probably all dead anyway."

"Ya think?"

"Yeah, there were still a bunch of dumb-assess, like my mom and me, that stuck around when the cops came in."

Amber let out a deep sigh. "Yeah, us too."

"You know when you look back on it…were we that naïve or just stupid."

"A little bit of both, I suppose."

"Oh well, enough of that, I don't like talking about it anyway."

"Me either, but I'd still like to see you rocking a dress with holsters."

"You know, next time we're in Canada, I might just try that look."

"Hell, why wait, when we get back to Jackson, let's find a couple of pretty dresses."

Reese gave her a profound look. "Definitely."

Amber pulled the Night Optics D-321B-AG binoculars out of the waterproof case. She powered the Gen 3 glasses on and carefully put the strap around her neck knowing these babies cost well over seven grand. The 3.6 magnification green hued vision was enough to see the shoreline across the river. She moved them up and down the river looking for a canoe or boat. There was nothing but a light chop on the river, so she raised them up and scanned the streets of Sarnia. She watched a car drive along the parallel street before making a right hand turn. She was disappointed when she didn't see anyone walking around. She would have liked to imagine what they were thinking and where they were going.

She continued to scan the streets before turning back to the river hoping to see a boat crossing the water with Scar and the boys in it. A flashing light to the south caught her attention. She moved the glasses over when she noticed two Canadian police cars cruising the street with their emergency lights flashing. Both were using spotlights to light up the side of the road. A chill ran through her. Were they looking for Scar?

"Reese, over there," Amber said pointing south across the water.

"What is it?"

"Couple of cop cars."

"Let me see those."

Amber pulled the strap off her neck and handed the binoculars to Reese. Without using the strap, she looked through them.

"They're looking for someone all right."

Amber flipped her goggles down while standing up and walking to the shoreline. She scanned the water for any sign of a boat. As she looked across the water, she noticed more flashing lights.

"Is that another one?"

"Yep."

Amber walked back to Reese, who still sat on the park bench. "I better call Meeks."

"Probably a good idea," said Reese, as she continued staring through the glasses, "these guys are out of their cars now and looking at the water."

Amber keyed the radio and reported in.

"Sounds like our boys might have escaped," said Meeks.

"Let's hope so," said Amber as she sat back down next to Reese.

"Keep me posted, over."

Amber put the radio away just as headlights lit up the darkness behind them on Griswold Street. She grabbed Reese by the arm and pulled her to the ground. "Someone's coming."

Reese spun around on her stomach and pulled her crutch off the bench. She raised the binoculars, but couldn't see past the bright headlights. Another car came up behind the first one. Both started coming down the street toward them.

Amber grabbed the radio. "We've got company, I repeat, we've got company."

It took a long agonizing second before Meeks responded. "Who are they?"

It took a few moments for Amber to figure out who they were. She clicked the button. "Cops and we're out in the open, we're busted here."

"Stay tight, we'll get ya help."

Amber looked around the wide-open field realizing they had nowhere to go and nothing to use as cover. Running wasn't an option because of Reese's leg, but it was too late anyway as the cop cars had gotten to the end of the street and stopped with their headlights pointing their way.

"We'll only get one chance at this," said Reese, pulling back the bolt on the Colt M-4 carbine.

"There's always the river," said Amber.

"Oh God, that's gotta be cold."

"Better cold than dead."

Reese turned to her. "I suppose."

"Be nice to know how many there are."

The two cars began moving again and as they headed toward the water, they began to put some separation between them.

"C'mon, just spread out a little bit further, please," said Reese.

The headlights from the cars now lit up the field on either side of the girls, which left some breathing room. However, they were actually in a worse situation because they were caught in the middle. Consequently, they now had two fronts to control and nowhere to go.

CHAPTER 60

SARNIA ONTARIO

Taking Quinn Johnson hostage proved to be a good move because he directed them to where they could pick up another boat. Had they not taken him hostage, they would have wasted precious time only to find their canoe was sunk and risked exposure as the cops would have expected them to go there.

Bassett continued to drive down Confederation Street before Quinn told him to take a left on the next street.

"I've got a buddy who has a boat."

Scar turned in his seat. "Will this buddy of yours let you borrow it?"

"Yeah, I mean you got guns."

Scar let out a scoff. "Let's get something straight, alright. I don't want to point a gun at some poor innocent guy. We came over here to buy food for a town that is starving, with money we no longer have. We escaped back there because you forced our hand."

"I'm sorry. I'll talk to him, I'm sure it'll be alright."

"Will it hold five people?" asked Burns.

"Five?" asked Quinn.

"Yeah, you're coming with us."

"But you said you'd let me go."

"Someone has to bring the boat back."

"Oh, yes, of course."

Bassett slowed down and took a left on Proctor Street. Quinn leaned forward and pointed to the house. "Back it in. There's a hitch on this thing."

An eighteen-foot skiff sat in the driveway. It was nothing fancy and with five people it would be a tight fit. The problem now was finding a place to launch it.

Scar opened the door and waited for Quinn to get out. "Don't force my hand, okay?"

"I won't."

An outdoor floodlight came on and the side door opened up.

"Quinn, is that you?"

"Hey, Scottie. How's it going?"

"Good, man, how's it going with you, eh?"

"Need a big favor from ya."

Scottie approached them holding a beer. He looked like he had consumed several before this one and was in a jocular mood.

"Scottie, these are some friends of mine and they need to get across the river."

"Hey," said Scottie toasting them with his beer, "Americans, huh? You guys want a beer, eh?"

Scar turned to him. "Wish we could join ya, but we're kinda in a hurry."

"Oh, that's too bad, but no problem...sure you can use my boot."

Scottie's drunken slur made Scar chuckle. "Sure would appreciate it."

Burns approached Scottie. "Hey, is there a launch site somewhere close?"

Scottie took a swig and thought for a moment. "Not if you're in a hurry."

"And if we are in a hurry?"

"Well heck, just take it down to Chemical Valley and throw it in."

Burns turned to Quinn for clarification.

"It's down at the end of the street. We can go through the gate and it'll take us right to the water."

"There's five of ya," said Scottie swerving his head, "you guys can easily pick her up but be gentle with her."

"She got gas in her?" asked Burns.

"Plenty."

"Well, let's go, boys, times a wasting," said an impatient Nordell.

Scar agreed and everyone approached the boat and hooked it up to the trailer hitch. It only took a minute before the boat was secure and they all thanked Scottie, who made a final offer of a beer.

Bassett eased off the brake to pull out of the driveway and back on Confederation Street. It was only another six blocks before they came to the end of the road and Quinn told Bassett to take a right turn on Christina Street. As soon as he made the turn, they could see a cop car in the distance with its flashing lights on.

Quinn leaned forward. "That's one of Wilson's."

"How do you know?" asked Scar.

"He's got his lights on, but we haven't heard anything on the radio, which means he's still keeping this quiet."

Quinn pointed to the left, and Bassett made the turn into a sandpit.

"Isn't this where we landed?" asked Burns.

"Yes."

"This is a dumb place for us to be," said Nordell.

"No, it'll be alright," said Quinn. "Go left here."

"Explain," ordered Nordell.

"We'll be on the other side, it's more than three hundred yards away from where you landed."

The big sand mounds reminded Scar and Burns of their two battles in sandpits. The first one resulted in a couple of hundred deaths by execution. The sight of gunmen shooting innocent women, children, and the elderly in the back was not an easy thing to handle for any of the Shadow Patriots. They had gotten there too late to prevent it but ended up killing the executioners. It was only a small victory considering all the people who had been murdered in cold blood. It was at that moment when they learned what the National Police were really up to when they came in to clear out a town of its citizens. It was also that day when they saved six girls, including Amber. The other battle was after they rescued the girls from the party house. Both battles resulted in the murder of many innocent lives and forever seared the atrocities of this war in their memories.

Bassett came to the water's edge and pulled the car around before backing it up. As soon as he stopped, Scar got out and looked around through the darkness. The white sand grabbed whatever light it could and reflected it off the ground. This was where night vision goggles came in the handiest. With the top of the line optics they had, they could see everything, and it always gave them an advantage over their enemy. General Standish had been gracious in supplying them with the best their military had to offer.

Burns unhooked the boat and the five of them manhandled it to the water. Burns jumped in the boat and after two tries had it started.

"Get in, Quinn," ordered Scar.

Scar waited for Bassett and Nordell before squeezing into the small skiff. He sat in the back with Burns, who piloted the small craft into the dark waters. The light chop rocked the small boat from side to side.

Scar leaned toward Burns. "You remember where we were?"

"Yeah, just up this way," he said pointing a little north.

They weren't but fifty feet away from shore when Bassett shouted out. "We got headlights over there."

Scar looked ahead. "Damn it."

"More than likely from Detroit," said Nordell.

"What about Don?" asked Bassett.

Scar considered his options. Whether they had Hadley or not, they still needed a vehicle to get back to Jackson. They were going to have to engage with whomever was over there. They didn't have much in the way of weapons and would have to come in stealth. He turned to Burns. "Come in a little to the south."

Burns nodded and steered the boat to the left. Everyone kept their eyes on the headlights, which grew bigger the closer they got. Scar continued to stare across the water when blood rushed to his face as muzzle flashes lit up the night sky followed by the cracking of gunfire.

CHAPTER 61

PORT HURON MICHIGAN

Hearing that cops had shown up where the girls were made Meeks realize they had more to contend with than he initially thought. The ones that drove by earlier hadn't come back yet. He was sure because he had a pair of spotters watching the bridge, and they reported that no one had crossed back over yet. This meant more cops were in the Port Huron area perhaps because they knew Scar and company had escaped. If that were the case, they'd try to get back across the river by whatever means available, even if it meant swimming. He radioed Eddie, who was a mile from Amber and Reese, to hurry to them. He decided to gather his force and go there himself when his spotter called back.

"Detroit is crossing, I say again, Detroit is crossing."

Meeks grabbed the radio. "How many?"

"All four."

Time slowed down as Meeks realized he wouldn't be able to help the girls. He threw his hands up at Taylor. "What the hell, Badger."

"We can't chance it," said Taylor.

"Damn it."

"I know, I know, damned if we do, damned if we don't."

Meeks' chest tighten as he grabbed the radio. Everyone get ready,"

Taylor wore a scowl on his face. "We're too far away to help the girls anyway."

Meeks nodded trying to convince himself of the same thing.

They jogged out of the woods and across the interstate to the big snowplows where the rest of the guys were already in place. He chambered a round in his M-4 and leaned against the front of the truck. Up ahead he had four guys lying in wait amongst the tall grass with another group behind him. He had assigned each group a sequential target.

The bridge was just a mile away, which meant the cops would be here in seconds. Meeks took a deep breath when lights broke over the horizon. One of the men shouted they were coming. Meeks patted himself on the back for putting the snowplows on the road. It gave them the perfect hiding spot while forcing the convoy to slow their speed.

The lead squad car was not Meeks' assigned target, his was the second car and he fought against all his instincts to not shoot. It flew by and Meeks turned the corner of the truck with his rifle to his shoulder for the second car. He pulled the trigger and muzzle flashes lit up the night as hot shell casings flew into the air. The magazine emptied and Taylor came around, stepping into the lane shouting as he fired point-blank into the car. The car veered to the right as it slowed down.

Gunfire continued as all the groups engaged their targets filling the squad cars with lead and killing anyone inside. Meeks slammed a fresh magazine in and came back around because the third car was still coming at them. He grabbed Taylor's jacket collar and yanked him backward. The third car then crashed into the side of the plow before bouncing away.

"Damn you, you son of a bitch," Taylor yelled pulling out an empty mag and throwing in a full one.

Tires squealed and Meeks turned around, as the paddy wagon drove over the grassy median and onto the opposite lane zooming past them. He raised his rifle up but backed off when he realized he could hit the backend where his friends would be sitting if they were in there. He yelled out when a shot rang out from the top of the roof across the road. Hollis found his target with a single shot into the driver's window. The van sped up but started to swerve heading back into the median. The driver had lost control and the van flipped over on its side.

Meeks' jaw dropped and he ran toward it with his rifle to his shoulder. The way the van flipped, at the speed it was traveling, was going to cause some serious injuries. His friends would have broken bones and concussions. This was the last thing they needed since they were hours away from their doctor in Jackson.

He approached the van in a cautious manner and looked in the windshield. The dead driver had blood running down his face. A bullet hole in his shoulder bled down his arm. The passenger waved his hand to surrender when Meeks came around holding a gun on him. He then rushed to the back and pulled open the door. Relief swept over him when he found it empty.

Taylor came running up. "I guess they did get away."

"Yeah, I guess they did. I got a live one up front."

They circled back around only to find the passenger had died.

"That's that," said Taylor. "We need to get to the girls."

Meeks looked at the men as they gathered around. Their job was finished, and they were ready to move out. They ran back to the vehicles, and Meeks hopped into the squad car. He then heard the cops on their radios asking for backup down by the river. Meeks' face went flush as he realized the girls didn't have much time.

CHAPTER 62

While watching the water for any sign of Scar crossing in a boat, Amber and Reese had spotted a few Sarnia cops taking an interest in the shoreline. Neither one of them noticed that Detroit cops were approaching from behind. Two squad cars came down Griswold Street and passed by the garage where they stashed their supplies. As soon as the cars reached the end of the street, they started coming across the tall grassy field toward the girls. They had nowhere to go as the cops split up and approached them on either side of their position.

"Let's back up," whispered Amber, as she turned the volume down on the radio before throwing the binoculars back inside the waterproof case and snapping it shut.

Reese nodded and they began crawling backward into the tall grass while dragging their stuff down a slight decline. The closer they got to the river, the sound of splashing water grew louder. It only took a few seconds before the water seeped into her boots, stealing what warmth remained before climbing up her legs. She gritted her teeth as the water started to soak the front of her shirt exploding goose bumps on her skin. It reminded her of when she and Meeks had been on the run and fell into a pond before the rain started. The cold water would make her shake and sap her energy like it did that night. How she and Meeks ever made it out of there was a miracle. She wanted to jump up and empty a magazine into the cars, but she'd be out in the open between the cars and didn't know how many cops there were. If there was one thing she had learned over the past couple of months, it was to be patient and not to panic. Take a few moments to assess the situation, find out their numbers, and remember you still had the element of surprise.

Car doors opened and slammed shut while Reese looked at Amber mouthing four cops. She raised her head and looked through the night vision goggles. The car headlights beamed across the water, which kept them in the shadows.

Reese froze when one cop started walking toward them. She didn't dare look away for fear of making a sound or moving the tall grass. Reese stared at the approaching cop and recognized him. He had been at the party house and had been with her on one occasion. She remembered he had been quick and didn't linger too long. It had been early in the evening and he had just gotten started. He was one of the ones who liked to visit as many girls as he could in one night rather than stay with just one or two girls all night. At least he didn't beat on her like some of them did. She remembered every single one of them and experienced the pleasure of killing several of them. This would be another notch on her belt. She wouldn't be satisfied until they were all dead. She felt Mister Hyde wanting to come out and play, but she tightened her muscles to contain him while fighting off the shivers that were spreading through her body.

The cop came closer and was now a mere ten feet away.

Reese could hear Amber's rapid breathing. She was fighting off the cold as well, but this would disappear as soon as they opened fire and the adrenaline took over.

"You see anything, Eric?

"No, man," said the cop, now standing right above Reese.

She nodded remembering the name. She didn't know all their names but remembered their faces.

"Maybe we should shut the lights off," said another cop.

Eric looked down at the shoreline.

Reese's eyes grew wide when the cop noticed something didn't look right. He stared right at her but was unable to figure out what it was. Reese tightened her grip on the Colt M-4 when he went for a flashlight on his belt.

The cop turned the light on. "What the hell?"

Reese sprang up pointing the rifle at him and pulling the trigger. The M-4 was in single shot mode, but the one round was all it took to bring him down. It hit him right in the gut and he cried out in pain. Reese took a quick look at him to see he wasn't going anywhere. She flicked the switch to full auto just as Amber jumped up and started spraying the squad car to her left. Reese took the car to her right and found an exposed cop, but she was too late and he dropped to the grass and scooted out of the way.

The cops began returning fire, and the girls slid back down into the water. Adrenaline raced through them allowing them to ignore the cold. Bullets whistled by, and a splash of water shot up in front of them. All the while the wounded cop continued to scream out in pain.

Reese wanted a moment with him to let him know who was about to kill him. She shook her head realizing that was Mister Hyde talking, and she no longer wanted any part of him. She raised her weapon and finished him off with a three-shot burst.

"How many did you get?" asked Amber.

"Just that one, you?"

"None. Bastards ducked out of the way."

"Where the hell's our back up?"

"Good question," said Amber, as she pulled out the radio. "Eddie, where are you?"

It took a few seconds before he returned. "Hold tight, we're running as fast as we can?"

Amber shook her head at Reese knowing they'd have to hold tight for at least another five minutes, which in a gun battle was an eternity. She rose up and fired a three round burst taking out the headlights. "Take those out."

Reese nodded and shot out both lights blinding the enemy and giving them a slight advantage with their night-vision optics. It wasn't much, but they'd take what they could get. The cops still knew where they were.

"I don't wanna, but we need to get further out," said Reese.

"Yep."

The further they waded into the water the more the current tugged at them. They only dared to go waist deep, which put them about twenty feet away from the shore. They moved out far enough to see the cops had opened their doors and were now using them as cover. If they opened fire now, they'd give away their new positions. Muzzle flashes began to appear and rounds ripped into the shore where they had just been. The cops began using automatic weapons and took turns firing a wide swath. Rounds started splashing in front of them again.

Reese shook her head at what they had to do. "Go, Amber, we've got to flank them."

Amber nodded and floated down the river.

CHAPTER 63

Burns pointed the eighteen-foot skiff toward the American shore and was fifty feet out when they noticed headlights shining across the water. Scar ordered Burns to come in a little south so they could sneak in to see who it was. No sooner had he altered course than muzzle flashes appeared. They assumed cops had snuck up on Hadley.

"We've got two returning fire," yelled Bassett.

"Can't be Hadley then," said Nordell, "unless he's got help."

Everyone stared at the shore when the return fire started lighting up the sky.

"It's more than one cop," said Bassett.

"They must be out looking for us," said Nordell.

Scar turned to Burns. "Can't this thing go any faster?"

"This is it."

Scar took a deep breath trying to calm down. This wasn't an ideal situation as they didn't have a lot of weaponry unless their stash was still in the garage. They weren't even sure which ones were the bad guys. They would be there in a few more minutes and he needed to figure out what to do with Quinn. Should he just let him go now or make him wait until they had more intel? Despite the help he had been giving then, he still didn't trust him.

The shore was about seventy-feet away when a barrage of gunfire fired echoed across the river. Whoever it was, wasn't taking any chances.

Burns landed the boat at a pier about a thousand feet from the gun battle. Bassett hopped out first, followed by Nordell, who motioned at Quinn.

"Tie the bastard up," said Nordell, "we'll come back for him."

Scar looked around and found a small tree to use. He ordered Quinn over to it and then used his own handcuffs on him.

"But you said you'd let me go."

"I will, just as soon as we figure out what this is."

Bassett tapped him on the shoulder. "Don't worry, we'll be back."

They started toward the gun battle to find it was cops firing from behind their cars. Scar led the way keeping low to the ground as they got closer. He looked out over the water but couldn't see who the cops were shooting at. It had to be Hadley, but why were there two shooters?

They were about five hundred feet away when something in the water caught Scar's attention. He froze while throwing his hand up motioning to the water. He pointed the Sig Sauer he had confiscated from the cops. He squinted his eyes and watched a shadow come out of the water. It was too dark to make out who it was, but the person squatted down and started walking toward the gun battle.

Bassett grabbed Scar's arm. "That looks like Amber."

"You sure?"

"I'd know that figure anywhere," smiled Bassett.

Scar cupped his hands to his mouth. "Amber."

The shadow stopped walking before turning around and recognizing her friends through the goggles. "I'll be damned." Amber ran to them. "Hell, am I glad to see you guys."

"What's going on?"

Amber gave them a quick rundown. "Reese is flanking the other side. She's got two to deal with."

Scar looked at the soaking wet Amber and figured her energy was drained. No telling how tired Reese was and if she'd be able to hold up. Scar asked for her radio and called out to Meeks. He didn't pick up, which meant he was being held up.

"Bassett, take the goggles, I want you to go around and catch up to Reese. We'll take out this one."

"You got it.

Amber took off the goggles and handed them to Bassett, who fastened them around his head in quick fashion before disappearing in the darkness.

The radio came alive and it was Eddie Perlee. "We're coming in behind you, so don't shoot us."

"Copy that," said Scar, putting the radio down. "Might as well wait for him before we take this one out."

They all turned to wait as Eddie and Harris came running toward them on their last breath.

Eddie shook Scar's hand, "Glad to see you're back." He looked at Amber, "Sorry we couldn't get here faster."

Amber nodded her head.

"Eddie give me those weapons," said Nordell. "Burns and I will handle this."

Nordell grabbed the M-4's and handed one to Burns. "C'mon, let's take this idiot out."

They ran toward the cop who was now using a flashlight to search the river. Nordell raised his weapon before Burns did and pulled the trigger. He continued to fire until he got within a few yards of the cop. Bullets slammed into the cruiser killing the cop who fell backward.

The cops from the other squad car began to fire at them just as Nordell and Burns reached the car for safety. Burns leaped up and fired a quick three round burst before ducking back down. Nordell followed him and did the same, suppressing the enemy fire.

"This is fun," smirked Nordell.

"Never a dull moment around you, Gunny," said Burns rising back up to fire again. As he came back around, he noticed lights coming toward them in the distance. "Looks like they've got back up."

Nordell took a quick look. "Oh good, more idiots to kill."

Burns let out a chuckle. "It's one way of looking at it, let's just hope it's not all of them."

"The more the merrier."

Four more squad cars came in fast, and they formed a formidable line facing them. Car doors opened up and they immediately started shooting at them.

"We're gonna need a lot more ammo," said Nordell.

"You suppose Eddie or Amber have any?"

"If they don't, we're screwed."

A barrage of gunfire pelted the squad cars flattening the tires and breaking the glass into spider web designs. The night erupted into strobes of light as deafening gunfire echoed throughout the area.

CHAPTER 64

Instead of putting weight on her bad leg and walking through the water, Reese began to swim. It would be faster and she wouldn't have to rely on the leg. She should never have come on this operation. She had become a liability and she would disappoint Amber. She shook the negative thought out of her head. "You can do this." The current was working against her, but she was a good swimmer. She'd done hundreds of laps in a cold high school pool. She pushed forward concentrating on her breathing and strokes. She just needed to go a little bit further.

She had two targets to take out and wanted to be in a perfect position before opening fire. She'd only have one chance, and if she failed she'd be exposed, out in the open with nothing to hide behind. The cold water drained her energy as she began wading toward the shore. The numbness in her injured leg actually made it feel better. She began to walk but noticed her movements were slower. She drew in a few deep breaths and dug down deep to push forward. She remembered her track coach always yelling at her. His voice became crystal clear in her mind, "Reese Saxby, don't you give up on me, don't you give up on yourself. You finish what you started, you hear me, Saxby?" "Yes, coach, I hear ya." "Good, you're almost there, now dig deep and keep pushing."

She reached the dry ground and shuffled forward before getting on her stomach. She stared at her targets while they exchanged fire from the other cop car. She figured Eddie finally made it to them. "Thank God. But, you still have a job to do."

She took a few moments to line up her shots. The two remaining cops were exposed and had their back to her. One turned around and she recognized him. He'd been with her on a couple of occasions and always had alcohol on his breath. Gin was his choice of drink, and it always made her sick to her stomach. The memory of it would forever turn her away from Gin. She was just about to pull the trigger when car engines came screaming down the street on her six. Her muscles tightened at the sight of more cop cars. She had no choice but to roll back to the river. She rolled over on her back; the M-4 cradled protectively in both hands and then kept rolling to until she hit the water. Again, the icy water hit her senses all at once as she rolled face first into the water. She stroked further away from shore and let out a big gasp as four squad cars blew past her.

The squad cars slid into position. Each held two cops, which meant she now had ten cops to deal with. She wasn't a bad shot, it's just that she wouldn't have enough time to take them all out before being spotted and her mobility wouldn't allow her to bounce around.

She continued to watch them while trying to come up with a solution when she noticed a figure out on the street waving at her. "Was that Eddie?" Whoever it was, he was looking right at her. She raised her arm out of the water and returned the signal. He motioned her to go up the river.

A new rush of excitement exploded through her and she found the energy to keep pushing. She kept her eyes toward the shore to watch the figure moving with her. She was finally far enough away from the cops to come out of the water. It dripped from her clothing as she reached the shore and Bassett came walking toward her.

"Out for a leisurely swim tonight?" he said as he extended his hand to help her out of the water.

"Yeah, waiting for you losers. What the hell?"

"Trust me, long story."

Reese let out a sigh of relief. "So, what do we do?"

"We can't have these guys chasing us all the way back to Jackson. Can you walk?"

"My legs are so damn cold they're numb. I can hardly feel 'em, so yeah."

"Okay, let's get closer. We'll start on those guys on the far end and work our way down the line."

Not wanting to let Bassett down, Reese ignored the numbness as they charged across the field. If nothing else, she could at least cover him while he went hunting. It was something he was good at even if he didn't have his tactical tomahawk. He had a knife, the element of surprise and night-vision optics.

Reese stayed behind him as they circled wide to the furthest squad car. Those two cops had a good line of sight to Nordell and Burns and kept them pinned down. However, the angle of their car would allow Bassett to take them out without warning the others.

"Stay here," ordered Bassett.

He streaked toward the cops with a knife in one hand and the confiscated Colt C8 carbine strapped across his back. Reese darted her eyes to the cops on the left making sure they didn't spot Bassett. He came in on the far side without being seen and wrapped his arm around the first target before slashing his throat with a knife. The cop collapsed to the ground as Bassett twisted around and plunged the knife into the side of the other cop before he even knew he was there. The shocked expression on the face of the cop who she recognized made her form a small smile of victory.

Bassett ran to the next cop car and repeated the same moves. Two more cops fell to the ground dead. Reese looked to the next squad car and saw that those cops spotted Bassett and were about to fire at him. She took aim and pulled the trigger bringing her target to the ground. This alerted his partner, who opened the car door to use as a shield. Bassett flashed a thumbs up, which Reese ignored realizing she just exposed her position.

A few bullets zipped past her from one cop before the others joined in. A round kicked up dirt in front of her. She rose up on her left knee, snapped the M-4 up to her shoulder, flipped the selector to fully automatic, and began raking the squad cars back and forth with suppression fire. She then fell into a roll and kept rolling, desperate to get away from her compromised position. Rounds whistled a greater distance off to the side as she frantically rolled away. Her ears were ringing from the gunfire and the rolling made her dizzy. She stopped but needed a moment before she could get her head back in the game. Bassett tried to distract the cops with his own volley of suppression fire. It worked for a few seconds before a car engine roared to life and Reese watched in horror as it turned toward her.

CHAPTER 65

The cops assaulted Nordell and Burns with a non-stop hail of gunfire that wouldn't allow Scar and the rest to get close to them. Errant rounds flew by forcing them to stay down on the ground. Scar grabbed the binoculars from Amber and scooted low to the ground and away from the shore before getting up to survey the situation. He wasn't focused on the cops but on finding Bassett and Reese. It took a few moments to find Bassett running toward the river to Reese. Scar nodded in satisfaction because the attention would soon be off Nordell and Burns.

He watched Bassett move like a gazelle leaving Reese to cover him. Scar concentrated on the sound of staccato gunfire, waiting for the tune to change. It didn't take long before Bassett found his first targets and then two more. Scar swept the glasses over to Reese who emptied a magazine and then rolled away.

The tune of the gunfire suddenly changed as the cops focused on Bassett and Reese. It was time for his team to move forward. Scar jumped up and ran back ordering everyone to move forward.

"Tell me you have ammo," shouted Nordell at Eddie.

Eddie and Harris pulled out loaded magazines.

"They're concentrating on Bassett and Reese," said Scar.

Nordell scowled, "We need to flank their position immediately."

Scar gave him a firm nod and then jerked his head up when he heard an engine roar to life. A cop car tore across the grassy field headed toward Reese. "Damn it."

Nordell rose up and emptied a full mag on the car forcing it to swerve to the right and away from her. It then kept going before spinning around to a stop. Two cops got out and used their new position to box in Reese and Bassett. The cops now had an advantage with their backs to the water.

"Burns, sweep left," ordered Scar.

He grabbed three full magazines before disappearing into the darkness.

"I'll go right," volunteered Amber knowing someone needed to go into the river.

Scar shot her a concerned look.

"I'm already wet," she responded with a slight shrug.

Scar conceded her point and watched her wade back into the water.

Amber thought, because she was wet, the cold couldn't be much worse. She soon discovered she was wrong. By the time she was in to her waist, the water was shooting needles back through her body. It was like having a porcupine quilt wrapped around her. She pushed it out of her mind by kicking her feet and swimming up the river. The current made it difficult and her legs grew heavy by the time she got into position. She was right behind the two cops who leaned on the hood of the squad car shooting at Reese and Bassett.

The loud gunfire was perfect cover as she crept out of the river dripping water. She kept the rifle butted against her right shoulder as she moved in closer to her targets. The cops looked at each other and seemed to be enjoying themselves. Amber let out a scoff and pulled the trigger. Blood splattered out of the first cop's head and flew onto the hood of the car. The second cop twisted around, confused as to why they were exposed, and then fell dead amid strobes of muzzle flash. Amber raced in keeping the rifle pressed against her shoulder pointing at her victims.

The glassy eyes stared at her while she turned toward Scar and waved a hand in the air. He returned the wave so she scanned the area looking for Reese. She spotted her in a prone position when she gave her the okay sign. Relieved, Amber jumped into the car and floored the pedal to pull up next to Reese. This effectively blocked any fire directed toward Reese, but she had now become a target herself. She crawled over the center console as bullets began pelting the car.

"Tell me again why I wanted to come?" asked Reese as she opened the passenger door to help Amber escape.

"Damn good question, sweetie."

"Thank God you got here when you did. Their aim was definitely improving."

Amber stood in a squatted position and scanned the area to assess the situation. Burns was just getting to Bassett, but wouldn't have a good line of sight to the remaining three cops.

Amber turned to Reese. "It's up to us."

Reese knew the score and nodded. They were only fifty feet away from the enemy and now had protection to hide behind while firing. Reese moved to the back of the car while Amber took the front. They had to wait for the enemy fire to subside before retaliating. When the rounds that were hitting the big car finally stopped, Reese yelled to Amber while rising up and applied pressure to the trigger. She swept the M-4 back and forth while in full auto. Rounds exploded into windows and one of the cops fell dead. Reese emptied the mag and squatted back down. Amber then jumped up but was more methodical with short and measured bursts.

Reese ejected her spent magazine and fished out another before Amber finished firing. She rose up again keeping her finger on the trigger guard while looking for another target. Not finding any, she counted the bodies. They were all dead.

"Damn girl, you took out the last of them."

"Did I? I thought there was another one."

"Nope, I already got him."

Amber yelled to Bassett and Burns. "That's it!"

She moved over to Reese and wrapped her arms around her thankful she was not killed. They weren't ready for this kind of battle and were lucky to have come out alive. Had Scar or Eddie not shown up when they did, they would have more than likely been killed. Reese began to shake from the cold as the adrenaline started to wear off. Amber began to shake in rhythm with her. That and the sudden tension release created a situation so silly they began to laugh hysterically.

"Aren't we a pair," cracked Reese.

"Yeah, the polar twins."

"More like wet puppy dogs."

Headlights broke over the horizon before vehicles came rushing down the street. Amber tensed up but soon realized it was Meeks and Taylor. She then got Reese to the passenger door of the car, helped her in, ran around the other side, started it up and turned on the heater.

CHAPTER 66

WINNIPEG CANADA

The girls slept as Winters drove over one farmer's field and into the next thereby entering Canada. He used the same route the Shadow Patriots had been using for the last few months. It was out in the middle of nowhere, and every time they had crossed over he had never seen a single person. The trip north had been uneventful and took just over twelve hours. They stopped a few times for bathroom breaks and to refill the tanks. Finley was still running a fever, and except for being wakened and forced to drink some water slept the whole way.

A shot of excitement raced through him as he crossed the border because he only had another fifty miles to go before he was able to see Sadie. Her innocence and spirit would be able to flush out any remaining sadness he had for Cara. He hoped his surrogate daughter was getting along well since he'd been gone. General Standish promised to keep her busy and get her back in school. He would spend as much time with her as he could during his short visit.

He looked down at Laney, who was leaning on Collette, who leaned against a pillow. They'd been sleeping since their last stop a few hours ago.

Winters hadn't discussed with them whether or not they wanted to stay in Canada. Life would be easier for them if they stayed, but if they wanted to go home he'd be more than happy to drop them off before heading back to Jackson.

He looked in the mirror at the van behind him. The morning rays bounced off the windshield, but he could see Collette's mom, Stacey, driving it. Despite her general negativity, she had been a big help in caring for Finley. Had it not been for her, Finley might not have made it. This gave him pause, as he feared losing another girl, especially this one. Finley would always hold a special place in his heart as the one who started his healing process. She broke through his melancholy and wrapped her positive spirit around him. You couldn't help but want to listen to her non-stop chattering about nothing. Not only was it entertaining, but also distracting, which was what he needed, especially with what he was going through and what he was doing that night. She helped him forget about Mister Hyde and the problems associated with that inner demon. Killing all those people and having him come out to play would not have been a good thing. A shiver shot through him thinking about the affect it would have had. He would not have had the patience to wait on the guy holding Collette hostage. No doubt, he wouldn't have taken a chance and would have shot them both just to be done with it. Had that happened, then the guys holding Laney and Finley would have killed them. He shook his head at the thought of their innocent blood on his hands. He would have given up any remains of his sanity to Mister Hyde and never look back.

The base came into sight, and Winters poked Laney on the shoulder. She opened her eyes and sat up, which woke Collette. They both stared out the window while rubbing their faces.

"How long were we sleeping?" asked Laney.

"Hmm, a few of hours."

"Wow, I really needed that," said Collette, running her hand through her short black hair.

"Wait, are we here?" asked Laney.

"We are," said Winters as he pulled up to the gated entrance of the James Armstrong Richardson International Airport. It was an expanded base, housing both British and Canadian air and ground forces. He recognized the guard on duty and rolled down the window. "Morning Sergeant, Cole Winters with the Shadow Patriots to see General Standish. I also have a girl in the van behind me with a gunshot wound."

The sergeant hurried back inside the guardhouse and made a phone call.

"Don't they know you?" asked Laney.

"Yes, but they still have to get permission. It'll just take a second."

"Sir, the infirmary is waiting for you, and Colonel Brocket will meet you there."

"Thank you, Sergeant."

The sergeant saluted as Winters pulled through the gate. He knew where the hospital was having been there many times. Seeing the building reminded him that Murphy was still here recovering from the gunshot wound he'd received in the sandpit after they rescued Reese and the other girls from the party-house.

He pulled around the building and into a parking spot. He then hopped out and directed Stacey to pull the van to the emergency entrance. A couple of orderlies came out with a stretcher and opened the back door where they moved Finley to the stretcher and carried her inside. The rest of the van passengers followed the stretcher leaving Winters with the girls out in the parking lot.

They approached Winters, who motioned them toward the entrance. They walked inside and found everyone standing in a waiting room talking to a doctor. The doctor finished reassuring Debbie that her daughter was going to be just fine.

Debbie approached Winters. "Thank you for doing this."

"Thankfully, we had a place to go to."

She nodded and turned back to her youngest daughter just as Colonel Brocket came around the corner.

"Captain Winters, it's good to see you," said Brocket with his obvious British accent.

"Colonel Brocket," said Winters, as he grabbed the outstretched hand and gave it a firm shake.

"I see you came here under duress."

"As always."

"Indeed, Captain."

Winters introduced Brocket to everyone and gave him a brief account. Brocket welcomed them and extended all the courtesies the base had to offer. He then had his assistant escort the moms with their kids to the hospital cafeteria to get something to eat.

Brocket turned to Winters. "General Standish will be available later this afternoon if you'd like to rest up beforehand."

"I would, thank you and I have much to report."

"I look forward to hearing it, Captain. In the meantime, you know your way around here, why don't you take these two young ladies to the big cafeteria. It sounds like they've earned a spot at the table."

"They have, sir. Believe me, they have."

Brocket turned to the girls and shook their hands before excusing himself.

Laney grabbed Winters' arm. "What's the big cafeteria? What does he mean by earning a spot?"

"He means you've fought in a battle and deserve to eat among warriors."

"Whoa, I love it," said Laney in an astonished tone.

"Are you really a captain?" asked Collette.

Winters got a kick out of their excitement. "C'mon let's go."

"Yes sir, Captain," giggled Collette.

"Please, just call me, Cole."

"But he called you, Captain. Aren't you a captain?" asked Laney.

"Not officially, but the guys in the Shadow Patriots chose to give me that title."

"So, you really are a captain then," protested Laney.

"I suppose so."

Collette grabbed Winters' other arm. "You need to stop being so humble. I like that you're a captain."

Winters shook his head as he led the chatty girls down the hallway and over to the cafeteria. They stopped chattering when they saw how big the place was and the hundreds of service men and women milling about.

Winters looked at the girls. "Pretty cool isn't it."

"Wow, this is amazing," said Collette.

He led the girls inside and noticed some of the soldiers giving him nods as they walked by. Most of the personnel knew who he was and what he was doing in the states. They also knew that if he was escorting these two girls, that they, too, were somehow involved. They had a strict protocol on who was allowed to eat in there. Everyone else ate in one of the other cafeterias. Winters recognized a few of the men who trained him and his fellow Shadow Patriots. They greeted him and said hello to the girls as they walked by. The girls were out of their element and didn't know how to act.

"Do they all know you?" asked Laney.

"Not everyone, but I think most do. Those men who just said hello, they're the instructors who trained us."

Winters got them in line and grabbed a tray for each of them. He watched their eyes grow wide looking at all the food that was before them. They hadn't seen this much food in a long time and they couldn't help but take a helping of everything. He found them seats, and they sat down to begin devouring their food. They giggled in ecstasy tasting all the different morsels.

Some of the service personnel smiled as they watched the girls relish their meals. It must have been an odd sight to see if you didn't know the girls' background. Winters knew it and knew how much this meant to them. They had earned a spot at the table and were taking full advantage.

CHAPTER 67

WASHINGTON D.C.

To anxious to get to work, Major Green skipped his morning jog and headed in early. He wanted to survey the damage to the garage and be there in case there were any phone calls from Lawrence Reed. He didn't get much sleep last night thinking about everything that had happened and how they were able to pull off such an important mission. They had just turned the world Reed lived in upside down. No longer would he believe everyone feared him. Not only were people conspiring against him but even his biggest benefactor, Gerald Perozzi, was now an enemy. Word would get around the district that he was no longer a power broker, and this would drive the man crazy.

What would be his first move? Would he be reactionary or more patient and put things into place first? Would he attempt to pull off a similar attack on Perozzi? He'd sanctioned many murders in the past, but this would be different because Perozzi maintained a formidable security team. Stormy reported how quickly and professionally they had moved in when Wagoner tried to arrest her. It wouldn't be easy to get to Perozzi, which is why he was glad it would be Reed. Besides being involved in the bombings of cities, the man ordered the killing of a United States Senator and made it look like an accident.

Green turned onto the street where his parking garage was located and entered it. The first thing he noticed was that nothing was out of place. There was no crime scene cordoned off and his bullet-ridden van was gone. Green parked his car and headed down the ramp to the office building entrance. Everything looked normal. Green kneeled down looking for any traces of blood from the bodyguard's wounds and found nothing. He looked at the walls where rounds had hit. All the bullet holes were gone. Someone spread new concrete over the holes and then repainted the whole wall the dark gray that matched all the other walls. It was as if nothing happened. Green pulled open the door and let out a guff realizing that Reed was a calculating man. He was going to pretend as if everything was okay and act like the shooting never happened. This would give him an advantage he already possessed but just didn't know it. He was doing this to make Perozzi think nothing happened when in reality, Perozzi didn't know that anything had happened. Green forced himself to control his facial expressions realizing this was even better than he could imagine. The only thing Perozzi would be thinking about was Reed was how he had tried to have Stormy arrested for some petty revenge play. Perozzi had to be happy about that because his interference made him look like a big hero. The only thing he had on his mind was getting her into bed. Unbeknownst to him, she was no longer going to work there, which would further increase his anger with Reed.

Green entered his office and hung up his jacket. He sat down and smiled at the blinking light on his phone. He reached over and dialed up his voicemail to hear the message.

"Major, this is Lawrence Reed. I want you to do me a favor and not mention to anyone what happened last night. It's a matter of utmost importance that you do this. I know I can count on you, and we'll talk in the near future."

Green leaned back in his chair curious as to what Reed was planning. He could only imagine the things he was putting in place at this very moment. He was going to make a play all right but it wasn't going to be anytime soon. Green decided that Reed was more calculating than reckless and wouldn't just fly off the handle. He couldn't wait to get out to Manassas and report to everyone. They had decided for the sake of operational security that no one would contact any of the others in case their phones were tapped or they were being followed. Besides wanting to report in, he also wanted to see Stormy and check on how she was doing. He realized he had become more attracted to her when he saw her taking down Perozzi's hired man. The way she jumped up and brought him to the ground was astonishing. Then watching the excitement flow out of her afterward and how thrilled she was had turned him on. Not only could she handle herself, but she also relished the fight. You didn't meet this kind of girl every day or ever.

Green got up and made a pot of coffee hoping his attraction wouldn't get in the way as they pursued a victory against Perozzi and Reed. He sat down in the chair and watched the water drip into the glass decanter. He'd have to keep his emotions in check so he could keep his head clear. Now was not the time to allow any kind of distractions to get in the way of their pursuit of taking down this phony government. Nothing was more important than re-establishing a government by the people and for the people.

He poured the coffee and sat back down before taking a sip. The coffee was strong and it reminded him of the coffee he shared yesterday morning with Stormy. Try as he may, he couldn't help thinking about her again. He smiled thinking how her place was a mess and reflected the way she was now living. Hectic and exciting. It made him realize it was the same for him. On the edge and taking chances. He took another sip of coffee and from the window he looked across Lafayette Park. Joggers were beating the path racing toward some imaginary finish line. His finish line was clear, but the path was full of obstacles still unseen. They had just hurdled over the biggest obstacle. Now they would have to wait and see what happens next.

CHAPTER 68

After finishing the food on their trays, Collette and Laney patted their stomachs a few times comparing who had the biggest. Neither of them had even seen this much food in a long time and couldn't wipe the smiles off their faces.

Winters laughed at their silliness. Then he heard a high-pitched voice coming from the entrance of the cafeteria. His eyes grew knowing whom it belonged to. He twisted around to see one of the instructors pointing his way.

"Cole," Sadie yelled as she came running over.

Winters' face lit up and he pushed away from the table to stand up.

Sadie charged in and jumped into his waiting arms. "You're here."

He squeezed her tight for a few moments soaking in all her excitement before letting her go.

"Why are you here? Where is everybody? How long you have been here?"

"I just got here and needed to get these girls fed before I came to see you."

Sadie looked over at the girls and as always took the initiative to introduce herself.

She held out her hand first to Laney. "Hi, I'm Sadie."

Laney looked at Collette before standing up. "Oh my God, she is so cute." Instead of grabbing her hand, she gave her a big hug. "I'm Laney and I've heard all about you and couldn't wait to meet ya."

Collette came around the table and did the same. "You are just too adorable, I'm Collette."

"You guys came with Cole then? What happened?"

"Cole, here, saved our lives," said Collette proudly.

Sadie beamed at Winters and then put her arms around his waist.

Winters looked around the room. Many of the service personnel stared at them with grins on their faces. Sadie had become quite a fixture on the base and because of what she went through with the Shadow Patriots, was the only kid allowed to eat in the big cafeteria. Her outgoing personality made it easy for her to make friends with most everyone.

They sat back down at the table.

"So, what have you been doing since I've been gone? They been keeping you busy?"

Sadie let out a big sigh. "I'll say."

"So, what have you been learning?"

With her hands animating she said, "Well, I've learned how to field strip and clean a Colt C7A2 rifle."

Winters leaned back in surprise. "Oh?"

Sadie giggled. "Don't worry, I'm doing school stuff, but if I get my lessons done early then I get to learn the fun stuff."

Laney grabbed Collette's arm. "I so like this girl."

"No kidding, she's, like, totally cool," said Collette.

Winters caught the eye of one of the weapons instructors, who shied away when he looked at him. "Glad to see everyone's been taking a liking to ya."

"I even got to shoot it... on full auto," she said slowly pronouncing the last words.

A proud grin spread across Winters' lips.

"I even hit the target with a nice tight grouping."

"Meeks will be happy to hear you're continuing the shooting lessons," said Winters referring to the first lessons Meeks gave her and Reese on the campus back in South Bend, Indiana. That was where Meeks gave her the Ruger SR-22 that Winters had now used on several occasions.

"How is Meeks? How's everybody?" Sadie grabbed his hand, "has anyone been...killed?"

Normally, this would be an odd question for an eleven-year-old to ask. However, she'd witnessed the destruction of her hometown while watching her mom being taken away, had a gun held to her head, sat in a jail cell, escaped Mordulfah's compound while bullets flew around her, and saw many people shot to death. Sadie was no ordinary kid and there was no sense in hiding the truth to someone who had been through hell.

"Everyone's good," said Winters, not sure where to start.

Sadie tilted her head waiting for him to continue.

Winters gave her a quick overview of what had happened leaving out certain parts, including the death of Cara. Her smile disappeared making Winters regret telling her all the things he had, but then she'd find out eventually.

"My big sisters are okay though?" she asked referring to Amber and Reese.

"Yes, and you'd be proud of them, they've been nothing but amazing."

"But Nate and Elliott?" she asked as tears began.

"Don't worry, they're going be alright."

She wiped her eyes and nodded. "I'm gonna make them get well cards."

"Honey, they would love that."

Winters wanted to get some rest before his meeting and asked Sadie to show the girls around the base.

"Sadie, my little brother, Seth, came with us," said Collette, "and also our friend's little sister, Kayley. She's your age. Would you like to meet them?"

Sadie's mouth fell open. "Kids my own age, alright!"

"They're at the hospital waiting room."

"I know the way," she said proudly.

Everyone stood up and Sadie gave Winters a hug before grabbing Collette's hand and leading the way.

Winters held Laney back and whispered to her. "Do me a favor and don't tell her about Cara. I want to tell her in private, okay."

Laney nodded

Winters watched Sadie lead the girls out of the cafeteria. He was proud of her and was happy she was taking full advantage of her surroundings. With her mom dead and her dad most likely dead, it was good she was being kept busy. It couldn't be easy for an eleven-year-old. He only wished he could be here for her and was tempted to stay a few days, but that would be impossible because he needed to get back to his men.

CHAPTER 69

GROSSE POINTE MICHIGAN

Winters opened his eyes and blinked a few times. He didn't want to get up because his body was so relaxed he thought it was part of the mattress. He rolled his shoulders and moved around the soft cotton sheets massaging the backs of his legs. Despite everything he'd been through the last few days, he had slept well. The excitement of all the fighting, driving the injured Finley to Canada and then seeing Sadie had overwhelmed him. He had fallen asleep as soon as he hit the sheets.

He took a couple of deep breaths then got up to arch his back before standing straight to grab a quick shower. As always, the hot water felt too good and he had to force himself to get out. He found a clean olive drab t-shirt in the closet and threw it on before heading down to the cafeteria. He entered the big room and found it almost empty, allowing him to grab a quick bite to eat. He had to laugh at himself for putting too much food on his plate like the girls had done. Truth be known, he hadn't seen this much food since the last time he had been here.

He looked at his watch noting it was time for his meeting, so he finished up and headed down the hallway to Standish's office. He had hoped to go by and see how Finley was doing before the meeting but ran out of time. He was ushered into the same conference room they'd used before with the blue swivel chairs. Both General Standish and Colonel

Brocket stood up as he entered.

"Captain Winters," greeted Standish, in his deep baritone voice.

"Sir, it's good to see you," said Winters, shaking his hand.

"I trust you slept well," said Brocket.

"Like I haven't slept in years."

"Battles wear the body down," said Brocket.

Tea was brought in and served as Winters began giving them an account of the last couple of weeks. Winters took a break from the story and took a few sips of the tea. He needed to gather up the courage to continue. He was just getting to the attempted rescue of Cara. His hands began to tremble and Standish noticed it.

"Are you all right, Captain?" he asked.

Winters took a hurried breath. "Yes, it's just that this next part is a little tough for me, but it needs to be told."

Standish put his hand on the table. "Take your time, sir."

Winters coughed and took another sip of tea trying to clear the lump in his throat. He took another hurried breath and continued with the story.

Neither Standish nor Brocket moved a muscle as Winters told them about storming Mordulfah's compound during the failed rescue attempt of his daughter.

"So, anyway, she huh, died in my arms," said Winters, trying to hold back the tears.

Standish glanced at Brocket before turning back to Winters and said in a gentle tone, "Captain, I'm so sorry."

Brocket repeated the sentiment.

He glanced at both of them and realized how uncomfortable the room had become. "It's okay, really, I'm still working through it, but I've actually pretty much come to terms with it. It's just that this is only the second time I've told it, so it's, ah, it's a little tough to get the words out."

"I certainly understand," said Standish giving him a reassuring nod.

"You see, it's the next part that of the story that makes it easier for me to deal with losing her."

His host exchanged puzzled looks.

Winters told them the second half of the story explaining how Cara's death was responsible for him rescuing his hometown of Sabine from a bunch of thugs. When he finished, Standish and Brocket both leaned back in their chairs shaking their heads.

"That's almost unbelievable," said Brocket, "without a doubt, something was guiding you."

"It's truly astonishing, Captain," said Standish.

Winters nodded and soaked up all the sentiment they offered. He found he still needed the affirmation and took great comfort in it. It would become easier over the coming days and more so as he got busy again.

"Anyway, those girls that came with me are true heroes. They were incredibly brave and unflinching in the thick of things. I could not have done it without them and certainly not in one night."

Standish took another sip of tea and agreed.

"I got a report a little bit ago from the doctor," said Brocket, "young Finley is doing well. They stitched her wound properly and have her on antibiotics."

Winters finished his tea and let out a deep sigh. That good news was another small accomplishment, which would help the healing of his heart.

"Now onto other matters," said Standish changing his tone.

Winters furrowed his eyebrows in anticipation.

"I received some news in regards to your men."

Winters didn't respond but found his chest tighten.

"Seems they killed a Sarnia cop last night."

Winters didn't know where Sarnia was and asked.

"It's across the river from Port Huron. They came across the river looking for supplies."

"Who did?"

Standish looked at the report. "Scarborough, Bassett, Burns, and someone named Nick Nordell."

"He's a retired Gunnery Sergeant, he lives in Jackson."

Standish nodded.

"So, what happened?" asked Winters

"Still gathering the details but it appears that one of the Sarnia cops decided to try and cash in on the reward that's on your heads. However, he must not have realized just who he had in custody because they managed to escape and get back across the river."

Winters rubbed his temples trying to comprehend all of this.

"Unfortunately, one of the cops was killed and several others are in the hospital, all with injuries to the head."

Winters tried to appear stoic, although inside he took joy in the fact that his guys managed to escape. "So, where do we stand? Where do my guys stand?"

Standish shifted in his seat. "I've been on the phone for the last hour sorting all of this out. What we know is your guys came over in good faith with money to buy supplies when the local cops asked for their papers. When they couldn't produce them, the cops arrested them and then found they had side arms, which is a big no-no. Your guys were up front with who they were and this is where greed came in and got in the way."

Winters grimaced, still not knowing what was going to happen to them.

"We're gonna sweep this under the rug. Blame it on some random criminals. This Sarnia cop is in a whole lot of trouble. Not only did he jeopardize the safety of his men, but he bribed border guards to allow your National Police into the country."

Relief swept over Winters. The last thing he needed was to be in trouble with a country that has been helping them. They needed Canada's help and couldn't have gotten as far they had without it. He then realized he would need to leave as soon as he could and get back to Jackson. If Scar risked going into Canada for supplies, then the situation must be more desperate than he remembered. With everything that had been going on over the last week or so, he hadn't had the time or the wherewithal to even think about the town's supplies.

He looked at General Standish and asked him for his assistance once again. He responded with his continued support to supply the Shadow Patriots with food, medicine, fuel, and most importantly, more weapons.

Made in the USA
Lexington, KY
27 February 2018